ECHO
NORTH

JOANNA
RUTH MEYER

PAGE STREET
PUBLISHING CO.

PAGE STREET
PUBLISHING CO.

Copyright © 2019 Joanna Ruth Meyer

First published in 2018 by
Page Street Publishing Co.
27 Congress Street, Suite 105
Salem, MA 01970
www.pagestreetpublishing.com

Distributed by Macmillan, sales in Canada by The Canadian Manda Group.

23   22   21   20   19   2   3   4   5

ISBN-13: 978-1-62414-715-9
ISBN-10: 1-62414-715-1

Library of Congress Control Number: 2018946119

Cover design by Sara Pollard, book design by Rosie Stewart for Page Street Publishing Co.

Cover image: Roots © Shutterstock/rolandtopor, Wolves © Shutterstock/ Gerasimov Sergei, Frame elements © Shutterstock/standa_art

Printed and bound in the United States.

Ripon Public Library

For my mom—someday, we're going to find the wolf's library
and explore it together, okay?

And to the spinners of stories: Robin McKinley, Edith Pattou,
and Diana Wynne Jones. Thanks for the magic.

PART ONE

ℭHAPTER ONℰ

I WAS CALLED ECHO FOR MY mother, who died when I was born, because when my father took me into his arms he said he felt the echo of her heartbeat within me.

My father didn't blame me for my mother's death, but he was often sad. He had me and my older brother Rodya to raise on his own. Two mouths to feed and no dark-haired laughing wife to come home to.

But he bore it all cheerfully. He gave me my freedom, and I loved both him and my brother fiercely. I was allowed to run barefoot in the summer, to tumble with the blacksmith's hounds, to skip my classes if I wished and go fishing with Rodya in the lake.

Not that my father wanted me to be ignorant. He taught me patiently from his books when we were at home together every evening. He read to me and asked me questions and answered all *my* questions. I couldn't have been happier. I'd never known my mother—my father and Rodya were my whole world.

And then my whole world shifted.

It happened the summer I was seven. Our village stood on the edge of a forest, and that year had been a particularly bad one for wolves attacking cattle and sheep in their fields. Old man Tinker had set traps all around the village, and my father told me to watch for them carefully. "Those traps could snap you in two, my darling, and what would I do without you?"

I promised him solemnly to take care.

But as I was coming back from picking wildflowers in the meadows, my embroidered skirts dirty about my knees, my kerchief forgotten somewhere amidst the waving grass, I heard a sharp, yelping scream—the sound of an animal in torment. I dropped my flowers, standing for an instant very still. The sound came again, and I ran toward it as quickly as I could.

Round the corner, caught fast in a steel trap that butted up against a fence post, was a huge white wolf.

I stared, frozen. For an instant, his pain seemingly forgotten, he stared back at me.

I could feel him, not just looking, but *seeing* me, as if he were searching out something deep inside my soul. I should have been terrified but I wasn't. I felt drawn to him. Connected to him.

Then I glanced down and saw the blood staining his white fur where the trap had caught his back left leg.

I was brave. I was foolish.

I went to help him without another thought.

I knelt beside him in the dirt and touched him, gently, my small hand sinking into his white fur; it was the softest thing I had ever felt, softer even than the velvet cushion on my father's favorite chair. I knew I was right to want to help the wolf. I was certain it was the most important thing in all the world.

I took a deep breath, grasped the jaws of the steel trap as firmly as I could, and *pulled.*

I couldn't shift it. Not even an inch. All I managed to do was jostle the trap against the wolf's wounded leg. He howled in pain and jerked away, a sudden whirl of claws and fur and snarling teeth. The trap was slippery with his blood and I dropped it back onto the ground. He lunged against the trap, desperate and screeching, but it held him, the metal jaws biting deeper and deeper, down to the bone.

The wolf grew more frantic with each passing second, and I started digging, tearing into the dirt around the stake and chain connected to those ugly metal jaws.

The stake loosened. The wolf gave one last desperate *yank* and pulled it free. For an instant, joy and triumph filled me up.

He leapt toward me in a blur of white, the trap and chain rattling behind him, and slammed into me with the force of an avalanche. Everything was all at once falling and fear, an impossible weight. Darkness.

And blinding, earth-shattering pain.

The weight lifted, but something wet and awful was smeared across my eyes and the world was distorted and bleared. It frightened me even more than the darkness had. Pain pulsed through me, lines of raging fire in my chest, my shoulders, my face.

Someone was screaming and I realized it was me.

I must have fainted, because when I opened my eyes again my father was kneeling over me, his form warped and strange. The light was fading orange and birds were singing in the wood. I was dizzy, my face and chest strangely numb. One of my eyes was swollen shut. Bits of rock and dirt had ground into my palms and behind my fingernails when I'd dug the stake from the ground—in that moment, it was the only pain I could feel.

"Let's carry her inside," I heard someone say. "She'll be all right, Peter. She's strong."

Peter was my father. The other voice belonged to old man Tinker. He must have come to check his traps and found me there instead. My father scooped me into his arms, and I passed out again.

The next time I tried to open my eyes there was only darkness, and something thick and suffocating pressed against my face. "Papa!" I screamed, "Papa!" I jerked upright and fell in a tangle to the floor and then my father was there, coaxing me back into bed, calming me down.

"Just bandages, little bird. We'll take them off soon. Hush, now. All is well."

I clung to him and he kissed me quietly on the forehead and sang me to sleep.

Later, I don't know how much, they removed the bandage from my right eye. It gave me an oddly skewed view of the world, but it was better than no sight at all. We lived in a house back then, and I sat for many weeks in my room on the third floor, watching through my little square window as the world below turned from the green and gold of summer to the red-brown blush of autumn.

A host of doctors visited me, and I didn't understand why. I crept downstairs and listened shamelessly outside the door to my father's study while they talked about me. I heard things like "never fully heal" and "the cuts were too deep" and "infection" and "lucky if she isn't blind."

And then one day, as the first of the winter snows blew soft across our village, the doctor came to take the bandage off the left side of my face. My father watched intently as the doctor peeled the cloth away, and I held my breath and waited for it to be over. Horror and shock flashed across my father's features, and for the first time, I realized what had happened to me might not be able to be undone.

"Cover your right eye," the doctor instructed. "Can you see out of the left one?"

I lifted my hand and obeyed. The light was very bright, but I could see. I nodded.

The doctor let out a breath of relief.

My father shifted where he stood. The horror had left his expression, melding into a distance that unnerved me. "Is there anything you recommend for . . . " he trailed off, looking help-lessly at the physician.

"Not unless God gives her new skin," said the doctor. I think he meant it as a joke, but my father didn't even smile.

I pushed past both of them and went out into the hall, pad-ding to the room my mother had once shared with my father. She had a handsome mahogany vanity, with a mirror above. I stepped up to it and looked in.

Four angry, jagged lines ran down the left side of my face, from my forehead all the way to my chin—the marks from the wolf's claws. My left eyelid was taut and scarred, my lips pulled up on one side.

I stared at my reflection, feeling dull and strange. I covered the right half of my face with one hand, studying the scars for a long while before switching to cover the left half and studying in turn the smooth, untouched skin.

Then I let my hand fall.

I heard my father's step and turned to see him watching me from the doorway. "It isn't so bad, little lamb. They will fade over time." But sadness lingered in his eyes. He swept me into his arms and I clung to his neck, sobbing, while he stroked my hair and wept with me awhile.

MY FATHER OWNED AND RAN the bookshop in our tiny village. He was excessively proud of it: it had a green door and a brass knocker and a large shop window with carved wooden shutters. "It's not a large living," he always said, "but it's enough."

PETER ALKAEV, BOOKSELLER was painted in bold red letters across the window. That was how I first learned to spell my last name.

The summer after the incident with the wolf, my father sold our house, and he, my brother, Rodya, and I moved into the apartments over the shop. I had my own little room with a tiny circle window that looked out over the street, and all the books I could ever want.

My scars whitened as I got older—they didn't fade. I learned very early that in the old tales of magic the wicked were always ugly and scarred, the good beautiful; I was not beautiful, but I wanted to be good, and after a while I couldn't bear to read those stories anymore.

The villagers avoided me. My fellow students crossed themselves when I walked by, or openly laughed at me. They said the Devil had claimed my face and would someday come back for the rest of me. They said he wouldn't have marked me if I didn't already belong to him. Once, I tried to eat lunch with a girl called Sara. She liked to read, same as me—she was always carrying around thick tomes of history or poetry or science, her nose permanently stuck between the pages. I thought that gave me the right to try and befriend her, but she spat in my face and pelted me with stones.

I was the monster in her story. She was the heroine.

I didn't try again.

Once, I wandered into the apothecary and bought a jar of

cream for two silver pennies because the proprietor swore it would make the scars vanish completely by the end of the month.

It didn't work, of course. Rodya found me crying in my bedroom and I told him what I'd done. He made jokes at the apothecary's expense until I finally stopped crying and forced a smile for him, but I still felt like a fool. I buried the empty jar of cream in a little patch of earth behind the bookshop—it had been intended for a garden, but no one had ever planted anything and it remained barren. I couldn't stand to confess what I'd done to my father.

By the time I turned fifteen, I had read nearly every book in the shop, and my father hired me as his assistant. "Her face might frighten the Devil who formed her," I overheard one of my father's patrons say, "but damned if she doesn't know every word of the classics and can be counted on to point a fellow to the right book, every time." This was one of the kindest things they said about me. There were many more less kind.

I withdrew more and more, trying to lose myself in running the shop. I organized the shelves and reorganized them. I wrapped books in paper and string for customers, I wrote letters to the booksellers in the city, sending for rare volumes we didn't have. I kept my father's account books in order, and when business was slow, I went to our upstairs apartments and scoured the rooms clean, one by one.

I kept busy, attempted to convince myself I was content. But no matter how hard I tried, I couldn't shove away my loneliness, couldn't bury it in my mind like I'd buried the jar of cream in the dirt where there ought to have been a garden.

CHAPTER TWO

A FEW MONTHS BEFORE MY SIXTEENTH birthday, my world inverted itself again.

It was full winter, snow clinging to the shop window and the stones in the street. My toes had grown numb, even in my felted boots, and I closed the shop a little early and went upstairs to our apartments, an anatomy book tucked under each arm. Anatomy was my latest passion—I spent hours every day pouring over medical notes and diagrams.

I bustled about the living space, closing the shutters, lighting the lamps, coaxing the fire into a nice red roar. I cooked beef and noodles and cabbage, then lit the samovar and started boiling water. Between tasks, I read one of my books, an anatomical study of the heart, careful not to spill anything on the pages.

I expected my father and Rodya at any moment. Rodya had apprenticed himself to the clockmaker in the village six months back, but he still came most nights for supper. My father had been gone on a mysterious errand since the morning. I hoped the snow wasn't delaying them overmuch, and I strained my ears to catch the sound of their footsteps on the stairs.

It was Rodya who came first, stamping through the door in his thick boots, shaking snow from his hair and shrugging out of his coat. I waved him to his customary chair by the fire as I poured concentrated tea into a cup and added water from the samovar to dilute it, then did the same for myself. I settled down adjacent to him on our threadbare couch. We would wait until our father came home to eat our beef and noodles.

Rodya yawned and sipped his tea. "Don't think Papa is coming tonight," he said conversationally, eyeing me over his cup.

"Coming from where? Do you know where he's been today?"

"At Donia's." My brother's lips quirked.

I stared at him blankly. Donia was the baker's widow, and had taken over the business when he passed, but I had no idea what that had to do with my father.

"Lord, sister! Don't you listen to the gossip?"

I met Rodya's dark eyes and frowned. None of the bookshop customers talked to me long enough to pass on rumors. "Rodya, just tell me."

"Papa is sweet on her."

"*What?*"

I dropped my teacup, yelping as the hot liquid splashed over my bare toes.

Rodya laughed as he laid his own cup down and knelt on the floor to help me clean up the mess. "Mother's been gone a long time, dearheart. Papa deserves to be happy again. I won't be here forever, and neither will you. Won't you feel better knowing there's someone to take care of Papa when we've gone?"

I scooped the shards of the teacup into my apron and bustled from the room to avoid my brother's question. When I'd emptied the pieces into the dustbin, I turned to find him watching me from his place in front of the fire.

"You won't be stuck here always," he said, reading my mind.

My throat tightened. "I haven't any options, Rodya. I never have."

"Echo—"

"I'll get our supper," I interrupted. "Since Papa's not coming."

We ate together in silence, and I stared into the fire and hated myself. The noodles had cooked too long and the beef was dry and the cabbage sour. But Rodya ate every bite.

He picked up one of my books from the end table when he'd finished, the one about the heart. I was nearly three-quarters of the way through it. "You could go away to the university," he said. "You're smart enough. Way smarter than me—maybe even smarter than Papa."

"They don't take girls at the university," I snapped.

"They're starting to," he objected. "And they'd take you. Why don't you write to them?"

Anger and hope warred in my mind, but it was the anger that spilled out. "And what then, Rodya? A whole city full of people to curse me as I walk by? To mock me and—and pelt me with stones?"

"No," he said fiercely. "A whole city full of people who will admire your intellect, who will see you for yourself."

I didn't have a chance to reply, because at that moment my father walked in, his beard dusted with flour and smelling of cinnamon, with the news he was to be married come spring.

"I'VE BOUGHT A HOUSE," MY father announced the next afternoon, beaming at me over his tea while I wrapped up a stack of books to ship off to a customer in the city.

"A house?" I was surprised.

"For Donia," he explained. "She spent so many years in the cramped rooms above the bakery, she isn't keen on trading them for our upstairs apartments. I was hoping you would help me fix it up, to surprise her."

We closed the shop early, bundled into our furs, and trudged four miles north from the village through the previous day's snow. Nestled into the very edge of the forest was the house, a wooden cottage with a stone chimney that had intricate woodwork around the roof and patterned shutters. The windows were broken, the paint chipped, the shutters sagging.

My father glanced over at me. "You have to see its heart, love. Look past the flaws." He fished a key out of his pocket and unlocked the door.

We stepped in, onto creaky wooden floors overstrewn with dirt and leaves that had blown in through the broken windows. The wallpaper was torn and faded, the carpet in front of the dead hearth threadbare. But even so, my father was right—it had a good heart.

He took my hand, like he hadn't done since I was a young child, and led me quietly through the whole house: parlor, sitting room, kitchen, then upstairs to the two bedrooms and private lavatory. We climbed one more creaky staircase to a charming attic room, with a sloped roof and large window overlooking the woods. It was in less disrepair than the rest of the house, and I got the feeling it hadn't really been lived in by the cottage's former occupants.

I loved it instantly.

My father could tell. "It's yours, if you want it. I doubt Donia will want to climb up this way very often."

I hugged him, because I knew he'd picked the room out specifically for me.

We tramped back down to the main floor. "Can we really afford it, though, Papa?"

He smiled. "I signed the papers this morning."

This wasn't quite an answer, but I reasoned with a little careful planning and penny-hoarding, we could make it work.

We walked back to the bookshop in the gathering dark, discussing what needed to be done to make the cottage livable. It started snowing again, but I hardly felt the cold, warmed by my father's love for me, and knowing that not even a stepmother could take that away.

AFTER WEEKS OF WORKING ON the house in shifts—mostly my father and me, with Rodya helping when he could—my father finally deemed the cottage ready for Donia's approval. Rodya took the afternoon off from the clockmaker's, and the three of us waited at the bookshop for her to join us. I was nervous and jittery. This would be the first time I'd really met my almost-stepmother. I'd invited her to dinner on several occasions, but she hadn't been able to come, too occupied arranging the sale of the bakery to pay for her late husband's debts.

She swept into the shop all bright and bustling, an expensive-looking fur coat fastened around her shoulders, a gold-embroidered sarafan just beneath. She reminded me of an arctic bear: tall and broad, with rosy cheeks and strong arms from years of kneading bread and shoveling loaves in and out of ovens.

She greeted my brother and father, and then approached me

with her arms outstretched. "Echo! Dear!" She embraced me in a careful manner, like she wished to give the appearance of affection without getting overly close to me. She kissed the air on both sides of my face. "Well. Let me look at you!" Her tone was too bright. Her eyes swept me up and down, lingering at first too long on my scars and then too briefly. She repeated: "Echo. Dear." It was in a more false-sounding voice than before.

My father's glance flicked anxiously between us, and I tried to smile to put him at ease. "Shall we go and see the house?"

We left the shop, my father and Donia leading, me and Rodya behind. It was Sunday, and winter was beginning to fade from the world. The air held the faintest hint of springtime—everything should have seemed fresh and new and hopeful. But my heart was a tumult of unease.

We climbed the hill that looked down onto the cottage, and Donia gasped in delight. "Oh, Peter, how lovely!"

She was more subdued once we actually entered the house. Her eyes swept around the rooms with relentless scrutiny, lingering especially long on the curtains I'd sewn and the rug I'd bought from the town seamstress and lugged all the way from the village. We followed Donia up to the attic room, where I had a sudden moment of panic she would claim it for her own.

But my father came to my rescue. "I thought this would do very well for Echo. What do you think, my dear?"

Donia glanced about again and gave a regal jerk of her chin.

"I can't think the room would have any other use—it's far too inconvenient. Yes, Echo may have it."

I looked aside at my father in time to see him wink at me.

Back downstairs again, Donia took one more turn through the lower floor, nodding as she rejoined us by the hearth. "It will do, Peter, it will certainly do!"

My father breathed a sigh of relief, suddenly all smiles.

Donia beamed at him. "It only wants a woman's touch. The curtains will have to go at once, of course—they're perfectly dreadful—and that rug, too. We'll need furniture." She raised her hand to forestall my father. "*Not* the furniture from your apartment, dear. New furniture, and new linens and carpets. We will have to manage with just that for now."

"Just that?" My father studied her quizzically.

"I'll need a writing desk eventually, all new wallpaper, certainly, and a piano. I was quite the songbird, you know, when I was small. I've longed for a piano these many years—"

"The wallpaper is new," I interrupted.

Donia fixed her dark eyes on my face. "I beg your pardon, Echo?" Her tone turned her meaning to: "How dare you speak to me!"

"The wallpaper is new," I repeated. "I picked it out myself, and I know where to get more to match, when we can afford it. I sewed the curtains—I thought they brightened the room considerably. I'm sorry you don't like them."

Donia frowned. Her dislike pulsed toward me with the

intensity of a heatwave, but she only said in a mild tone, "You ought to have consulted me first. They are not at all to my taste."

"Though I'm sure Donia greatly appreciates your efforts," my father put in, gently.

Donia glanced at him, then back at me. Her jaw tightened. "I'm sure I do, however misguided. Now, Peter. About the furniture." And she turned her back to me.

Rodya tugged me firmly outside.

We paced around the back of the house and sat on the stoop. I stared at the patch of earth where I'd spent a whole afternoon pulling out brambles, planning to grow vegetables when the weather got a little warmer—if Donia allowed it, that is.

Rodya bumped my shoulder with his. "Don't mind her, Echo. She's just jealous of Papa's affection for you."

I chewed on my lip and stared into the woods, straining for glimpses of green on the bare, black branches. I thought I saw a flash of white between the trees, the sudden gleam of an amber eye. But then I blinked and there was nothing there. "She hates me because of my face."

"That isn't true."

"Of course it is." I tugged my kerchief off my hair, closing my eyes and leaning into the wind. The scars still hurt sometimes, a twinge of pain when the weather was turning.

"You have to stop disparaging yourself. No one gives a damn about your scars."

"*I* give a damn," I said fiercely.

"Then stop. There isn't a single thing you can do about them, and you're too brilliant a person to waste your life bowing and scraping to dimwits in the bookshop. No matter how much you might deny it, Echo Alkaev, you are extraordinary. You have been since the moment you were born."

I reached up to touch my scars, but Rodya caught my hand and laid it in my lap again. "Write to the university. Please."

I refocused on Rodya, tracing every line of his dear face, and hope sparked inside me. "I'll write them," I promised.

CHAPTER THREE

THE DAY MY FATHER MARRIED Donia, spring bloomed in earnest across the countryside, verdant leaves bursting bright, birds trilling jubilant choruses from the treetops. It was also my sixteenth birthday, which my father had momentarily forgotten when fixing upon the date—Donia hadn't let him change it when he did remember.

I rose early, creaking open my tiny window to let in the fresh air, brushing my hair and braiding it. I had a brand-new sarafan that my father had refused to tell me the price of: it was a soft orange brocade embroidered with gold thread down the front and around the hem. I slipped it on over my white blouse, which lay cool and delicate against my skin, and buttoned all twenty-five buttons. I slid into my felt boots and stepped out into the hallway to peer in the circle mirror hanging on the wall. I avoided mirrors as a general rule—I didn't have one in my room—but that day I stood studying my reflection for quite a long time.

My eyes stared back at me, the deep blue echo of my mother's. My hair was dark. My scars were white, pulling up the skin of my face so I almost looked like I was sneering.

For the first time since the bandage had come off, I lifted one hand to cover the scarred side of my face, looking at the smooth side, the perfect side. I wondered what my life would have been like if the scars had never existed. If I concentrated hard enough I could see myself: unscarred, untouched.

And then I moved my hand to cover the right half of my face, and forced myself to stare at those ugly white lines. That was what I was. All I ever would be.

"You look lovely, Echo."

I jumped and turned to see my brother watching me from his room. He looked tall and handsome in his new shirt, embroidered in red, his dark hair combed neatly and the beginnings of his beard shaved clean.

I dropped my hand, ashamed of myself.

We walked together to the brand-new wooden chapel on the outskirts of town, and I couldn't help but think of the crumbling stone chapel on the hill where my parents had been wed, barely a penny between them. Somehow that seemed more romantic than newly hewn wood, the paint hardly dry.

The ceremony was simple. Donia looked exquisite in her glittering gown and impossibly elaborate veil. I focused on my father's face, on the joy shining out of his eyes when he saw her.

The celebration that followed filled nearly the whole village. There was food and music and dancing, and the afternoon spooled quickly away. Rodya offered to dance with me, but I didn't want to monopolize him, and retreated to the outskirts of the festivities. I sat in the grass under a huge old oak, nibbling shortbread and watching Rodya flirt with the village girls and dance with the ones he particularly fancied.

The dancers whirled past me in shimmering skirts, their quick-stepping feet keeping time to old man Tinker's violin. I wished I was among them, but none of the boys asked me to dance—and why would they? I was little more than the cloud on the horizon no one wanted to see.

I slipped away without wishing my father and Donia well on their honeymoon. I told myself it was just weariness, that I longed for solitude. But really the villagers overwhelmed me, with their whispered words and lingering glances. My loneliness and shame threatened to swallow me.

The afternoon was beginning to turn toward evening by the time I arrived at the cottage. I went to sit on the back stoop, hugging my knees to my chest and trying not to feel forgotten.

The wind teased through my hair, and it smelled of earth and wood and springtime. Ahead of me the forest teemed with life, and away to the west the sun began to slide down the rim of the sky. I was staring into the woods, my eyelids growing heavy, when I caught a flash of movement between the trees. All at once I saw a huge, white wolf staring at me from the border of the forest, and I swear to God in heaven that his eyes met mine, that his eyes *knew* mine. I had the sudden wild thought that it was the same wolf I had rescued all those years ago from the trap, and I rose involuntarily to my feet.

I took one step, two, toward the woods and the wolf. He didn't move or blink or even seem to breathe, just watched me. I wasn't afraid and I didn't know why—the thought that I should be afraid didn't even enter my head.

I stared at him, and he at me, and we were frozen there together for one moment of time that seemed to stretch on into eternity.

And then a twig snapped behind me and the wolf jumped and whirled round. In the span of an eye blink, I lost him among the trees.

I turned to see Rodya coming toward me, his hands in his pockets. "Echo!" he said, concern pressing into his forehead. "Are you all right? You look as though you've seen a ghost."

I glanced back to the wood, straining for one last glimpse of the wolf, my pulse still raging. But there was no visible sign he'd ever been there. I drew in a deep breath and forced a smile for my brother. "I thought I saw something in the woods, but—" I shook my head, "It was nothing. I promise."

He put one hand on my shoulder. "If you're certain. Come inside, won't you? I've something to show you."

I followed him into the house, and tears sprang into my eyes when I saw he'd laid out cake and tea for me on the red rug in front of the fire.

"Happy birthday, Echo," said Rodya, smiling.

I hugged him tight and then we sat down and ate every crumb of nutcake and drank every drop of tea. Rodya lit a fire, as even in the heart of springtime the nights were still chilly. He stretched out on the rug and fished something out of his pocket that was wrapped in a square of cloth. He handed it to me.

I unfolded the cloth and my mouth dropped open: in my palm lay a delicate clock on a chain, gears whirring and hands ticking softly, all encased in a gold-plated shell engraved with a compass rose. "Oh, Rodya," I breathed.

"Do you like it? I made it for you."

I nodded, at a loss for words. I couldn't stop staring at it. As I watched, the hands whirled around the clock far too quickly and then jerked to a sudden stop.

I glanced up to see Rodya frown.

"It's never done that before," he said. "I'm sorry, Echo. I'll take it back to the shop and fix it for you."

"No, no, I'd like to keep it awhile, please? I don't mind about the time."

He laughed. "Oh all right, I'll fix it next week. Here." He scooted behind me and fastened the chain around my neck. The little clock hung solid and cold through the brocade of my sarafan.

"The best part is, if you open it—" Rodya pushed a little pin down on the side of the clock face so that it sprung open to reveal a tiny compass inside. The needle pointed steadily north. "So that wherever you go, you'll always be able to come back to me. At least *that's* still working."

I threw my arms around his neck and hugged him.

He extricated himself from my embrace, laughing, and asked me if I'd written to the university yet.

When I admitted I hadn't, he pulled ink and paper from his shoulder bag. "I thought not," he said gently. "Let's write it together."

So right there on the red carpet in front of the barking fire, we composed the letter, and my hope swelled nearly to bursting.

Two blissful weeks passed, during which I was mostly left to my own devices. I kept busy running the bookshop and overseeing the delivery of Donia's furniture, making sure it was placed in the correct rooms in the proper arrangements as she had specifically instructed me.

Every evening, I strayed a little into the woods, deep enough to be just out of sight of the house, but not so far I wasn't certain of my way back. I felt drawn there, like a string had been tied to my heart. I couldn't stop thinking about the white wolf, about the comprehension in his eyes as he stared at me, at the connection I felt between us. I thought maybe the string was tied to him.

The night before my father and Donia were scheduled to arrive home, I paced a little deeper into the woods than usual, and settled myself beneath an ancient elm that was knotted and gnarled yet still bursting with leaves. I rested my head awhile against its trunk, and when I looked back into the clearing the wolf was there, not ten paces from me. His eyes were amber, flecked with gold, and the edges of his white fur ruffled in the light wind. He came toward me, his back leg dragging a little behind. He was near enough when he stopped that I caught his scent: wild honey and deep grass and dark earth.

As before, he simply stared at me and didn't come any closer.

"What are you?" I whispered, and his ears twitched at my voice. I wanted to reach out to him, sink my hand in his thick fur as I'd done as a child, but I stayed where I was.

Around us the forest faded to the deep silvery-blue of twilight. Somewhere I heard an owl cry, the sudden rush of wings in the growing dark.

The wolf dipped his head to me, like he was bowing to a queen, then he turned tail and slipped away into the wood, leaving me to stare numbly after him.

I stumbled home in the dark, the stars obscured by the trees and a thick layer of clouds, to find smoke coiling up from the chimney.

CHAPTER FOUR

M Y FATHER AND DONIA WERE HOME earlier than expected, and hard on their heels, in a rattling wooden cart, came a piano.

"A wedding present from your father!" Donia explained, beaming at me, as two men with bulging muscles carried the thing into the house.

I was shocked. I had no idea how my father could possibly afford such an elaborate instrument. It took up half the parlor, with ornate scrollwork on the legs and stand and a brightly colored painting detailing all the angels of heaven on the underside of the lid.

Donia sat down and started playing immediately, and I had to choke back my surprised laughter—if she'd ever possessed any skill, she had clearly lost it.

My father winked at me as Donia stumbled up and down the keys, hitting so many wrong notes it was hard to imagine there were any right ones. I was glad I'd be away at the bookshop most days so I wouldn't have to hear her practicing.

Rodya's visits to the house dwindled down to almost nothing after my father and Donia's return. He popped in frequently at the bookshop to ask if I'd heard back from the university, and would apologize profusely for not coming more often to the cottage. One particular afternoon, when spring was slipping headlong into summer, he hung his head and admitted sheepishly: "I can't stand that woman."

I laughed. "She's not that bad."

"Liar," he retorted.

It was true, so I laughed even more.

I found the evenings at the cottage increasingly difficult. Donia was an excellent cook, but her taste in ingredients ran as expensive as her taste in everything else, and I was forever trying to persuade her to buy cheaper ones.

On the rare occasions I was home and Donia was not, I sat down at the piano and experimented with trying to play. I taught myself one of Donia's pieces and made the mistake of playing it for her and my father one evening after supper.

I stumbled over a few notes, but for the most part the tune came out nicely, and I could tell my father thought I had done well. Donia, however, was livid.

"I don't recall giving you permission to touch this delicate instrument!" She jerked up from her seat, stepped over to the piano, and slammed the key cover down, narrowly missing my fingers. I snatched them out of the way just in time.

I sat there on the piano stool, trying not to hate her. "I'm sorry, Stepmother. You like music so much I thought it would please you to hear me try."

My father left his seat and came over to us. "Donia, my dear, there's no harm in letting Echo learn to play a little. You could perhaps even teach her some things."

"There is no question of that!" cried Donia. "You heard how she tripped and stuttered through the notes! She isn't bright enough to pursue music."

I stood from the stool and brushed by both of them, pausing in the doorway to look back. "I'll take an axe to it then, shall I? It would be more pleasant than listening to *you* play."

And then I went up to my room and read about dressing wounds until my candle burned down to a stub, refusing to unlock my door no matter how many times my father knocked, telling me to come out and apologize.

Guilt gnawed at me for a few weeks after until, at long last, I relented and asked Donia's forgiveness. She just sniffed and said

I wasn't to touch her things without her permission ever again.

The piano mostly gathered dust after that.

A FEW WEEKS LATER, LETTERS from my father's creditors began to arrive, most to the bookshop, some to the cottage. At first, I didn't realize they weren't the usual bills or notices. They all demanded immediate repayment of a staggering amount of money. One threatened fines. Another, prison. I tried to talk to my father about them but he continually put me off, saying that these city creditors were just making thunderstorms out of raindrops.

One morning, I went into the back room of the shop to shelve some books, and caught my father unearthing my mother's jewel case from its hiding spot beneath the floorboards. It was empty except for her treasured emerald ring and a gold necklace.

He bowed his head, and the next moment he was crying silently on the floor, his shoulders shaking. I knelt beside him, wanting to comfort him as he had so often comforted me.

"We're ruined, Echo," he said when he'd grown calm enough to speak. "Utterly and completely."

"Because of the furniture? Because of the piano?"

"It's the house. I thought I could manage the payments, and perhaps I could have if business were better, but—" He sighed. "I just wanted your stepmother to be happy. I've borrowed much more than I can ever possibly pay back."

"What can we do?"

He took the necklace and the ring out of the jewel box. "We'll sell the necklace. But this—" He offered me the ring. "I always meant for you to have it."

I bit my lip and stared down at the ring, sliding it quietly onto my finger.

He clasped my hands in his larger ones. "Rodya told me about the university. I think it's wonderful, Echo. I'm so proud of you."

"I haven't heard back from them yet."

"But you will. I know you will."

I hugged him, kissing his cheek as I drew back. "Tell me exactly how much you owe."

MY FATHER BROKE THE NEWS to Donia over supper.

"We'll have to sell the piano, my love."

Her chin quivered. "Must we?"

I clamped my teeth down on my lip to keep from reminding her that she hadn't even touched the thing in weeks.

My father took her hand across the table. "We must," he said firmly. "And we will have to live just a little smaller for a while. Forgive me, my darling. I ought not to have bought more than I could pay for."

Donia sniffed noisily. "You certainly shouldn't have."

"He wasn't the one who—" I began, but my father raised his hand to stop me, which was probably wise.

"The fault is entirely mine," he went on. "But you must try and bear it. It will only be for a year or two."

"A year or two!" Donia shrieked.

"That is nothing for so strong a love as ours," said my father.

I hated that he loved her so much and she thought only of her own comfort.

We sold the piano and one of the couches, too. My father appeased his creditors with the money he received by mortgaging the bookshop, piece by piece. Late in the summer, the shop belonged entirely to the bank and he had to pay rent out of our earnings. At the best of times the shop had never turned an enormous profit, and with a poor harvest the previous year, the villagers hadn't many leftover pennies to spend on books.

We couldn't pay the rent.

On the first day of autumn, my father closed the shop for good. He explained his next plan to me and Rodya and our stepmother that night over supper.

We sat in front of the fire, sipping tea and eating lentil soup flavored with a bit of ham, and Rodya looked more worried than I'd ever seen him. His apprenticeship would be over by the end of the year; he'd be free to open his own shop in another village, unless the clockmaker decided to hire him on. But most likely he'd be leaving us.

"I've decided to take my collection of rare manuscripts and

illuminated maps into the city," my father said. "If I can find the right buyer, our worries will be forestalled a long while."

Donia pursed her lips. "Why didn't you think of this before, Peter dear?"

My father studied her. "Because it is our very last hope. If it fails, my darling, there is nothing left."

Rodya and I spent a few minutes trying to persuade him to let one of us take his place, but he would not be shaken. He promised to post a letter to Donia if he thought his inquiries would take more than three weeks.

We stayed up late into the night, talking together and sipping tea in front of the fire, and for the first time, it felt like the four of us were a true family. I didn't want it to ever end.

But at last Rodya rose and took his leave, and my father and Donia went to bed. I dozed on the floor by the fire, hanging on to the feeling of peace and togetherness.

In the morning, my father came downstairs, laid a blanket over top of me, and kissed my forehead. "I'll see you in three weeks, little lamb."

I fell back asleep and dreamed of the wolf.

BUT MY FATHER DID NOT return in three weeks.

He sent no letter—we had no word from him at all, and by the time a month had expired, Donia was falling to pieces and fear stabbed sharp in my mind.

Another fortnight passed. I went to see Rodya at the clockmaker's, perched on a stool across from his worktable. I watched him repair the workings of a table clock in the rosy glow of his lamp, soldering a new piece of brass onto a broken gear, then filing it down into teeth to replace the missing ones. He blew the shavings from the gear and fitted it into the movement. "The roads have been bad because of the rain, Echo. His letter could have gone astray."

Rodya flicked his gaze to mine, then back down to the clock movement.

Suddenly I heard the worry in his voice.

He lay down the clock and took the loupe from his eye. "If there's still no word from him by the end of the week, I'll send inquiries into the city. But I'm sure he's fine."

There was no word by the end of the week, and Rodya's inquiries came up empty—none of the city booksellers had spoken with or seen my father.

Autumn faded and the first winter snows came, thick and heavy, making the roads impassable. There was nothing for it but to keep our heads down and wait for spring.

Donia took to her bed, complaining constantly of a fluttering heart and immobilizing headaches. I brought her tea and assumed the responsibility of cooking, which meant more and more water in our already-thin soup, and less and less sugar for our tea.

I cleaned the house from bottom to top and then back down again. I organized the shelves in my father's study. One evening, fresh snow swirling white at the windows, I had a bout of generosity and decided to organize Donia's writing desk—it was drowning in paper, envelopes and dried-up bottles of ink. I methodically emptied the drawers and began sorting through everything, deciding what to keep and what ought to be discarded.

I didn't mean to snoop into Donia's personal correspondence. But one of the letters in her drawer fell out onto the carpet, and when I snatched it up I saw the first line by accident.

I read the rest in a blaze of shock and anger.

Dear Mrs. Donia Alkaev,

Suzdal Bank has made the requested deposit on your behalf in the amount of 30,000 roubles, with interest to be paid quarterly into your account. For withdrawal requests or any further assistance regarding the sale of your late husband's property, please write to the address below.

Thank you for choosing Suzdal Bank for your financial requirements.

Yours very sincerely,

Fedor Novak

Enclosed were several lists of figures with cramped notes written next to them. It was dated a month past the wedding.

As far as I could tell, the sale of the bakery had more than canceled Donia's late husband's debts—if he'd had any at all—and she was sitting on a sum of money that staggered me. Why had she not told my father? Why had she let him go off to the city with his precious manuscripts, allowing him to think it was our only hope?

"What exactly do you think you're doing?" came a sudden voice behind me.

I wheeled to see Donia, in all her menacing arctic-bear size, glowering down at me. She was wrapped in a brocade dressing gown, her hair hanging in limp curls on her shoulders. Her eyes were red like she'd been crying, and that made me more angry than anything.

"You *viper*," I spat, jabbing the letter into her face. "You plunged us into debt when you could have paid for everything! Why did you keep it from us? Why did you keep it from *Papa*?"

She glanced at the paper impassively. "What I do with my money is not your concern."

"If you've killed him—" My voice pitched unstable and high. "Donia, if you've killed him I will never forgive you."

"Fortunately for me I give little thought to your forgiveness. His death is not on my hands, nor my conscience."

I crumpled the letter and let it fall to the floor. "Why did you even marry him?"

"I wanted a comfortable life—I knew your father would provide that for me. And there are rewards in heaven, I think, for becoming stepmother to the Devil's child." Danger lurked behind her gaze. "Which reminds me. This came for you today." She pulled an envelope from the pocket of her dressing gown and held it up: it was postmarked from the city, addressed to me, with the seal already broken.

Hope and horror rushed into me. I grabbed for the envelope but Donia snatched it back, crossing the room and holding it over the roaring fire.

"Give me the letter, Donia."

She smirked. "It's only fair that I read your mail since you took it upon yourself to read mine. Would you like to know what it says? Of course you would." She unfolded the letter. "'Dear Miss Alkaev, We would be happy to receive you at the university in the spring, provided you have with you upon your arrival three references from persons of note in your chosen field and the fee—in part or total—for your initial term . . .'"

I shrieked and lunged for the letter, which Donia thrust suddenly into the fire.

She caught my arms to keep me from scrambling after it, and I was forced to watch as the paper crackled and curled and fell away to ash.

"You didn't think I would let you attend the university, did you?" said Donia calmly. "Even if you managed to come up with the fee, they would take one look at your monstrous face and shove you back into the gutter where you belong."

I stared at her, breathless and numb and hot. "The only monster in this place is you."

I turned from my stepmother without another word, stopping only to grab the lamp from the desk, my shoulder bag and furs from their hooks on the wall before stepping out into the frigid night.

CHAPTER FIVE

I TRUDGED INTO THE FOREST, the lamp banging against my knee, snow blowing thick and wet into my face. It was bitterly cold, but across the boundary of the wood the wind blew less sharp. I wandered on, fighting back anger and tears and a blinding sense of helplessness. I couldn't stop seeing the letter from the university devoured by the fire, ashes falling white in the hearth. Donia's words repeated endlessly through my mind: *They would take one look at your monstrous face and shove you back into the gutter where you belong.*

One look at your monstrous face.

One look.

But wasn't she right? Why did I expect the university to be any different from my little village? There was no place for me there, and if my father was truly gone, there was no place for me anywhere. I refused to stay another minute with Donia, and I couldn't burden Rodya. He needed a life of his own, unhindered by me.

I walked without purpose or destination and my thoughts ran in circles, vipers swallowing their tails—there was no end to my despair and self-loathing. The lamp burned steadily through its oil and the snow fell on and on, heavy even through the trees. All was awful and empty and brittle, biting cold.

And then my lamp winked out.

I stopped short, realizing the folly of my actions with sudden clarity. I fought off the burgeoning panic and scrabbled in my shoulder bag, where a packet of matches and a half-burnt candle were wedged beneath a couple of books. I jammed the candle down into the chimney of the lamp and lit it, the glass shielding the flame from both wind and snow. Light flared once more in the wood and I turned back the way I came, but my footprints had already vanished.

I tried to retrace my steps anyway, bending my head down against the wind, but it was snowing so heavily I could barely see past the candle flame. I didn't really know what direction I was headed—I could be wandering in circles, or deeper into the wood.

I kept going, my whole body numb with cold, watching the candle shrink too quick before my eyes. The drifts came up to my knees. I shoved my way through them—as long as I didn't stop moving, there was still hope.

What do you even have to live for? whispered a needling little voice in my mind.

One look at your monstrous face.

I scrubbed angry tears from my eyes and thought about my father and Rodya, about a white wolf watching me through summer trees. I wasn't ready to give up. Not yet.

I pressed on, snow seeping under my collar, ice stinging my eyes. The candle burned down to a stub and guttered out, so I abandoned the lamp in a snowdrift, grabbing the packet of matches and lighting them one by one. I walked on in those brief flares of light, the tiny orange flames burning down to my fingers or hissing out in the wind.

The matches dwindled. I forced myself to wait between striking them, until the clamor of the dark made my head wheel and I knew I couldn't go a step further without another precious spark of light.

And then there was only one match left. I cradled it to my chest, forcing each foot in front of the other. My right hand grazed against a tree trunk, and I sensed space opening out around me—the wind swirled angrily, unhindered by the wood, and the snow fell even thicker. I hesitated a few moments, wondering if by some miracle I had found my way back through the forest, and the cottage stood just out of sight.

My fingers trembled as I lit the last match. Light flared.

I stood in a clearing in the midst of the wood, and a man lay in a crumpled heap in the snow not three paces ahead of me. I recognized his jacket, his pack.

It was my father.

I cried out and moved toward him, as quickly as I could through the drifts. The match burned out but I didn't care, sinking to my knees beside my father, feeling his neck for a pulse and finding it, faint but steady beneath his skin.

"Papa," I breathed, "Oh, Papa I found you." I threw my arms around him, hugging him close.

"You need light," came a sudden voice, gruff and strange. "There is a lantern in his pack."

I jerked my head up. "Who's there?"

"Light the lamp, and you will see."

Bewilderment sparked through me, but I wasn't afraid—my father was *alive*, and my elation at finding him overshadowed everything else. So I obeyed the voice, digging through my father's pack until I found a handful of matches and a lantern heavy with oil. I crouched on my heels, lit the lamp, raised it up.

The white wolf stood among the trees, his fur blending into the snow, his amber eyes huge and bright. He padded toward me and I gripped the lantern tighter, its metal digging cold into my palm.

"We do not have much time," said the wolf, stopping just a pace away.

I screamed and dropped the lamp. Every impulse raged at me to run. *How could the wolf be speaking to me?*

But I couldn't leave my father.

"You will be sorry if you lose the light," the wolf said gruffly.

I snatched the lantern before all the oil could spill out; it shook in my trembling hand, metal rattling, light jouncing. I set it gingerly on level ground. I must have been dreaming—I must have fallen asleep in the wood and was freezing to death, my father and the wolf phantoms invented by my dying mind.

The wolf's breath rose like smoke from his nostrils. "I am not a dream, and neither is your father. But we're running out of time." He came another step nearer.

I grabbed my father's hand, trying not to panic at the bluish tint of his skin. Desperately, I massaged his fingers. "What are you?" I whispered to the wolf. "Why are you here?"

"I have come to ask you something. Something I have not had the memory or the courage to ask you until now."

Too cold, too cold. I put my ear against my father's chest, listening for his heartbeat. I fought back my burgeoning panic.

"You must answer quickly," said the wolf. "I do not think I could get through again, not this way. It is *her* wood. She does not like me to leave it."

I flicked my eyes up to him. I didn't understand what he was saying, and I didn't care—I had to get my father warm. "What do you want from me?"

"A promise."

"To do what?"

"To come back through the wood to my house. To live with me there for a year."

My voice shook: "Why would I do that?"

"Because if you do, I will save your father's life and send him safely home. He's been trapped in the wood for weeks, maybe months. I found him, led him out. If not for me he would already be dead, or worse—he would be at her mercy."

My head was wheeling. *I had to get him warm.* "I don't understand."

"The power to save him is in your grasp," said the wolf. "Choose. Come with me now—or let your father die."

The bluish tint to my father's skin looked darker than before, and his pulse grew erratic under my fingertips. Something twisted hot and sharp beneath my ribs—there was only one choice I could make.

"I'll find my way back to you, Papa." I bent to kiss his forehead. "I'll find my way back."

I forced myself to stand, forced myself to look the wolf in the eye. "I promise to come with you. Now save him."

The wolf dipped his head. "Follow me." He paced to the edge of the clearing. I tore myself away from my father and went after him.

"You said you'd save him!" I looked back to the halo of

lamplight where my father lay crumpled in the snow, his life ebbing away. Horror and hope woke wild inside of me, along with a strange unwavering conviction I didn't understand. Snow fell wet and cold against my cheek, evaporating in the heat of my tears.

The wolf stepped in front of me. He raised his white muzzle to the sky and barked a sharp, harsh word I didn't recognize.

The wind rose wild, tearing at my furs and my hair, spitting ice into my face sharp as glass. And through the howling wind, came the sounds of a jangling harness, barking dogs, a man singing in the snow. I knew that voice—it belonged to old man Tinker.

My heart jerked.

The wolf glanced back at me. "Get out of sight."

I ducked behind the trees and held my breath.

Tinker's sled drew close, barreling between the trees. The dogs yapped and a lantern bobbed from a pole. He pulled up next to my father in a spray of white and climbed down, assessing the situation with a single shrewd glance. He hefted my father onto the sled and piled furs on top of him. Then he uncorked a bottle of what could only be brandy and tipped a few swallows down my father's throat.

Tinker stepped onto the sled again and called to his dogs and then they were all of them gone, hurtling away into the snowy dark.

I ran into the clearing, shouting after them, but they didn't hear.

And the wolf was at my knee.

"I have kept my promise, my lady. Now you must keep yours. We must go quickly—she senses already that you are here. We will have to run. Can you?"

Another gust of wind tore through the clearing, knocking me backward. The trees began to groan and wail, and I thought they must be dying, breaking in pieces, splintering inward.

"Run!" barked the wolf above the roar. "Don't lose sight of me!"

He sprang away into the darkness and somehow I leapt after him, my lungs already screaming out for air.

I ran, the wood and the wind and the dark wheeling round me, my eyes fixed on the white flash of the wolf. He was ever ahead, just out of reach. There was nothing but gnawing, bitter cold, the burn of my lungs, the bursting of my heart. Somehow, the snow didn't hinder me.

I ran, away from the grasping fingers of the bony trees, away from the cruel wind that sought to snatch me up and shatter me against the stars.

I ran for a lifetime, and another after that, while the centuries spun away and time slipped into eternity. I became part of the wood, and the wood part of me.

But still I ran after the wolf, the trees shrieking, the wind coiling around me, ice biting deep into my soul. Exhaustion dragged me down. In another moment I would stumble, and fall, and be devoured.

I cried out, lunging for the blur of white in front of me. My fingers grasped the scruff of his fur, my arms locked tight around his neck. And then he was carrying me, barreling on into the horrible dark. I screwed my eyes shut, sobbing for breath. The wolf wasn't fast enough. The wind would catch us, the trees would tear us apart. We would be forever lost.

But then—

Chattering birds, rustling leaves, the smell of rich earth and green growing things.

Warm fur, pressed up against my cheek.

I opened my eyes. My arms and legs were wrapped around the wolf, my fingers tangled in the scruff of his neck. Fear tore through me and I let go, tumbling from his back onto a soft carpet of wildflowers. I scrambled to my feet.

The wolf looked at me impassively. We stood in a quiet meadow, tall grasses waving among the flowers, bees buzzing in lazy air currents. The wood lay leafy and ordinary behind us, not even a hint of snow in sight. Ahead rose a lone hill, sharp and brown against the sky. It was midmorning, or a little past.

"Where are we?" I whispered, my voice hoarse and my lungs aching. The enormity of what I had done threatened to overwhelm me. All I could see was my father, hurtling away on Tinker's cart.

"The house under the mountain," returned the wolf. "*My* house."

And he stepped toward the hill.

CHAPTER SIX

T HE RUN THROUGH THE FOREST HAD sapped all my strength—I was wholly drained and hollowed out from leaving my father. His absence tore at me. Half of me was on the sled with him, rattling through the winter wood. The other half was struggling to comprehend the promise I'd made to the wolf—was struggling to comprehend the wolf at all. My head spun. How could any of it be real? Talking wolves and angry forests. *Magic*. It wasn't possible.

And yet there I was. There *he* was, watching me with those amber eyes.

The warmth of my fur cloak was suddenly stifling. I shrugged out of it and draped it over my arm, overwhelmed by the birdsong and wildflowers and spicy tang in the air. It couldn't possibly be springtime, and yet it was certainly no longer winter. I wrapped one hand around Rodya's compass-watch and found, to my surprise, that it was ticking steadily—it hadn't worked once since he'd given it to me.

"How long were we in the wood?" I asked the wolf.

"A week or two," he answered, not looking back as he went on toward the hill. It loomed large enough to block out the sun.

I went after him. "But how can that be?"

"The wood works according to her will, and no other."

"What does that mean? Who is 'she'? Who are *you*?"

He didn't reply, just paced through a screen of knotted trees and vines growing out of the base of the hill. I followed, ducking underneath a low-hanging branch; long leafy tendrils brushed cool and sticky past my face. Beyond lay a dank hollow that smelled of decay and worms. The sunlight seemed very far away.

I could hardly breathe. "Where are you taking me?"

"Come," said the wolf, somewhere ahead.

There wasn't room. There *couldn't* be room, but I stepped away from the vines and into solid darkness.

A great booming voice echoed around me, howling in a language I didn't know, and a frigid current of wind grasped my shoulders, snarling my hair. I screamed and tried to fight it off, but the wind wrapped around me like coils of a snake, seeping under my skin, sewing ice into my bones.

And then the wolf was beside me, pressed up warm against my knee. "Another moment and we'll be through."

We walked together, wind and blackness clawing all around, and passed into what felt like a cool, echoing hall. The howling stopped and the wind seemed to vanish. A door shut behind us, a key turned in a lock (who or what turned it? Not the wolf, surely) and then a lamp flared, banishing the dark.

We stood in a long, low corridor, with stairs at one end and a wooden door at our backs. The lamp was set high on the wall, where the wolf couldn't have reached it even if he did have hands, which pointed to something—or someone—being with us back there in the dark. I shuddered.

I stared at the wolf, noticing as if for the first time the enormity of him, the power in his white frame, barely contained. The danger. There were nicks in his ears, ropy scars on his back left leg, and places on his flanks where his fur didn't lay smooth, evidence of more scars I couldn't see. His power of speech made him seem almost human, but he wasn't human at all. He'd manipulated me with my father's life hanging in the balance—I wasn't about to forget that.

The wolf glanced back, amber eyes and bone-white teeth flashing in the lamplight. "Welcome to the house under the mountain, my lady." And then started up the stairs.

For all my tangled fear and anger, I had no desire to be left with whatever lurked behind that door, so I followed him.

His nails clicked on the stone steps, my felted boots whispering behind. I focused on the white flag of his tail, trying not to feel as though I was marching to my death. "What was that back there, outside the door?"

"The gatekeeper—the North Wind, or what's left of him."

"The North Wind? What does that *mean*? *Who are you?*"

He looked back briefly, but kept climbing until he passed out of sight.

I stood gaping for a moment, then yelped and leapt up the stairs after him. I caught up just as he came to another door, which swung open by itself and closed quietly behind us.

Beyond was a grand hall that might once have been a ballroom. It had high paneled ceilings, formerly elegant wainscoting, and intricately patterned wallpaper that was faded and torn.

The wolf walked faster and I matched his pace, wooden floors creaking beneath our feet. "I abandoned my father to come with you. Why won't you answer me?"

His words were clipped and cold: "Not here."

A yellow gown lay puddled in the corner, ribbons ragged, one worn shoe discarded beside it. I thought I heard whispers, rustling gowns, tinkling laughter.

But then we stepped into another corridor, and silence closed around us.

The wolf drew a breath and flicked his eyes up at me. "I do not like that room."

"Why?"

"It reminds me of something I lost."

On we went, down more halls, around corners, up stairs. We passed countless doors, some plain, some carved, some wavering impossibly, like they were made of liquid glass. Lamps flared to life just ahead of us, casting eerie shadows over the floor.

"Wolf. Please—tell me who you are. Tell me why you brought me here."

He sighed, as though he was weighed down with an impossible burden he could no longer carry. "I am the keeper of this house—I am bound to it, and it to me. I am old, my lady. I am dying. At the end of the year I will fade, and if the house does not have a new master by then, it will fade with me."

Whatever I expected him to say, it wasn't that. "You brought me here to . . . take your place?"

"If you choose the house. And if the house chooses you."

"But I have to get back to my father—my family!"

"And so you can at the end of the year, my lady, if you so choose."

"Will you give me a choice?"

"There is always a choice."

"You didn't give me a choice tonight—I couldn't let my father die."

The wolf shook his white head. "Tinker would have come, whether you made your promise or not. He was never in any danger."

And then he stopped in front of a red door, carved beautifully with lions and birds and trees. "Your room, my lady, for the duration of your stay. Dinner will be ready as soon as you are settled."

"But—"

He was already gone, the tuft of his tail showing around the corner, leaving me to reel with the knowledge I had abandoned my father and sacrificed a year of my life for absolutely nothing.

I HAD NO INTEREST IN investigating the room behind the red door. I paced the corridor after the wolf instead, but he was nowhere to be seen. Frustration twisted through me. The wolf had tricked me, and for what? To trap me in this strange and terrifying house? I could have been home with my father. I could have been *safe*.

But I blinked and saw my university acceptance letter crumbling to ash. If it weren't for my father, would I even want to go home?

Down the hall to the left, lamps flared suddenly to life, stretching out of my sight line. I walked that way, hoping they would lead me to the wolf.

I passed countless doors and wandered up seemingly infinite hallways and staircases. Icy currents of air whispered past my neck. Laughter and music echoed faintly from behind some of the doors, while from others came the scent of wine and honey and autumn flowers, or the winter tang of a crisp starry night after a snowfall. The whole house seemed to brim with memory and sorrow, with lost dreams and forgotten joy. I ached with a sadness that wasn't my own.

Magic teemed around me—I didn't know how to process it all. Part of me still wondered if I was freezing to death and delusional in the wood, but it was all too *real*. I paced through a white marble hallway and brushed my fingers along a vein of gold running through the walls; it pulsed warm, humming with life. Donia would hate this place. My father would be awed. Rodya would try to make sense of it all, reduce it to cogs and gears. I could do little more than try and accept it, shifting my understanding of the universe to include something that, in this house, was as natural as breathing.

And then I found myself opening a tall door and stepping into a high-ceilinged chamber hung with glistening chandeliers and furnished only with a long table, draped in a linen cloth. The wolf was perched awkwardly on a chair at one end of it.

"My lady," he said with a regal dip of his white head. "Come. Eat."

A second chair was pulled up to the right of the wolf's. I caught the aroma of braised meat, and realized how hungry I was, my stomach growling. I went and sat down. The table overflowed with food: platters of venison and bowls of fruit, soup tureens and a mountain of sugary square cakes layered with jam. An elegant place setting lay before me: a china plate intricately painted with blue and red birds, silverware wrought to look like tree branches on a lace napkin, and a crystal-studded glass of shimmering pink liquid.

I cast an eye at the wolf. There was no place laid out for him. "Is the food poisoned?"

"Poisoned? Certainly not. I have not the table manners to entertain a lady of your worth—I had my dinner elsewhere."

I noticed suddenly that his back and tail and ears were flecked with blood. I shifted uneasily.

He dipped his muzzle at the waiting feast. "You are hungry. Eat."

Tentatively, I obeyed him, my hunger outweighing my suspicion. I sampled little bits of everything: the meat was tender, the fruit summer-sweet, the soup hot and rich with flavor. The glass of pink liquid tasted lightly of honey and berries, and fizzed pleasingly on my tongue.

The wolf watched me eat. His stare was disconcerting—he rarely blinked—and I couldn't stop looking at the blood in his fur. I laid my fork down before I was quite full. From some distant room came the sound of a woman's bright laugh, but the next moment it was gone.

I thought of the long, long way from my bedroom to the dining hall, the infinite doors, the horror of the gatekeeper. The blood in the wolf's fur. "Is the house . . . safe?" That wasn't quite my whole question.

"It is like any wild thing that has been tamed, my lady. It is sometimes safe, and sometimes not. But that isn't the point."

"What is the point?"

"To remember that it is wild, and to be on your guard."

I knew he was referring to more than the house, just as I had been. "Was that you in the wood, last spring? Why didn't you speak to me then?"

He shifted in his chair, his fur brushing against the table-cloth and leaving little flecks of red on the linen. "There are times when I have been too long away from this house. I forget reason and speech. I become truly . . . wild. But when I saw you I remembered, a little. Enough to return to the house, where I remembered everything."

"What did you remember?"

"That I needed you, my lady."

His amber gaze pierced through me, and I found I could no longer meet it. Silence slipped between us. The flames in the candelabras danced; the light hurt my eyes. I felt like I was falling.

"My lady, you're crying."

I touched the scars on the left side of my face and my fingers came away damp. "I miss my father. You took me away from him." But that wasn't why I was crying. I didn't know why.

One last shrewd glance and he leapt down from his chair, stumbling a bit. "Come, my lady. The night grows short, and the house becomes . . . less tame the nearer we get to midnight."

He paced toward the door, limping.

I wiped my eyes and followed, the sounds of shattering crystal and frenetic laughter clamoring in my ears. "What happens at midnight?"

"The magic ceases to function, and the house is unbound." He nudged the door open with his nose. "You had better hold on to me, my lady. To be safe."

Tentatively, I wound my right hand in the scruff of his neck, and we went out into the corridor together.

It was almost wholly dark, a single lantern flickering partway down the hall. Somewhere in the distance there came a high, keening wail.

"Stay close," said the wolf. "Nothing can harm you."

He was warm against my knee, a stark contrast to the frigid air around us. I couldn't help but wonder: When the house was unbound at midnight, would the wolf also become wholly wild? I took a deep breath and tried not to think about the blood in his fur.

The darkness narrowed in as we walked. It seemed to stare at us, it seemed to *listen*. The floor creaked beneath our feet. Somewhere close by, doors sighed opened and snicked shut again. Keys rattled, voices laughed. Bells jangled loudly and chains dragged over stone. I caught the scent of a winter forest, damp wood and cold so sharp it burned.

And always the wolf, solid and strong beside me, padding quietly and confidently on. "What is your name?" he asked after awhile.

I fixed my eyes on the single lamp burning ahead of us that we never seemed to reach. "Echo. For the echo of my mother's heartbeat."

We climbed a set of stairs, turned a corner. Someone sobbed in the dark.

"I heard a story once, about a girl with that name."

My breath caught hard in my throat. "How did her story end?"

"I do not remember."

"What is your name?" I asked.

"I do not have a name."

"Then what am I to call you?"

"Whatever you like."

We passed a row of doors that smelled of smoke, and a little ways beyond another row that smelled of rain. Currents of light began to swirl in the air, like colorful fireflies with long tails. I reached out to touch one. It was warm, and soft as a willow. "What are they?"

"The lamps. They are the last things to become unbound. Hurry."

He quickened his pace and I nearly had to run to keep up with him. Something spiny wound around my ankle and I yelped, falling against the wolf.

But then I looked up and saw the carved red door, the very normal lantern on the wall beside it glowing steadily.

"Just in time," said the wolf, and he stepped inside.

I scrambled to my feet and followed.

CHAPTER SEVEN

THE ROOM BEYOND THE RED DOOR was comfortingly ordinary. It boasted a grand four-poster bed rather too big for it, a dressing table, and a tall wardrobe. A small circular window was set high on the back wall—the first window I'd seen, I realized, since entering the wolf's house.

The wolf eyed me strangely, tension in his frame that hadn't been there a moment before. "My lady, there is a . . . stipulation . . . to your stay here."

Ice flooded my veins, and once more I grabbed the compass-watch, taking comfort in its constant ticking. "What stipulation?"

He paced in front of the door, immense power evident in his

huge frame, the specks of blood on his fur darkened and dried. I was safe from the house in here, but was I safe from him?

He stared at me, and I was transfixed by him, neither willing nor able to look away. "You must allow me to stay in this room with you every night," he said. "And—and there is something you must swear you will never do."

I could barely breathe, my heart overloud in my ears. "What is that, Lord Wolf?"

For some reason, he flinched at the address. His voice dropped into an even lower growl. "You must swear that you will never light a lamp and look at me during the night. Not once. Not ever. And if you do not agree to this—" His eyes narrowed to slits. "If you do not agree, I will even now thrust you from the room and leave you to the mercy of the house, and the wood. Will you swear?"

The wolf loomed large in my sight line. I wouldn't last half a moment outside of that door, and he must have known that. But how cruel to offer me a choice when I really had no choice at all.

"My lady." His voice was softer somehow. "I will not harm you. You are safe with me. I hope you know that."

I didn't know that—and I had the scars to prove it—but I also didn't have the luxury to deny him. Slowly, I dropped to my knees so I could look the wolf in the eye. I bowed my head to him as if he were a king. "I swear, Lord Wolf, that I will never light a lamp and look at you in the night."

He dipped his white muzzle. "Thank you, my lady." He broke

my gaze and loped away from me. "I shall turn my back while you dress for bed. Then you may blow out the light."

As if it were the most ordinary thing in the world. As if my promise was a matter of course. For a moment more I stayed on my knees, anger threatening to swallow me, and then I got up and began fumbling with the ties of my blouse. I had no nightgown, and so I stripped off my boots and skirt and blouse as quickly as I could and crawled into the huge bed in nothing but my shift.

"Are you dressed?" asked the wolf.

I drew the bedclothes up to my chin, the anger dissolved into misery. "Yes."

He came around to the other side of the bed and curled up on the floor in front of the wardrobe, one eye open, staring up at me. "You will not forget your promise?"

Our earlier conversation echoed in my mind:

"What happens at midnight?"

"The magic ceases to function, and the house is unbound."

Did that mean he would become unbound, too? What would happen when I blew out the lamp—what would happen if I lit it again?

"I will not forget." I blew out the light before I lost my nerve.

Darkness flooded the bedchamber. I lay there with my eyes wide open, acutely conscious of the wolf on the floor; I was blind in the dark, but I could hear him breathing, the rustling scrape of fur against carpet as he adjusted his position.

"It is like any wild thing that has been tamed. It is sometimes safe, and sometimes not."

My scars twinged with remembered pain, and I shifted uneasily. What was to keep the wolf from leaping into the bed and devouring me in the dark?

"Remember that it is wild, and be on your guard."

Or perhaps it was the darkness itself keeping the wolf at bay, some lingering remnants of magic that kept him tame in the night, but only if he stayed in this room, and only if the lamp remained unlit.

Down below me, his breathing evened out: He was asleep.

But sleep didn't come as easily for me. I couldn't stop thinking about my father, about the hatred in Donia's eyes, and my university letter crumbling to ash. About that moment in the wood when the wolf first spoke to me. Everything that had happened afterward was impossible—maybe I really *was* freezing to death in a snowbank.

And yet the pillow was smooth against my cheek, the quilt soft and warm. The sound of the slumbering wolf somehow comforting.

Was my father all right? Had he made it home?

Part of me ached for him, but I wept into my pillow, hating myself, because the other part of me—the largest part of me—wasn't even really sorry. I'd left him, but I'd left Donia and the villagers and the stifling constraints of my old life, too. It gave me a strange sense of freedom.

Somehow, I fell asleep.

I JERKED AWAKE IN THE dark, skin drenched in sweat. Something was pounding on the bedroom door, trying to get in. No, something was *roaring* outside the door. Heat radiated toward me. Instinctively, I reached for the lamp, then remembered what I'd sworn and yanked my hand back.

"Wolf," I stammered, straining to see him down below the bed in the blackness. "WOLF!"

He drew a sharp, gasping breath. "Echo?" His voice was strange and slurred with sleep.

"Something's out there."

There came a *thud* on the door, the sound of a rushing wind and high eerie laughter. The whole room seemed to shake.

"Wolf?"

"It is all right, Echo. Nothing can harm us in here." What I'd thought was the strangeness of sleep I realized was an accent, a weird emphasis on his i's and a's.

Harsh, insistent knocking sounded on the door, growing louder and louder, mixed with the roar of some unknown beast.

"Do nothing," said the wolf. "Do nothing. It shall pass."

I shuddered and shuddered, sitting straight against the headboard and drawing the covers up to my chin. The compass-watch ticked steadily underneath my shift—I hadn't taken it off.

Laughter echoed in the hallway, whispers in an unfamiliar language. Fear crawled through me. I wished it wasn't so dark, and my mind jerked once more to the lamp on the end table.

"It will get in," I whispered. "It will destroy us."

"We are protected. As long as we don't open the door. As long as—as long as you don't light the lamp. She is . . . she is tempting you. She is testing your strength."

"*Who* is?"

"The force in the wood. The force . . . binding the house."

The room trembled as something hit the door with an earth-shattering *bang*, like it had been rammed with a tree trunk.

"You must get your mind off of it. The fire cannot harm you. *She* cannot harm you."

I twisted my fingers together, tangling them in the blankets.

Another *bang* at the door. The wood creaked and splintered. A deafening *crack*, heat pulsing on my skin. I was shaking so hard I thought I would burst apart.

"Tell me about your father," said the wolf.

"What?"

CRAAAACCKKKKK.

"Your father!" He had to shout above a sudden roaring wind. "Tell me about him."

I dug my fingers into the mattress. "He's good and kind.

Even to me. Especially to me."

"Why wouldn't he be kind to you?"

"Because of what I am!"

"And what are you?"

"I'M A MONSTER!"

"You are no monster!"

The wind shrieked and screamed and twisted around us. I gripped the bed frame, shuddering.

"Tell me more about your father!"

I grasped for words behind my fear. "He loves my stepmother, but I don't know why. He never—he never laughed at me. He never signed the cross to ward off my Devil's face."

"Your face was not carved by the Devil." The wind died all at once, the roaring shrank away, and the wolf's next words echoed overloud in the sudden silence: "IT WAS CARVED BY ME!"

The room stretched between us. The heat seeped away, as if conducting a strange slithering retreat back under the door.

"Then it *was* you, that day with the trap."

"Yes."

"Why were you there?"

"I was watching you."

"Why?"

"I have always been drawn to you, Echo Alkaev. Even when I couldn't remember why."

It wasn't a proper answer, and yet his words pulsed strangely in my heart, like their meaning lay just beyond my grasp. If he hadn't been there that day, my face would be soft and smooth. The village would have accepted me. Donia wouldn't despise me. I would have a future. But somehow, somehow, I didn't hate him for it.

I chewed on my lip, slipping back down into the bed and laying my head on the pillow. "Is it over?"

"I do not know. But I will guard the door till the morning. Nothing will harm you."

And I believed him.

I fell into twisted dreams, trapped in a winter wood, the wolf running one way, my father in Tinker's sled hurtling the other. Everything was burning, and blood poured fresh from the scars on my face. Donia's eyes gleamed in the dark, and she laughed as she shoved me into the fire. *"It is all a monster like you deserves,"* she cackled. *"The Devil made you, and the Devil can take you back again."*

I wept in the snow and crumbled to ash, for I was only pages in a book, burned and lost and gone forever.

When I woke it was morning, gray light flooding through the window.

The wolf was gone.

CHAPTER EIGHT

W OLF?"

I stepped from the safety of the bedchamber, but
the hallway was empty. It stretched ordinarily, innocuously,
to the left and right, the lamp flickering steadfastly from the
wall. There was no hint of last night's fire, of anything magical
whatsoever.

"Wolf?"

Fear weighed me down like sodden clothes in a river. He'd
said he would guard the door—how long had he been gone? How
long had he left me to the mercy of the house?

"Wolf!"

I ran, left toward the dining room, down carved ivory stairs and up narrow, creaky ones, round corners and through passageways I swore I'd never seen before. I passed door after door shimmering in bright shades of blue or green or violet. One door seemed to be made of grass; another, flowers. I ran past fiery doors and snowy doors, through a corridor of rain, down a spiral staircase that chimed a different bell-like note with every step. *"Wolf!"*

But I couldn't find him.

I collapsed, gasping for breath, against a gem-studded wall. Emeralds dug into my back and a whispering breeze tangled warm around my ankles. Somewhere in the distance a woman laughed, and a sighing harp filled the spaces between. I was lost in a labyrinth, searching for the monster at the end of the maze.

And then I looked up and saw a black door at the end of a dim, narrow corridor. I'd had no desire to open any of the other doors, but this one beckoned me. It was smooth, and hard as obsidian.

It opened soundlessly at my touch. I stepped into an inky black chamber that seemed to stretch forever into darkness, baubles of multicolored crystal in all shapes and sizes hanging from some unseen ceiling. There were birds and bears, abstract coils, globes that pulsed with light—it was like a field of curious stars suspended in the moment of their falling.

The baubles brushed my shoulders as I passed through, some warm and some icy cold, some so sharp they sliced through my blouse and left hot lines of pain in my skin.

I reached the back of the room where I wasn't even expecting there to be a back and found a tall, whirring object that had a glass face and a thousand spindly spider arms grinding and clicking. I recognized the object, for all its strange otherworldliness, as a clock. The glass face held something inside of it, and peering closer I saw it was a lock of pale hair, tied with ribbon, and a dark smear of dried liquid that could only be blood.

Horror crawled down my spine, and I turned to find the wolf at my back, his fur standing on end, fresh crimson spots marring the white.

A growl tore from his throat. He lunged at me.

I yelped and scrabbled sideways, grabbing one of the swinging crystals to keep from falling. But it was knife-sharp and I let it go, gasping. Blood seeped from both palms.

"Get out," snarled the wolf. "GET OUT!"

He lunged again and I leapt past him, ducking under the baubles, stumbling in my haste. The crystals tangled in my hair and I had to claw myself free.

And then I was back out in the corridor with the wolf hard on my heels, the black door slamming behind us.

I cringed away from him but he just stood there, sides heaving, ears pinned back against his head. "You must not go there," he spat. "Swear you will never go back. *Swear it.*"

I trembled, but faced him. "What *is* this place?"

"Swear it!"

Beyond the black door came a faint tinkling music; my shoulders and hands pulsed with pain.

I stared at him, at the blood in his fur, the flash of his teeth, the coiled tension in his body.

"SWEAR IT!"

But I'd had enough of making promises I didn't understand. I turned and fled.

I RAN BACK DOWN THE corridor, my heels pounding into the floor. The gem-studded wall had vanished, and I bolted instead into a tunnel of twisted branches and leaves, spongy moss beneath my feet, swirling red and gold as if it were patterned carpet.

The wolf came hard behind me, anything he might have been shouting lost in his guttural barks and my thundering heart.

"Somewhere safe," I pleaded as I barreled out into a glass passageway, veins of blue and silver liquid tracing intricate patterns under the transparent floor. "Somewhere safe."

I half fell down a nearly invisible glass staircase and into a blue wood door inlaid with bits of colored glass. It swung soundlessly inward and snicked shut again when I'd tumbled through. Three heartbeats, ten, thirty.

The door stayed closed, and the wolf didn't follow. I scrambled to my feet and took a steadying breath—had the house somehow answered my plea for sanctuary? A sense of calm settled over me.

I stood in a huge, airy room. High paneled ceilings stretched twenty feet or more above my head, illuminated by a dozen sparkling chandeliers. Several elegant couches were arranged in the center of the chamber on a blue-and-gold carpet emblazoned with birds. Set into the back wall was a second blue door.

It might have been a drawing room in some grand house, except for the dozens and dozens of mirrors that obscured every inch of the walls. Some were rectangular, some oval, some oblong, most of them as tall as me. They refracted the light from the chandeliers, making it hard to look directly at them, and giving the whole place a glistening, dizzying quality. Silence reigned so complete my ears rang with it.

I had no desire to leave the serenity of the room and face the wolf—or the house—so I moved left away from the door, brushing my fingers along the mirrors as I passed. All of the frames were made, unusually, of leather, some soft and supple, some old and cracked. I couldn't place why they seemed familiar until I noticed that every mirror had a little gold description plate, many at the top, a few at the bottom or tilted sideways along either edge. Book spines—they reminded me of book spines.

I peered at a few of the description plates, which said things like: *The Monster of Montahue: In Which a Prince Slays a Beast Only to Find it Within Him* and *The Doorway to All Things: In Which a Magical Hat Causes Much Havoc* and *The Soldier's Gift: In Which Heaven Fights for the Emperor, a Firsthand Account.*

Were these mirrors books? Had I stumbled into a library? Wild house and unpredictable wolf aside, I didn't care *where* I'd promised to stay for a whole year, as long as there was something to read.

Beyond the blue door at the back of the hall was an even bigger chamber. This one was lined with a maze of ebony shelves stretching out of my sight line, all chock-full of mirror-books, hundreds upon hundreds, maybe even thousands of them.

I stared, my mouth hanging open, and retreated into the first room, overwhelmed.

How did one read a mirror-book? It seemed foolish not to try—if I left the library I might never be able to find it again in the seemingly infinite, ever-changing house. And I still didn't want to face the wolf. The library was a welcome distraction.

I selected a mirror at random and stepped up to it. The nameplate read: *The Hidden Wood: In Which a Princess Confronts the Queen of Fairies.*

I thought perhaps the story would parade magically in front of my eyes as I watched, but nothing happened. My reflection stared back at me, my scars stark in the light from the chandeliers. I wished I could scrub them away, leave them like so much dirt in the bottom of my washbasin. My jaw hardened, and I stretched my hand out to touch the mirror.

The glass—if it was glass—wavered, rippling out like water in a pond, and a sensation of coolness washed through me.

The next instant I was standing at the edge of a tangled, overgrown wood, briars curling up tree trunks and cutting into rough bark. Horrid black blossoms peered at me from between the thorns, and they reeked of death. A cold wind soughed through the trees; a bird with black wings squawked overhead.

A pale-haired girl came along the forest path, a basket mounded with mushrooms swinging from her arm. The bird flew down and settled on her shoulder. She ran one finger along its glossy head, singing a note that the bird echoed back to her. She laughed and fed it a mushroom.

The girl passed out of sight among the trees, and without even thinking about it, I stepped into the wood and followed her.

The forest enveloped me, the scent of moss and sap and a hint of those horrible black flowers cloying and sticky in the air. Leaves crunched under my feet. The wind coiled icy around my neck.

The girl walked quickly—I nearly had to run to keep up with her. She followed a deer path through the wood, singing and feeding the bird mushrooms as she went. After a while she came into a clearing, where a little stone cottage nestled among the trees, wind flapping cheerily through bright, flowered curtains. To the side of the house a garden marched in neat green rows; a hedgehog sat in the midst of it, munching noisily through the lettuce.

I blinked, and was suddenly inside the cottage, watching the girl make tea and sit down to drink it at a tiny, narrow table. The bird never left her shoulder, and I thought its eyes flashed green, though I couldn't be sure.

"Where . . . am I?" I asked carefully, not wanting to startle the girl but needing answers.

She smiled at me, not startled in the least. "The House in the Midst of the Wood, of course. My mother left it to me, after she died." A shadow of sadness crossed her face. "I'm a Guardian, just as she was."

I squeezed into a tiny chair across from her. "What do you guard?"

"The wood. It was made as a prison for the queen, you know, but she's powerful. She can find cracks. I can't let her loose—she would devour the world." The girl ran her finger around the rim of her mug and offered the bird a handful of cake crumbs. "So I tend the forest. I cut down the blossoms that grow from her poison, and care for her creatures who managed to escape. And I plan how I might defeat her, when the wood can no longer keep her at bay."

"And how—how do you plan to defeat her?"

The girl's eyes caught mine, a fathomless sea-green. She shook her head, sorrow weighing heavy on her thin shoulders. "The only thing that can stand against her is the old magic, and it's all gone. I gather what ragged bits of it I can—the wood sheds it, here and there. But the weavers of old magic left this world long ago. They imprisoned her here. They didn't think she could ever get free."

The bird squawked and flapped suddenly to the window. The girl flung her head up. "She's here. She's coming."

"But—"

And then the world changed around me. I stood with the girl in an ink-black forest, the wind whipping her hair about her shoulders. She held a torch in front of her, outstretched like a sword, and a tall spiny creature that looked like the black-flowered briar come to life shrank back from the light, hissing through thorny teeth.

"A sentinel!" cried the girl. "A vanguard! The queen is coming. We stand against her *now*."

The bird flapped its wings and grew in front of my eyes, until it stood as tall as a man. It wrapped one wing around the girl like armor, and its feathers glinted iron silver in the torchlight.

But then the spiny creature plunged its arms into the earth, and a hundred creatures in its exact image sprang up to stand beside it. They dripped black petals onto the ground like blood. I choked at the stench.

The girl hurled the torch into the air and somehow it ignited, sending a wall of flame toward the thorny creatures. She dropped to her knees while the enormous bird stood guard, his iron wings shielding her. From her pocket she drew a spool of shimmering thread, which she began to unwind. Using only her hands and one of the bird's metal feathers, she wove a glittering net that grew and grew and grew, until it was large enough to encompass the queen's army. The spool ran empty of thread, and the girl stood to her feet with a great cry. She cast the net at the creatures.

But it wasn't enough. The thorny army broke the threads, shredding the net. They surrounded the girl and the bird, they tore the bird's wings from its shoulders, and wrapped the girl in briars. The bird stood stiff as any soldier, blood dripping down its iron feathers, but the girl wept. The thorny creatures dragged her away in briar chains.

I blinked and saw the girl, bowed and bleeding before the Queen of Fairies. The queen was tall, and formed of the same stuff as her army: her limbs were thorns, her gown black flower petals, her hair decaying leaves. Her eyes glittered red-orange, embers of fire in her brambly face. "You thought to defeat me!" she mocked the girl. "And see what has become of you—you will *die*, and the world will be mine, and all you've done and fought and lived for will be for *nothing*."

The girl wept in the dirt, clutching one last iron feather as if it were a knife.

But the queen saw, and plucked it out of her hands. "Your precious bird cannot help you now." And she plunged the feather into the girl's heart.

I gasped as the girl's eyes grew wide with shock and pain and she collapsed on the ground. Blood spread crimson beneath her body.

The queen threw the feather down and strode past the girl with obvious disgust, whistling for her army.

I couldn't stop shaking—whatever this was, however I had come here, if this were a story, I didn't want to read it anymore.

But I didn't know how to break free. I ran away from the girl into the wood, leaves slapping moldy and wet against my face. The forest lightened slowly to the silver hue of dawn, and I stumbled at last into the clearing where the girl's cottage stood. The hedgehog was curled up tight and sleeping amongst the radishes.

I collapsed on the front stoop, hugging my knees to my chest as tears leaked down my face. The girl was dead, the queen had won, and I was trapped here more completely than I had been in the wolf's horrible house.

"Are you all right?" came a sudden voice just above me.

I jerked my head up to see a young woman standing by the garden, the hedgehog cradled in her hands. *Beautiful* didn't begin to describe her. She was luminous—willowy and tall, with straight silver hair that hung nearly to her knees and an enormous pair of eyes the color of summer violets. She wore a diaphanous blue gown, and her feet were bare. I got the feeling she didn't belong here any more than I did.

"Are you all right?" she repeated.

I nodded dully, at a loss for words, and she let the hedgehog loose in the garden again and came to sit beside me. "I haven't seen you in the books before—is this your first one? I'm Mokosh."

Her words took a moment to sink in. "What do you mean?"

She shrugged, her lips quirking. "Not many people have

access to book-mirrors—there used to be scores of readers like us, but there are hardly any left. I've only met one or two others my whole life, and I read a *lot*. Where is your library? Mine's in my mother's palace. You must be a princess, too—or at least a duchess?"

I blinked at her loquaciousness. "I'm not—I'm not anyone important."

"Of course you are. Ordinary people don't have access to magical libraries."

I didn't know what to say to that.

She leapt to her feet and pulled me up as well. "You do know the rules, don't you?"

"What rules?"

"There are rules for reading ordinary books, aren't there? Start at the beginning, read in order, no skipping around, and *certainly* don't read the last page until you get there."

"Well, yes."

She wrapped her arm around my shoulder and propelled me away from the cottage, down a winding path that cut quickly through the wood and spilled out onto the cobbled streets of a tiny village.

"It's the same thing in the book-mirrors," Mokosh explained. "You can't change the course of events—the story *always* follows its intended path, and it's impossible for readers like you and me to die here, so you don't have to worry about battle scenes or the plague."

"The *plague?*"

"But *you* don't have to follow the story—you can explore the world around it, instead. Just walk away from the main character— as you must have, or we wouldn't have met—and you're free to do as you please. There are limits, of course—you can't go anywhere the author never imagined, but if the book is even somewhat well written, there are layers of places to visit barely touched upon in the story." She gestured at the street in front of us. "For example, this place has an excellent pub. Come on."

And then she was tugging me forward again, past the village square, where a fountain shaped like the iron-winged bird spilled water into a stone basin. Thorns coiled up between the cracks in the stone.

"Oh, don't worry about that," said Mokosh, noticing my terrified stare, "The story will reset after it gets to the end, and everything will go back to normal. And besides—it can't hurt *us*. Ah, here we are."

She pulled me through a low doorway, into a small, square room, that was lit with flickering candles and smelled of roast chicken. Patrons sat close together at long wooden tables, drinking beer or eating bits of greasy meat with their fingers. At one end of the room stood a makeshift stage where a storyteller sat in multicolored robes, waving his hands in the air and causing little silver sparks to appear above him.

"The winds," said Mokosh with a disgusted glare at the storyteller, "always inserting themselves into the narrative somehow."

She found us a seat in a relatively quiet corner and ordered beer and cakes. "In any case, I'm glad to have a friend in the books now—it gets ever so lonely at home. You'll come reading often, I hope? You never did tell me about your library."

Glancing down the length of the room, I found one of the patrons watching me. He was seated several tables away and had a thatch of shockingly light hair, neatly trimmed, a handsome, pleasing face, and eyes the color of a midsummer sky. His jaw was clean shaven, and he wore a red surcoat with dark embroidery around the edges.

His eyes locked on mine, and it seemed like the whole tavern grew still. Then he glanced down, and the moment was lost.

"Or your name," Mokosh was saying.

I jerked my attention back to her. "I'm Echo. And my library is in an enchanted house. I'm still trying to figure it out—the house." I considered. "*And* the library. The only reason I found it is because I got lost." I glanced over to the blond man's table again, but he had vanished.

Mokosh nodded sagely. "I'm happy to make your acquaintance, Echo. And I'm sure your house and your library have rules, like anything else. You'll begin to understand them and become an expert in no time!"

"I don't even know how to leave this book-mirror," I confessed.

Mokosh laughed. "Why, that's the easiest thing in the

world! You must only make a request to your library." She stood and addressed the dirty tavern wall in a language I had never heard before. It sounded like water falling on stones. A mirror shimmered into being, suspended on nothing. "I step through, and I'm home. Now you try."

I chewed on my lip, wondering why the serving boy who had just delivered our beer and cake wasn't gaping at the appearance of a magical doorway. I stood and looked at the stones of the fireplace, right beside Mokosh's glimmering door. "Library, I'd like to stop reading, please."

Another mirror appeared, its surface wavering like water before growing still. I stepped up to it, but didn't reach out my hand. I stared at my reflection, stared and stared.

Both sides of my face were smooth, the skin perfect, unscarred, as if that day with the wolf and the trap had never happened.

I touched the left side of my face—it felt just as smooth as it looked. I thought I would be sick.

"Do you look different than at home, Echo?" said Mokosh softly.

I turned to her, blinked back tears, nodded.

"The worlds in these books are not real, you know. Readers project their preferred versions of themselves inside them, whether they're aware of it or not."

I looked back at the mirror. This was my preferred self, something I could never be in real life. Bitterness coiled hard in the pit of my stomach.

I didn't want to be there anymore. I couldn't bear it.

I stretched my hand out to the mirror, and that sensation of coolness once more rushed through me.

Then I was back in the library, my hand just drawing away from the glass.

CHAPTER NINE

"MY LADY."

I yelped and wheeled. The wolf stood behind me, his amber eyes flashing.

I scrabbled away from him, my shoulders bumping up against another book-mirror.

The wolf didn't move. "I mean you no harm. Please." He sat back on his haunches, ears tilted forward. "Forgive me. The room—the room behind the black door . . . it helps me remember. If I don't go there, I forget myself, and the wildness creeps in. But it is dangerous, the most dangerous room in the house. It will hurt you—it already has. Please don't go back. I'm begging you."

Pain pulsed anew through my shoulders and palms—something else the book-mirror had erased. I swallowed, feeling my scars stretch tight along my jaw, and tried to push away my sense of loss. "I won't go back."

He dipped his white muzzle. "Thank you."

I balled my hands into fists. "But I'm not going anywhere else with you until you explain—*properly*—what's going on. And until I know for sure my father made it safely home."

He made a soft *whuffing* noise, which I realized after a moment was his version of laughter. "We are in the right room for that, my lady. Follow me." And he stepped through the second blue door into the storeroom.

I followed him down several aisles between the shelves of book-mirrors, to a little locked cupboard on one wall. It was made of a smooth dark wood, carved with whorls.

"There's a key underneath," he told me.

I reached below the cupboard and fished out the small brass key hidden there, then fitted it into the lock and pulled the door open. Inside lay a small hand mirror encased in ivory. I took it out, glancing to the wolf for instructions.

"It will show you anything you wish to see, anything in this world, at least. You must only give two pieces of yourself to make it work."

I sank quietly to the floor, my skirt pooling out around me, and laid the mirror in my lap.

"It need not be something big, so long as it is part of you."

I plucked out a strand of hair, and unfastening the broach from my collar, I pricked the first finger of my right hand. A spot of blood welled up, and I pressed my finger and the hair together against the surface of the mirror.

"Tell the mirror what you wish to see," said the wolf.

I swallowed. "Show me my father, please."

The mirror's surface wavered and went milky white, the blood and hair swirling inside until both were lost.

A dark forest came into view, a lantern bobbing on a pole. My father was trudging through the snowy wood, holding the lantern pole, Rodya and Tinker with their own lights just behind him. "Echo!" they called into the darkness, *"Echo!"* But the howling wind spat their words back at them.

The mirror shifted, showing my father and Rodya climbing the steps to the house, shaking the snow from their boots. My father wept into Rodya's shoulder. Donia appeared at the door, her face drawn and tight. "Foolish girl, to go out into the wood in the snow and the dark!"

But Rodya squeezed his hand. "We'll find her, Papa. Don't worry."

"I saw her," my father whispered. "She was there in the wood, just before Tinker came with his sled. I know I saw her."

Rodya's lips thinned, worry in his eyes. He didn't believe him. "You need rest, Papa. Come upstairs."

Tears leaked down my father's face. "Leave a lamp in the window for her—so she can find her way back to us in the dark."

Rodya lit it himself, settled it on the windowsill.

Only then did my father allow himself to be taken up to bed.

Donia lingered, waiting until Rodya had fallen asleep on the couch all bundled in blankets before she blew out the lamp.

"Good riddance," she said to the dark. But her hand shook.

I jerked to my feet and flung the mirror away like it was a snake; it bounced and skidded across the floor. My heart screamed inside of me.

"My lady, is all well?"

"I have to go home."

His eyes peered into mine. "Is your father not safe?"

I dug my nails into my palms, fighting bitter tears. "He doesn't know where I am. He thinks I'm lost in the wood."

"But you are not."

"He doesn't *know* that. Let me go back. Let me tell him I am safe."

The wolf's fur stood on end. "You must stay here, my lady. You cannot go home—I am sorry."

"At least let me write him a letter."

"There is no way to send it."

"*You* could bring it to him." I was getting desperate. "I swear to you I'll stay however long you wish, if you just bring him a letter."

The wolf seemed all at once to loom large, his voice grating and firm. "I cannot get back through the wood, and neither can you. It is impossible. Your father is safe, my lady. You must let it go."

"But—"

"Enough. There can be no letter. Now come. We have business with the house—your first lesson on how to care for it."

He turned and trotted out of the library, as if I should forget all about my father. I ground my jaw. I didn't care what the wolf said—I would find a way out of the house, somehow. Wait until he was occupied. Slip away. I refused to let my father fear the worst.

The wolf peered back through the library doorway. "Come. The house needs us."

I took a deep, steadying breath and followed.

The glass staircase and corridor had vanished, replaced by a dark passageway that smelled of earth and worms. Bare dirt ran hard beneath our feet; crude torches flickered eerily from the walls.

The wolf barked a harsh word into the air, and the passage turned a corner, ending at an open door that yawned into a chasm of darkness. There were scorch marks around the frame, streaks of soot on the floor. The air reeked of smoke, and amidst the darkness, specks of ash danced like snowflakes.

I had no desire to get anywhere near the doorway. "What is this place?"

"The fire behind our door last night was my fault," said the wolf. "I was too long away from the house, and it broke loose from its binding. We have to bind it anew."

"What do you mean?"

"Come down here with me. I will show you."

Reluctant, I knelt beside the wolf in front of the doorway. Laughter echoed from deep inside, tangled with a high keening wail. Ash dusted the hem of my skirt.

"Reach down, through the doorway," the wolf instructed. "You will find the binding. But don't lean too far." He plunged his head into the blackness beyond the door.

After a moment, I stretched my right hand in, not knowing what I was feeling for. Something small and spiny scuttled over my arm, and I clamped my teeth together to keep from screaming. I reached further into the empty dark, in and in, and my fingers closed around something thin and smooth and silken.

I pulled it out.

A shimmering scarlet cord lay in my hand, so light it seemed to be made of air. It twisted and sighed as if it were alive, and not content to be still.

The wolf emerged with a similar cord in his teeth, and dropped it into my other hand. "Don't let go," he said. "I must call the fire back, and then we will bind it." He stood on his back legs, propping himself upright against the wall with his front right paw. *"Return!"* he bellowed down the passageway. "By the laws of the old magic, I command you to return!"

Two heartbeats passed, then another two. The cords shivered in my hands; it was like grasping wind.

And then a wall of flame came rushing down the corridor, twisting and writhing. Screaming.

"Hold on!" the wolf cried.

I screwed my eyes shut and ducked my head, clinging to the scarlet cords with all my might.

The fire reached me, enveloped me; I screamed at the clawing heat. But it didn't devour me, and in another instant it had gone by. I opened my eyes to see it vanish into the darkness.

"Shut!" ordered the wolf, and a heavy oak door slammed against the door frame, smoke hissing out through the cracks. The wolf dropped onto all fours, panting a little, and came to stand beside me. "Now to keep it from breaking free again. House! Bring the binding kit."

A blue leather pouch and matching braided belt appeared out of thin air and fell in a heap at my feet. I squawked in surprise, and dropped the scarlet cords.

"Open the pouch," said the wolf.

I gave him a wary glance, but obeyed. Inside was a gold thimble and needle, a pair of gold scissors in the shape of a bear, and a spool of shining thread that looked for all the world like strands of coiled sunbeams.

"Thread the needle," said the wolf. "I will teach you the binding stitch."

"The binding stitch?"

"To keep the fire contained."

"I don't understand."

He blew out a breath. "Old magic, my lady. It's what keeps the house from falling apart, no thanks to *her*. She had the power to collect it in the first place, but not to keep it together."

"Wolf." I was running out of patience. "*I don't understand what you're talking about.*"

He just nudged the pouch closer to me.

I sighed and picked up the needle. It was strangely heavy and warm, and it buzzed in my hand. The spool of thread was just as light as the scarlet cord, if not lighter. I unwound a bit—it seemed to have no substance at all—and it stretched out toward the needle all on its own, slipping through the eye. I put the thimble on and was startled to find it soft inside, like it was lined with velvet.

"Now for the binding stitch," said the wolf. "Take the scarlet cords, and stack their ends on top of each other, then draw your needle up through both cords. Loop it around to the bottom and do it again, over and over until the binding is secure."

I hesitated a moment, then did as he asked. The needle chimed like a tiny bell as I sewed, the golden thread whispered, the scarlet cords sighed. I could *feel* the moment the binding stitch was complete, the cords and thread fused tight together. I glanced at the wolf, and he nodded, so I used the bear-shaped scissors to snip the end of the thread. The girl from the book-mirror flashed into my mind, weaving a shimmering net to use against the queen's thorny army. Old magic—it sent a thrill through me.

The wolf seemed satisfied. "That should hold. We will be vigilant about tending the bindings—the fire will not break loose again." He tilted his head to one side. "The pouch and its contents are yours, my lady. I would be honored if you would wear them."

For a moment, I just stared at him, then returned all the sewing items to the pouch and put on the belt, cinching it tight around my waist. I liked the weight of the pouch at my hip; it felt natural, somehow.

The wolf's lips curled up in what I took for his version of a smile. "I have always hated this part of the house. Let's walk somewhere more pleasant. Come."

He trotted off down the dirt passageway. I had no desire to go anywhere else with the wolf—I couldn't stop seeing my father, sobbing on Rodya's shoulder—but I wasn't sure how to slip away without him knowing. And old magic or not, I didn't want anything more to do with the door I'd just bound. So I gritted my teeth and ran to catch up.

I walked next to him, glancing down to see that the cuts on my palms had healed where the scarlet threads had touched them. The same sensation of coolness that had poured through me when I stepped into the book-mirror tingled in my hands.

"Garden!" the wolf barked at the air.

The floor shimmied a little beneath our feet, and the dirt passage turned into a normal hallway, lanterns on the walls, green-and-blue patterned carpet stretching out before us. We went up a stair and around a corner, then down two more stairs to a small white door. It opened at our approach, and was so low I had to duck my head to pass through.

I stepped into full daylight, the almost unbearable brightness making my eyes stream. I stood still a moment to let them adjust, overwhelmed by the cacophony of birdsong and bumblebees after the heavy silence I had grown used to inside. The air was alive with the heady scent of roses; water burbled from some hidden fountain.

I blinked the tears from my eyes. The wolf had brought me into a terraced garden, wide grassy steps cut into the hill that were bordered with white stones. We had come out, somehow, at the very bottom of the hill, and the entire garden rose above us. A narrow walking trail wound up the steps, and on either side of the level ground stood an impenetrable iron fence. My eyes traced the length of it, but I saw no gate. I wondered if it was to keep the wood out, or the wolf in, or both.

The wolf watched me intently, as if it were important to him that I was impressed by the garden.

I was in no mood to be impressed. "Tell me what's going on, and what exactly I did back there."

He let out a breath. "We will talk as we go. Come."

We mounted the first step and climbed past a lily pool, water splashing silver over bright, darting fish.

"The house is wild, as I told you before. It's brimming with magic, some of it lovely and some of it more dangerous than you know."

The book-mirrors. The bauble room. The laughing, shrieking fire. I nodded and climbed on.

"All the rooms exist, but none of them *here*, if you understand me. They are never in the same order unless you command the house to make them that way."

"Command the house?" Roses nodded at us in the breeze, vines twining up a trellis set against the hill. I got the feeling they were dancing to music I couldn't hear.

"If you would like to see the conservatory, you must simply tell the house 'Conservatory,' and that is what you will find behind the next door."

That must have been why the wolf had yelled "garden" after we left the bound door. "But how did the rooms *get* here?"

"The . . . person who . . . arranged . . ." He growled, the words not coming out, then tried again. "A collector amused to gather bits of things . . . she . . . likes meshed them all together. A room here. A . . . life . . . there."

I frowned. "Her" again. "Someone with great magic chose things to bring here. Gathered by . . . enchantment?" The word felt like ash in my mouth.

"Yes."

We had climbed nearly to the top of the terraced steps. Around a bend in the path, a waterfall spilled from the brow of the hill. The wolf slipped through it, disappearing behind a curtain of spray.

I followed, holding my breath at the touch of cold water on my skin, and then I was through. A cozy room lay hidden beyond, a pair of armchairs facing out toward the waterfall. Between them stood an end table that sported a lamp and an ancient-looking tea set with chips in the china.

"But who *is* she?" I pressed.

He clambered up into one of the chairs, sitting on his haunches and draping his paws over the arm like someone's overgrown house pet. Donia would have a conniption if the wolf sat on her furniture like that.

I tucked myself into the other chair.

"She is . . . the wood is . . ." The wolf looked at me, his sorrow palpable. "The wood is under her will, as is the house. But I can't . . . I can't *talk* about . . . in this house. . . ." He looked at me helplessly.

I thought about the way I could barely say "enchantment." "You *can't* talk about her. Not here."

He nodded.

"And the gatekeeper? The North Wind?"

"My guard."

"Then you're a prisoner."

If the wolf was human I swear he would have shrugged. "Of a sort."

"Then what am I?"

"You are my guest. The house's next potential caretaker."

"And have you had . . . guests . . . before?"

The waterfall roared; the air in the cave grew suddenly cold.

The wolf's eyes found mine. "It has only ever been you, my lady."

I unfolded myself from the chair, and paced over to the water-fall. I plunged my hand into it; icy cold seared through me. I blinked and saw my father, holding his lantern high in the snowy wood. Looking for me. Waiting for me. Fearing the worst.

The wolf padded up beside me. Why did I still feel drawn to him?

"I will teach you how to care for the house. How to command it. You don't have to be afraid."

"I'm not afraid of the house." I realized it was true.

"Are you afraid of me?"

For a moment I peered down at him, trying to parcel out my feelings. "I don't know."

He dipped his head. "I will endeavor to give you no further reasons to fear me. Now, come. There is much to show you before the day is gone."

He stepped back through the waterfall.

And I followed.

CHAPTER TEN

WE RETRACED OUR STEPS THROUGH THE garden and into the house, where a blue tiled corridor lined with miniature apple trees waited for us. I told the wolf I was tired and hungry, that I didn't want to see anymore of the house just then.

His amber eyes burned into mine, but he didn't call my bluff. "Ask the house, and it will bring you a meal. If you have need of me, call."

And then he left me, the apple trees rustling as he passed them by.

I waited as long as I could bear, then started walking in the opposite direction. "House," I said, feeling foolish, "Could I have a meat pie?" The air shimmered, and around the corner I found a plate waiting on a low table; the tantalizing aroma of stewed meat wafted up to greet me. I grabbed the pie and ate as I walked, so quickly I burned my tongue—I was starving, and even Donia had never made something so delicious.

Heartened by this success, I addressed the house again: "Could I have my knapsack, and supplies for the journey home?"

There was another shimmer in the air and around the next corner I found my knapsack hanging on a peg, full near to bursting. I slung it over my shoulder and made my last request: "Bring me to the gate. Show me the way out."

The air shimmered a third time, and there came a rumbling sound from somewhere underneath me. "Please," I said.

The apple-lined corridor gave way to an ordinary carpeted hallway, then a staircase winding down into darkness. I remembered how long it had taken the wolf and me to reach my room from the gate. "The shortest way, if you please," I added. The floor jerked beneath my feet and I fell the rest of the way down the stairs, coming to a stop at the plain wood door. The lantern pulsed from its place high on the wall.

I took a breath, and opened the door.

Blackness enveloped me. "Let me through," I whispered, in case the house held any sway down here. "Let me through."

Wind raged around me, whipping through my skirt, clawing at my hair. I could feel its power, its *anger*. But I could feel its sorrow, too. Icy claws scraped my neck, thorny fingers grasped my ankles, dragging me down, down. An invisible weight crushed my lungs, swallowing my breath away. I thought of the girl in the story. "By the laws of the old magic," I gasped, "let me through, let me through."

A high mournful shriek echoed in my ears. The weight on my chest lifted. Gentle hands steered me through the darkness, and then I was tumbling through trailing vines, out into the sunlight.

I blinked up at the sky, scrambling away from the hill, toward the wood. I looked back, something in me wrenching at the thought of leaving the wolf there, alone forever. *You could go back to him*, said a voice in my mind, *when you've told your father you are safe*.

But I knew I wouldn't. Whatever I'd thought connected me and the wolf didn't really exist.

And yet.

I stood there longer than I meant to, torn between the wolf and my father.

But at last I forced myself into the wood.

It was perfectly ordinary, at first. Leaves crunched under my feet, the wind blew cold and smelled of damp earth. There were no animals, no birds. Just me and the trees. Rodya's pendant thumped against my chest, the ticking of the clock speeding up suddenly before stopping dead. Its silence was deafening. Ominous.

I tramped on as the shadows lengthened and the light began to fail, pushing away my uneasiness, telling myself I was almost through, almost home with my father again, even though I knew that was impossible—the wolf and I had been trapped there two weeks, my father longer.

I tried not to think of the girl in the story, of the thorny creatures and the cruel queen. I tried not to think of the wolf, of how angry he would be when he discovered I was gone.

I tried not to dwell on the possibility that I had made a terrible mistake, coming here.

Ahead of me, the trees began to rustle, even though there was no wind. Their bare branches twined together, twisting down over the path and blocking my way.

I turned right, walking faster.

The trees moaned, their voices deep and horrible, like strings ripped from cellos, or trod under boots.

I broke into a run, my heart slamming into my rib cage, one hand holding tight to the compass-watch. I ducked underneath hanging branches that tore at my clothes, trying to catch me, hold me, but I tore free.

All around, the trees bowed low, knotting their branches together, cutting off my path.

And suddenly there was nowhere left to run.

A sapling sprang out of the ground and reached its twiggy fingers toward me, pinning my ankles and wrists, cinching tight around my chest. It stabbed toward my throat but I wrenched my head to the side, screaming.

More branches wrapped round me, until I couldn't move, couldn't breathe, couldn't see. They dragged me down and down, into smothering blackness, and I was swallowed by the wood into the dark of the earth.

Spots swam before my eyes. My life slipped away.

My father would never find me. Never know what had happened.

And then, heat, pressing in. A sudden thrust upward, the binding branches falling free.

I collapsed on the ground, gasping, so much grit in my eyes I couldn't see.

Fire raged round me.

Smoke crawled high.

And the wolf was there, white against the flame, a torch gripped in his teeth.

The wood shrank back from him, screaming.

I reached out for the wolf; my fingers grasped his fur, locked around his neck.

He dropped the torch.

And then we were hurtling through the wood for the second time in as many days, me clinging to his back, shutting my eyes against the horror, against the dark.

He had found me. Somehow, the wolf had found me.

He carried me through the meadow and into the hill, past the gatekeeper and into the house. Up to the bedroom behind the red door.

I collapsed onto the bed, dirt and leaves falling black on the sheets, blood smearing red. I sobbed into the pillows, sobbed and sobbed. I couldn't stop. But it wasn't because of the pain raging in every part of me.

The wolf climbed up beside me, rested his head next to mine.

"I'm sorry," I said. "I'm sorry."

But he blew a breath of warm air into my ear and said, "Dear one, do not be sorry."

"Echo. Echo."

I swam back to consciousness. Pain seared from every point in my skin; my vision was blurred and too bright. Some part of me realized that the wolf had never said my name before. I liked the sound of it in his gruff voice.

"You're bleeding, Echo. We need to see to your wounds. You have to come with me."

Somehow I pulled myself up, half falling out of the bed and leaning heavily against him. My blood seeped into his fur. Blackness threatened to overwhelm me.

"Stay with me. Just a little further."

Down the hall, through a carved stone doorway, into a cavernous, echoing chamber. I had the dim impression of pillars and arches, silver light flooding through a wide window, a chaos of wheeling stars beyond. There was a sensation of peace and stillness, solemnity and great age. And underneath it all a feeling of tremendous power.

My head spun. I collapsed onto the floor, succumbing to the pain.

A breath of wind passed over me. I peered up to see the wolf bowing before a man who seemed to have wings growing out of his shoulders.

And then the man was kneeling over me. His wings wrapped around me, his fingers brushed whisper soft over my wounds. The cool sensation of magic buzzed under my skin. The pain faded.

"Sleep, dear one," he said. "Until we meet again."

My mind floated away from my body.

I slept.

WHEN I WOKE IT WAS morning and I was back in bed, Rodya's pendant tickling once more against my heart. The wolf slumbered down on the floor, bathed in a circle of sunlight from the window. I watched his chest rise and fall.

He must have sensed my gaze, for he opened one amber eye, and then the other. "Good morning, Echo."

I rubbed the sleep from my eyes and sat up in bed, remnants of my encounter with the wood coming back to me like tatters of faded dreams. "How long have I been sleeping?"

"Only since yesterday afternoon."

That was a relief. "What was that place?"

He stood and stretched, back legs first, then front ones. "The Temple of the Winds. We are lucky one of them was near; they are not always. They have many things to attend to. The temple itself is not always there—it exists apart from the . . . collection. It is ancient. Nearly as ancient as the world itself."

"Was that . . . was that the gatekeeper? The North Wind?" I couldn't quite reconcile the angry force under the hill with warm wings and whispering magic.

"The North Wind does not properly exist anymore. His power was unbound from him long ago. That was the West Wind."

"Old magic," I said softly.

The wolf nodded. "The Winds command some of the oldest magic there is."

I brushed my fingers over my newly healed skin, then reached up to touch my scars. I wished the Winds had been there that day in the field so many years ago. "I'm sorry," I told the wolf. "I shouldn't have tried to leave."

"I am sorry, too. I am afraid you are stuck here, my lady, until the year runs its course and the power in the wood fades along with me." His eyes blazed bright.

His words echoed in my mind: *I am old, my lady. I am dying.*

I thought about the strange spidery clock in the bauble room, and wondered if it was ticking down the remainder of the wolf's life. "Thank you. For saving me from the wood."

He dipped his muzzle. "You are welcome."

For the first time, I wondered if there was a way to save him.

And I realized I wanted to find it.

CHAPTER ELEVEN

I GOT DRESSED BEHIND A SCREEN that appeared when I asked for it, in a cloud-soft blue gown I pulled out of the wardrobe. It had satin ribbons tying up the cuffs, and embroidered silver birds around the waistline in an unbroken circle of wide wings.

"Come," said the wolf, when I was dressed and had eaten my breakfast of nut bread with sliced pears and spicy orange peel jam. "I will take you on a proper tour of the house, or at least as much as we can manage in one day." He paused at the door and cast a glance at my dressing table, where I'd laid the braided belt and pouch. "You will need your tools."

I put the belt on and followed the wolf into the corridor.

"Think of the house as a quilt, the rooms as patches," he told me as we went along. "There are two kinds of bindings: the kind we did yesterday, to keep whatever is in a room *in*, and the kind that keeps all the rooms bound to the house. Those bindings rarely fail, but they can unravel, and so must be checked regularly."

We walked down a stone hallway, sapphires gleaming from inside the rock, and came to the door I had bound the day before. The fire crackled noisily behind it, but I tugged on the mended scarlet cords, and they held firm. The wolf gave me a nod of satisfaction, and I swelled with pride.

We walked along a grassy hallway and stopped at all the doors that lined it. One was carved with the image of a flower; another, a spider; another, a bear. To my surprise, the wolf told me to open the spider door.

Inside was a vast hall, overgrown with moss, sunlight streaming in through a tall, broken window. Silver spiders the size of my palm were gathering the sunlight and spinning it into elaborate webs that hung all around the room. In one corner sat a spinning wheel and a basket heaped with empty spools. I gaped, awed. The whole place buzzed with magic.

"The spiders make the binding thread," said the wolf, with a toothy smile. "Sometimes you can convince them to wind the spools for you, too, but it makes them a little cross, so mostly you have to do it yourself."

"How often does the thread run out?" I asked.

"Sometimes every day. Sometimes once a year. It depends."

"On what?"

"How the house is feeling," said the wolf, as if that were obvious.

I shook my head in bewilderment, and we went on to the bear door. That room contained, unbelievably, the inside of a huge circus tent, where a trio of white bears sang a sort of song in strange throaty voices.

"I like to bring them honey every day or so," said the wolf. "It soothes their throats."

I stared. "Do they do anything besides sing?"

"Not really."

"Don't they get exhausted?"

"How should I know? They are the singing bears. That is what they do."

Behind the flower door lay a venomous garden. Roses bloomed purple, dripping poison. A wicked-looking vine grew up from the center of a crumbling well. The sky was mottled with dark clouds, and the air stank of mold and decay. The vine turned toward us, reaching out with dark tendrils.

"House!" cried the wolf, "Axes!"

And then an axe appeared before each of us and we grabbed them (the wolf with his teeth) and started hacking away at the vine as if we had done it a hundred times before. When the vine was cut down to a stub, oozing black, horrible-smelling sap from its wounds, we hurtled back into the hallway. I gladly took out my needle and bound that door tight. "We have to keep an eye on the vine," said the wolf. "Binding or not, it'll seep through and devour the house."

On we went, down dusty hallways and leafy ones, up some stairs that seemed to be formed from dragon scales, others of paper. Monsters beat against one door, thudding, hissing, wailing. The binding was fraying; I used the needle and thread to knit it back together. There was a door made of silver that shimmered and sang. Behind it lay a whirling, twisting *something* that I didn't comprehend. "A gateway to another world," said the wolf. "But we cannot go there; the journey would rip us apart."

There were more normal rooms, too. We passed through an armory, where racks of weapons, chain mail coats, and shields lined the walls, all emblazoned with a white bear on a blue field. There was a treasury, countless parlors, a storeroom, a small conservatory lined with windows and filled with perfectly ordinary plants. There was even a laundry.

Every so often, I saw evidence that a young woman had once lived here: a wooden-heeled shoe, discarded in the hall; the loose beads of a bracelet gathering dust in a wall niche; a spilled bottle of perfume in front of one of the doors that smelled of sunshine and wildflowers. I wondered where the owner of these things had gone, and if the wolf had brought me here as her replacement. But every time I opened my mouth to ask him about it, we were somehow at another door, with another binding to check, another task to do.

The day spun away, and the infinite, terrifying, wonderful house began to weigh on me.

"You are tired," said the wolf, concern in his voice.

I leaned against the wall to catch my breath. I had just bound a room that randomly grew or shrank with no warning, and had nearly been trapped behind a door the size of my thimble. The wolf had dragged me out just in time. "I don't know how you've lived here for so long all alone," I said, wheezing. "The house is—the house is—"

"Unwieldy?" the wolf supplied. His teeth flashed in a smile. "That is why I am glad you are here. It is very hard to hold a needle in one's mouth, you know."

I laughed—I'd been wondering how he'd managed binding the doors on his own.

He nudged my hand with his white muzzle. "I want to show you one last room."

BEYOND THE DOOR LAY A tall, sparse chamber, with wooden floors and a window looking out over the forest; the sky was deepening toward twilight.

I gasped. In the center of the room was a dark mahogany grand piano, the lid lifted to reveal gleaming strings. It was the most beautiful thing I had ever seen.

"I thought you would like something to practice on, while you are here."

"I don't really know how to play," I replied, wondering how he'd think to bring me there. But I paced toward the piano anyway, sank onto the blue velvet bench. I pressed a few keys. Notes awoke from the heart of the instrument, echoing all the way up to the ceiling like embers in an underground cavern.

The wolf came to sit beside the bench. He tilted his head at me, as if debating something. "The last mistress of the house was a musician. I could teach you what I learned from her."

I thought about the shoes and gowns and discarded bracelets. I wondered who the former mistress of the house could have been, and why the wolf had told me the night before that I was his only guest. Whatever the case, I very much wanted to learn. I touched the smooth wood of the piano, and couldn't stop my smile. "I would like that."

I HAD A BATH AFTER dinner, in a copper tub filled with magically heated water, then pulled on a soft nightgown and thick knitted socks. It was only after I climbed into bed that the wolf trotted in. I was about to ask him where he'd been since dinner, but the blood in his fur made it clear he had visited the bauble room.

"My lady, it is almost midnight." His voice was rough, distant, as he curled up in his customary spot on the floor. "You had better put out the lamp."

He sounded like he was in pain, and my throat constricted. I blew it out.

Darkness flooded the room. I pulled the blankets up to my chin, listening to the steady sound of his breathing.

"Good night, Wolf."

"Good night, Echo."

I woke a few hours later to a quiet chattering sound. I realized it must be the wolf, his teeth clacking together as he shuddered with cold on the floor.

I half sat up in bed. It was warm under the coverlet, but the air outside the bedclothes was icy sharp. For the first time, I noticed the room had no fireplace.

"Wolf?" I blindly tilted my face to where he lay shivering.

"All is well, Lady Echo. Go back to sleep."

"But you are cold."

Silence. Then, "It will pass, by the morning."

"Morning will be a long time in coming."

"Sleep, Lady Echo."

I thought of how he'd lain next to me after he'd rescued me from the wood. It wasn't as big a thing, but I couldn't leave him down there; he hadn't left me. "Come up here with me. The bed is big enough. You'll freeze down there."

"I am fine."

And yet his teeth went *chatter, chatter, chatter.*

"Wolf, please. It is so much warmer up here."

A long, long pause. Then: "Very well, my lady."

There came a shuffling, scrabbling noise as he got up, the creak and sag of the bed hinges.

I was careful to scoot over to the side to give him enough room; I feared to touch him in the dark.

I heard him burrow under the blankets, felt the weight of him on his side of the bed.

"Echo?" He sounded lost and sad.

"Yes, Wolf?"

"Thank you."

"You're welcome."

And then we fell asleep.

Somewhere in the night, I thought I felt the wolf's warm breath on my cheek. I turned toward him, reached out, but my fingers touched only blankets.

His voice was the barest thread in the dark: "I am sorry, Echo. I am sorry for everything."

My head was too thick with sleep to answer.

I knew nothing more until morning.

CHAPTER TWELVE

WHEN I WOKE I WAS ONCE more alone, no sign of the wolf but the mussed bedclothes. I wondered where he'd gone.

All the gowns in the wardrobe were too elegant for every-day wear, so I asked the house for a new blouse and skirt. They appeared out of thin air, laying themselves over the bed, the skirt a dark green wool with gold leaves embroidered around the hem, the blouse of cream linen, so finely spun it felt like silk.

"I'd like some breakfast," I said when I had dressed. A little table unfolded from nothing and settled by the door, with a low cushioned stool beside it. I sat down to honey-sweetened porridge, plump sausages, and tangy orange slices.

"May I have some tea?"

A teapot and cup arrived an instant later, and I poured out a cupful and took a sip. I nearly spat it out.

What *was* this? I raised the cup and took a hesitant sniff—it smelled like dirt with a hint of charcoal, which would explain the taste. I laid it hastily down again, and wondered if it was possible to teach a magical house how to make a proper cup of tea.

Breakfast over, I stepped out into the hall. "Bring me to the wolf," I said, and started walking. The floor shifted under my feet, and I found myself trudging through a corridor of fine white sand. It slipped into my shoes and clung to the hem of my skirt. I turned a corner and came face to face with the obsidian door. Whispers and music echoed from behind it—the wolf was in there. Remembering.

I put my hand on the smooth black surface. I couldn't shake the feeling that there was more to my being there than simply to help him care for the house. Could I stop him from dying? Halt the hands of that strange clock and free him somehow? There had to be answers somewhere in this rambling collection of magical rooms. When the wolf wasn't with me, I could look for them.

And where better to look for answers than a library?

I tapped my fingers against the obsidian door and turned away, telling myself it was my promise to the wolf that was keeping me from going back inside, and not my gnawing fear of the strange and terrible room. I gave the house its next command.

I WASN'T BRAVE ENOUGH TO try a book-mirror that might turn out as tragic as *The Hidden Wood*, so I chose one with an innocuous description about a rich young fop who liked to go on fox hunts. Perhaps I would get lucky and find Mokosh again—she had an enchanted library, too, after all, and she read so much, maybe she would have insight into the wolf's situation.

I touched the mirror; magic curled through me.

The next moment I was barreling along on horseback in the midst of a company of riders, wind singing in my ears, banners snapping bright overhead. Laughter rang loud on the summer air. My mount's mane whipped back into my face and my stomach leapt into my throat. I could barely catch my breath but found I was laughing, too.

A bugle sounded just ahead; hounds bayed. The landscape was a rush of green on every side.

One of the riders looked back at me and gave a loud *whoop*—to my surprise I saw it was the blond man from the tavern in *The Hidden Wood*. Was he a reader, too? If he remembered me, he gave no sign.

The tide of the hunt hurtled onward, and I caught sight of our quarry: the orange blur of a fox, dashing madly across the countryside, losing ground.

The men around me hollered louder. They raised silver spears high; the sun made the metal flash and dance.

The blond man didn't have a spear.

Out of the corner of my eye, I saw another company of riders thundering up. One moment they were still a ways off, the next they surrounded us, a wall of glistering plate armor and naked blades. Swords pressed suddenly against all of our throats—mine included—and I glanced over at the blond man in an attempt to quell my panic. He was grinning widely around the blade at *his* throat. This might be a story, but pain bit into my skin; blood trickled down my neck.

A woman rode through the soldiers in her own plate armor, a blue cloak fastened around her shoulders, a silver crown pressed into her black hair. She looked young, no more than twenty or so, but there was a hardness in her eyes that made me tremble. The hunting party recoiled from her, some of them swearing, some of them begging.

The woman just swept them all with her cold gaze and waved one hand at her soldiers. The blades withdrew, but only an inch. "The punishment for hunting in the queen's wood is death." Her voice was as brittle as wind rattling icicles.

"We were nowhere *near* the wood, your majesty!" cried one of the young men. He had ginger hair and a scruff of a beard; blood dribbled down his neck to stain his blue doublet. I wondered if he was the book's main character.

The queen didn't acknowledge him. "Tomorrow at dawn,

your lives will be mine." And to her soldiers: "Take them."

A sword hilt jabbed into my back, and my horse lurched forward along with the other members of the hunt. The queen's soldiers ringed us tightly and herded us toward the dark line of a wood. Trees marched like soldiers, their trunks stark against the susurration of the wind in their deep green leaves. I shuddered at the memory of clawing branches, of smothering dark. But this wood was just a story. The queen was just a story. They couldn't hurt me.

Still, fear coiled tight and sank its claws in.

The wood loomed near. The blond man glanced back once or twice, like he wanted to talk to me, but the soldiers didn't abide conversation. If any of the men spoke, the soldiers knocked them in the head with their sword hilts or, in one case, sliced off the offending speaker's ear. I gaped in horror as blood gushed down his neck, wondering how on earth I'd thought this book-mirror innocuous.

We rode into the wood, where dark leaves and darker branches shut out the sunlight and the sky. The men wept. The man who'd had his ear cut off passed out from blood loss, slumping in his saddle—I doubted he would make it to morning. Maybe the soldiers would let me look at the wound. Maybe I could do something for him.

It's just a story, I told myself firmly.

But it didn't feel like just a story.

The ginger-haired young man's eyes grew hard, the line of his jaw determined. Like he'd expected this. Like he'd prepared for it. Had he come on purpose to infiltrate the queen's fortress?

On we rode, on and on. The wood grew darker and colder the deeper we went into it. Glowing eyes watched us from behind the trees. Whispers and high eerie screams flitted around us. The soldiers at the front of the group lit torches, but the bright flames did very little to banish the dark.

Then all at once we broke past the line of the trees. A black tower rose before us, stretching hundreds of feet into the air—I couldn't see the top of it. Beyond sprawled a massive city, green lights winking in countless windows.

The soldiers could no longer stop the men from speaking. Their whispers whirled round me:

"The queen's fortress."

"The Dead Tower."

"Her creatures' dark hovels."

"She'll eat our hearts."

"Drink our souls."

"Destroy us."

"Would that we had never been born."

The ginger-haired young man sat tall in his saddle, like he was unafraid.

But his hands shook.

And then we rode up to the gate and the soldiers were yanking us from our mounts, shoving us through a gaping doorway, pulling us down a winding stone stair. The air grew colder, colder. It stank of decay, and blood.

The men wept.

My teeth chattered, my fingers and toes wholly numb.

We were taken in different directions, shoved through doorways or dragged further on. I was yanked down into a stone room, my wrists chained to a rough wall. I could sit, but it pulled my shoulders nearly out of their sockets, so I crouched instead, my thighs burning.

This book had turned out to be a huge, huge mistake. I thought about leaving, but I kept hoping Mokosh would eventually appear—last time, she hadn't come until after the confrontation with the queen. And I was curious about the blond man—I wondered where the soldiers had taken him. So I waited.

After a while, moonlight filtered in through a window slit up near the ceiling, illuminating another prisoner chained to the adjacent wall. He was fiddling with his wrist cuffs, a scrape-scrape-tink of metal against metal, and he lifted his head, and *grinned* at me.

It was the blond man.

"You look uncomfortable," he said, yawning.

I squinted in the dim light and saw that he was using a dagger to pick the locks on his wrist cuffs. First one, then the other, made an alarming racket as they clattered to the floor. He seemed nonplussed. He stood, stretched, then paced over to me.

"You aren't in any *real* danger, of course," he said as he started on my cuffs. "Readers never are. But it's good to come prepared." He gestured significantly with the dagger.

My left cuff fell off, then my right one. I rubbed my sore wrists and sagged gratefully to the ground.

My companion flashed another grin as he sheathed his dagger and pulled a cloak seemingly out of thin air, which he handed to me. I draped it around my shoulders, more than a little bewildered. "Who *are* you?"

He sketched a little bow. "Hal, at your service."

"Echo," I told him.

"Pleasure to meet you, Echo. Now, stay close and try not to make any noise. I don't know about you, but I have no intention of sticking around until dawn."

I gulped, and followed him over to the cell door. The lock seemed to give him more difficulty than the cuffs had. He fiddled with it for a long while, muttering and cursing under his breath.

I studied him as he worked. He looked younger than I'd first thought, just a year or two older than me. He was lanky and tall. His blond hair curled over his ears; his shoulders were strong beneath his white linen shirt. He wore tall black boots and tight pants, and he smelled like rich earth and sun-warmed stones.

"I read a book once about a girl called Echo," he said, jiggling the lock. "The ordinary kind of book. She was in love with a god who loved only his reflection, and she wasted away into nothing until she was just a voice in the wood, calling his name for all eternity."

"That's horrible."

His lips quirked. "I suppose it is. Ah. There!" The lock sprung free, and Hal creaked the door open. He peered out into the passageway, then beckoned me to follow.

We crept out into darkness. Somewhere, water dripped, a man sobbed, another prayed.

"This way," Hal whispered. He grabbed my arm and tugged me through a narrow door. The ceiling was so low I had to duck. I felt like a mole, burrowing through the earth. "Not much farther now."

The passage grew too close and tight for any conversation, so I focused on following him, my heart yammering away in my throat.

And then, just when I didn't think I could take it anymore, we burst out into cool starlight, whispering trees, freedom.

Hal pulled me to my feet, his warm hand circling mine an instant longer than necessary before he let go. I shook dirt from my hair and spun in a circle, laughing.

He grinned. "We should escape from certain death more often."

I glanced behind me. "I do feel sorry for the others. Does the queen kill them all, in the morning?"

"If I knew, would you want me to tell you? I wouldn't want to spoil your reading experience." He winked at me.

I gave him an exasperated glare. "If I'd thought this story wouldn't have a happy ending, I would have read something else."

His blue eyes locked on mine, suddenly serious. "Must

you always know a story ends happily before you feel equal to beginning it?"

I stared at him, my heart pulsing insistently in my neck. I thought of my promise to the wolf in a snowy wood, of knife-sharp crystals and a whirring clock behind an obsidian door. A moth flickered past us in the moonlight, and I wondered what kind of story I was in. "Sometimes the adventure is enough."

Hal smiled. "Adventure is all I live for. Come on!" And he grabbed my hand and tugged me out of the path of our escape tunnel, just as the ginger-haired man and two others from the hunting party came wriggling through. A half-dozen of the queen's soldiers arrived in the clearing, hoofbeats thudding on hard earth. They drew their swords and circled the escaped prisoners. Hal pulled me behind a tree. We crouched there together.

One of the soldiers hauled the ginger-haired man up by his doublet and spat in his face. "You don't deserve to live until dawn. The queen is coming for you *now*."

"Let her come! I am a prince of my people, and the moon's faithful servant. She cannot touch me."

"He's right," whispered Hal. "But he's the only one who knows it."

I glanced over at him—his grin was back. "You *have* read this book-mirror before!"

"It's one of my favorites," Hal confessed. "The queen has been terrorizing this kingdom for centuries. If anyone crosses her, she kills them. It's a very involved process. She slits your throat and then drinks your soul out of your ear—it's how she stays so young. But the prince has been preparing for this his whole life. He's drawing her out to meet him here, in the moonlight, where he is more powerful than she is. It's all very exciting, if rather ridiculous."

I couldn't help but laugh. "*You* are rather ridiculous."

He winked at me again. "Are you ready to run?"

"What?"

That's when one of the soldiers spotted us, his blade flashing toward our hiding spot.

"Run, Echo!" cried Hal. He grabbed my hand and we dashed into the wood. I gulped mouthfuls of air, giddy and frightened, the soldiers hard on our heels.

I tripped on a protruding root and tumbled away from Hal, who looked back just as the soldier grabbed him. "It was nice meeting you, Echo!" he called, gleeful as ever. "I hope to see you again!" And then he shouted a word at the sky and winked out of existence.

The soldier cursed, and turned to me.

"Library!" I said frantically, "I'd like to stop reading now!"

The mirror wavered into being, much slower than the soldier. He seized my shoulder, hauled me to my feet.

I wrenched out of his grasp and threw myself toward the mirror.

I fell hard on the library floor in a tangle of arms and legs, my lungs still screaming for air after all that running.

CHAPTER THIRTEEN

LIFE IN THE HOUSE UNDER THE mountain began to settle into a quiet rhythm.

Each morning I woke to an empty room, ate breakfast alone, and then stepped out into the corridor where the wolf was waiting for me. We paced round the house together, checking bindings, feeding snakes, watering plants. We loosed golden birds with red wings from their cages, allowing them their freedom for the day—we only had to remember to lock them in again at night, or they would turn into dragons and try to burn the house down. ("It's not their fault," said the wolf. "I like to give them what happiness I can.")

The binding thread in my pouch dwindled rapidly, so the wolf brought me into the spider room, and showed me how to carefully detach the webs, spin them into thread, and wind them onto the spools. We always made sure to bring the spiders a treat, so they wouldn't get too cross: honey or fruit or little pieces of cheese.

After the first few weeks or so, the wolf would sometimes not appear, and I tended the house on my own. I enjoyed the work, the needle like a natural extension of my arm, the thread singing between my fingers.

Often the wolf and I had lunch together in the room behind the waterfall. Or rather, *I* had lunch while the wolf sat draped in his armchair and woefully watched me.

"What do you even eat, anyway?" I asked him one afternoon.

He said vaguely, "I go hunting," and refused to elaborate further.

After lunch, we went to the music room, where, slowly, the wolf was teaching me how to play the piano.

It was curious, learning from him. He clearly knew a great deal (I tried not to think about the last mistress of the house, who he'd learned from), but he was limited by his lupine frame and couldn't demonstrate anything. He gave me specific verbal instructions, but sometimes I didn't quite understand what he was after.

"Curl your hands, Echo, with your fingertips pointed downward and your thumb crooked out to the side. No. No, not like that. It is your fingertips *only* that are to touch the keys. Yes. Now press the key, feeling the weight fall from your arm and through your wrists and into your fingers."

He paced back and forth behind the piano bench when he was talking, occasionally popping his head up to check my hand position.

He taught me how to read musical notation, which was like a different language, little spots on the page transforming into the heartbeats of living, breathing music. There were more sheafs of music in the piano bench every time I stepped into the room—I suspected the wolf asked the house to supply them.

We had lessons daily at first, and then gradually spread them out to once a week to allow me time to practice. A few times I saw the wolf listening outside the door as I worked through the exercises he'd given me, but he never stayed, slipping away again just before I finished. Sometimes I stepped into a book-mirror titled *The Empress's Musician* and practiced the title character's harpsichord while she was busy kissing her teacher in the palace gardens. I liked playing in there; it was quiet, sun streaming in through tall windows and dust motes swirling up to dance in the light.

By the third week of my stay in the wolf's house I was able to play some simple Behrend pieces. I liked Behrend—he wrote in strict contrapuntal lines, and I appreciated the intellectualism as much as his brilliant, crisscrossing harmonies.

After that, the wolf began to give me works by Czajka, who wrote gut-wrenching pieces of endless perfection—his melodies soared to the heights and depths of the human condition, grabbing hold and not letting go until the last lingering note. As my fingers began to catch up with my brain and I was able to do Czajka greater justice, I found myself breathless at the end of his pieces, heartbroken, like I had passed through all the sorrows of the world and hadn't made it out unscathed.

I think the wolf liked Czajka best, because he parceled out those pieces sparingly, like they were precious drops of sunlight in winter. I preferred Behrend; he didn't make me ache.

Every day after my piano practice, the wolf disappeared into the bauble room, and I was left with a handful of hours to fill before dinner.

I spent those in the library.

I grew bolder, after my first few excursions. If I didn't like where a book-mirror was going, I stopped reading, or told the library to skip ahead, or to mark my place so I could come back later. I was still determined to help the wolf, but as the weeks passed, reading became more and more about the adventures themselves; finding a way to free him retreated to the back of my mind. The book-mirrors were exhilarating—I'm not sure I could have stopped reading, even if I'd wanted to.

I was pleased to stumble upon a collection of nonfiction book-mirrors, and stepped into several about doctors. I watched them operate on patients, help mothers give birth, mend broken bones, stitch wounds—it fascinated me endlessly, and somehow made my dream of attending the university not feel so far away.

I attempted to familiarize myself with more music history to complement my piano lessons, but the only book on Behrend I could find was a fabricated account of his romance with a painter's daughter who supposedly inspired many of his later works. It was hard to check references in a book-mirror, but the story was so melodramatic I doubted there was much truth in it.

Neither Hal nor Mokosh seemed interested in nonfiction. I looked for both of them in every book-mirror I read, but Hal proved especially elusive. I saw Mokosh when I went to a concert where a made-up musician performed actual Pathetique Nocturnes on an absurd but interesting keyboard-type instrument built into the side of a mountain. We waved at each other across a sea of unusual concertgoers—antelope and elephants, an enormous crane, a pair of unicorns, all perched on chairs too small for them and listening attentively. I had to get back to the house for dinner and didn't have a chance to speak with her.

Mokosh was also there at the coronation of a young king, who had fought against all odds to win back his country from a powerful darkness. The South Wind crowned him on a hill in the blazing sunshine, and all the people cheered.

"Echo!" cried Mokosh, moving through the crowd to grasp my sleeve. Her violet eyes sparkled. "I'm so glad I caught you. I'm sorry I haven't come reading much—my mother has kept me so busy! Come have tea with me?"

Before I could stammer out a response, she laughed and tugged me away from the hill, where she showed me how to create a doorway from that book-mirror into another one. We stepped through, and found ourselves in a tea parlor high up in the branches of an enormous tree. Stained glass made of butterfly wings winked from the windows and firefly chandeliers spun from the ceiling. The tea party attendees were mostly owls and squirrels. We huddled round a table and sipped tea from acorns, nibbled tiny cakes, and laughed until our sides ached at the ridiculous stories the owls told.

Every night, before I left the library, I took the hand mirror out of the cupboard in the back room, and asked it to show me my father. He always put a lantern in the window for me before he went to bed. Donia always snuffed it out. Winter spun on, and one night, my father didn't light the lantern.

Instead, he wept in front of the fire. "She's gone, Donia. Gone. She's not coming back again."

Donia stroked his back while he cried and I had never hated her more.

The next night, there was no lantern. Two nights after, my father smiled at dinner.

It was small of me, but after that, I didn't look anymore. I didn't want to see my father moving on without me. I couldn't quite bear it.

Every evening I had dinner while the wolf watched me eat. We locked up the golden birds on our way to bed, and just before midnight, I climbed under the covers and blew out the lamp, and the wolf clambered up beside me. I had the house make him an oversized shirt, for extra warmth in case the covers weren't enough.

Sometimes, in the early hours of the morning, I thought I heard him crying.

But that didn't make sense.

Wolves didn't cry.

ONE MORNING, I ASKED THE house to take me to the wolf, and it led me out into the garden. Several months had passed, and over the fence and past the meadow the wood was thick with verdant leaves.

In the village, the arrival of spring saw melted snow and mud everywhere, irises and daffodils bursting bright from the ground, a taste of sunshine and sweet breezes, the ability to shed our winter furs. Villagers were a little freer with their coins, which meant more book sales, and luxuries like butter and sugar and red meat for our table. That year, it also meant the end of Rodya's apprenticeship—I was terrified that he would take a job in another town while I was with the wolf and I would never see him again.

I paced into the garden, wandering up the first few steps, and caught the sudden scent of blood tangling acrid with the flowers.

Around one of the rosebushes, the wolf was bent over a freshly killed rabbit, ripping its throat out.

I froze, my stomach wrenching.

Before I could creep away and leave the wolf to his meal, he looked up and saw me watching, his white muzzle drenched in blood.

For a second, we stared at each other. Then his tail drooped between his legs and he dashed away from me, on up the steps like a blaze of lightning.

I ran after him.

I found him huddled in the back of the waterfall room, desperately rubbing his bloodied mouth with his front paws.

"Wolf." I approached him slowly, knelt down beside him, took his paw in my hands. "Wolf. Stop. You don't have to do that."

He turned away from me, his ears pinned back.

"Wolf." I tugged a handkerchief from my skirt pocket, and gently, gently, wiped the blood from his muzzle.

His amber eyes couldn't meet mine.

"It doesn't bother me, Wolf. Really. I know you can't have much of a taste for soup or noodles. I understand."

He paced to the waterfall, staring out into the spray. "I did not want you to see me like that."

I sat beside him, put one tentative hand on his back. The water danced and sparkled, catching in his fur, clinging to my eyelashes and framing the world with diamonds. "I don't mind."

"*I* mind," he said.

My free hand went unconsciously to my scars; I traced their

bumps and ridges. I understood. But it made me sorrier for him than I had been before—I thought of the clock in the bauble room, ticking down the rest of his life, and felt guilty I hadn't been trying harder to find a way to save him.

"You should come reading with me," I said. "There's a few hours yet, before dinner. We can go to a fancy party and put frogs in the soup bowls, frighten all the guests."

He let out a little huff that was some mix of a sigh and a laugh. "I fear I do not care for reading."

"Oh, but you've been to the library here, haven't you? It's very peculiar. Not like a normal library at all."

He *whuffed* with real, wolfish laughter. "I have, but the library has nothing for me."

"You must not have found the right story yet. I can help you!" I wrapped my arms around his neck as if to tug him to the library that moment.

But he shook me off, suddenly cold. "I do not wish to go reading, my lady. I will see you at dinner." He barked, "Rain room!" at the house, and disappeared through a door that appeared in the wall of the cave.

I sat alone as the sun set beyond the waterfall, unaccountably dejected.

The wolf didn't come to dinner. I ate by myself and took the long way back to the bedroom, locking the gold birds in their cages, letting them eat seeds from my hands.

It wasn't until I had climbed into bed and turned out the lamp that the wolf joined me; the door creaked open and shut, his nails clicked across the floor, the bed hinges sagged.

Minutes ticked by in the dark, and at last I said, "I didn't mean to offend you."

He didn't answer for so long I thought he wasn't going to. But then: "You did not offend me."

"Wolf?"

"Yes, Echo?"

I crumpled the covers in my hand. I listened to the sound of his breathing. "I wish you would let me help you."

"You are helping. The house is in better spirits than it has been in years."

"No, I mean help *you*. Help this year not be your last."

He rustled in the bed; his fur scraped the sheets. "You cannot help me, Echo. You never could."

"But—"

"Go to sleep," he said.

I shut my eyes.

But sleep was a long time coming.

CHAPTER FOURTEEN

O UTSIDE THE ODD HUMOR OF THE house under the mountain, spring had turned to summer, and summer was deepening. Already, the year wended away. It would be autumn again soon, then winter, and my year would be fulfilled. I didn't like to think about that—I wasn't ready to think about it, so I pushed it to the back of my mind, and focused on music lessons, reading, and tending the house.

I was practicing one day on the Empress's harpsichord when I looked up to see Hal leaning in the doorway.

He jumped a little, caught staring, and for a moment we blinked at each other and didn't say anything. He was dressed simply: gray trousers and a loose-fitting white shirt, with embroidery about the neckline.

I'd been struggling to make my fingers understand my first ever three-part Behrend contrivance after semi-mastering the two-part ones. As delighted as I was to see Hal again, I was embarrassed he'd been listening.

Hal recovered his nonchalance before I had a chance to collect myself. "There are much better instruments than this to be found," he said, folding his arms across his chest and walking over to the harpsichord. "I could recommend hundreds of titles with gorgeous pianos shut up in back rooms."

I sat a little straighter on the bench, offended into speech. "I quite prefer the harpsichord, thank you."

His lips quirked up. He leaned over me and played a few careless notes in the upper register. "If you say you prefer it because you read somewhere that Behrend originally composed his pieces for harpsichord, you clearly haven't thoroughly pondered the topic."

"Beg pardon!" I yanked the key cover down, forcing Hal to jerk his hands out of the way to keep them from getting crushed.

He grinned, unabashed.

I stood from the bench and paced over to the window. The music room looked out over one of the Empress's many gardens. I glimpsed the edge of her gown peeking out behind a hedge, along with the elegant shoe I knew belonged to her wretched musician. I was so glad I'd never followed the book along its intended path.

Hal came over and plopped himself down in the window seat, yawning as he languorously stretched out his legs. "While it is *true* that Behrend composed for harpsichord, the piano had barely been invented when he was alive, and the quality of pianos built in those days was severely lacking. They hadn't perfected the instrument yet. Many scholars believe that if Behrend were alive today, he would eschew the harpsichord immediately in favor of the piano."

I gaped at him, fumbling for a scathing retort and coming up empty. All I knew about Behrend was what the wolf had told me, the brief biographies printed on the back of his sheet music, and that ridiculous book-mirror about the painter's daughter. If I'd had an ordinary library at my disposal I could read up on my music history and refute him, but as it was . . .

I shrugged, attempting indifference. "I like how it sounds."

He smiled. "Fair enough."

I studied him, wondering how I could be so glad to see him and so irritated with him at the same time. "You haven't been reading lately." My words came out more accusatory than I actually meant them.

"Yes, I have. You're just a hard person to find."

I tapped my finger against my breastbone. "You've been looking for me?"

"Of course I have! Books are very dull without someone to share them with."

Heat flooded up my neck.

He winked at me, unfolding himself from the window seat and standing in one smooth motion. He bowed with a flourish. "Fancy a walk, Echo?"

I glanced once more out the window. "As long as we avoid that awful Empress."

He laughed. "I wouldn't have it any other way."

We left the music room by way of the rose garden, passing through the hedgerows and out onto a wide hill, where tall grass rustled in the wind. The air was alive with honeybees and the scent of wildflowers, and huge white clouds scudded through the sky; their shadows stretched long over us.

"Where are you from?" I asked Hal, trailing my hand over the tops of the grass. It was feather soft, but it itched.

"From?" He raised an eyebrow at me, as if that was a difficult question.

"Where are you when you're not reading?" I clarified.

"Oh, I'm always reading." He dashed ahead of me and I ran after him, half tripping the rest of the way down the hill.

Ahead of us, a wide lake sparkled in the sun, and beyond it was a wood.

It seemed there was always a wood.

"You can't *always* be reading. You have to be from somewhere."

Hal walked up to the edge of the lake and pulled his boots off. The water lapped over his toes.

I watched him for a moment, then followed suit. I yelped at the icy touch of the water and Hal waggled his eyebrows at me.

"Well, where are *you* from?" he said.

"The village. Although right now I live in the house under the mountain."

"Sounds very pretentious."

I gave him a little shove and he nearly toppled over. "*You're* the pretentious one, with all your opinions about harpsichords."

"They're not opinions, they're facts."

I shoved him harder, laughing, and that time he lost his footing, grabbing my arm before I could leap out of the way and yanking me down with him. We tumbled into the lake with an enormous *splash*. I surfaced first, sputtering, and pulled Hal up after me. We couldn't stop laughing.

"I'm not sure," said Hal a while later. "Where I'm from, I mean."

We were stretched out on our backs in the grass, still damp, but warm from the sun. Overhead the clouds knotted together and grew dark, the wind blowing colder than before. It smelled like rain.

"How long has it been since we met on the hunt?" he asked.

"A few months at least."

He folded his hands behind his head and I found myself staring at his eyelashes, which were long and light. "For me, it seems like yesterday."

"You haven't . . . been anywhere since then?"

"I've just been reading. There was the book about the hunt,

and then one about a boy and a glacier, and then something about sea monsters. Definitely a few wars. A handful of dragons. And—" His brow creased in concentration. "I think there was a woman made of clouds. Or cats. I don't quite remember, it was very peculiar. And then this one."

"So you just go from book to book."

"It seems so."

He rolled on his side, propping himself up on one elbow. There was a light dusting of freckles across his nose.

"You must have a family," I said.

"There's always just been . . . this." He gestured at the sky. "For as long as I can remember."

I studied him, thinking about the nature of the house under the mountain. Was Hal trapped in the book-mirrors somehow? Enchanted between their pages like a rose left to press and then forgotten? The library had been collected with the rest of the house. Maybe Hal had accidentally been collected with it. Although he could just as easily be stuck in Mokosh's library, or another library entirely—there was no reason it had to be mine.

He sighed, so suddenly sad that my heart wrenched. "What about you, Echo? Tell me about your family."

And I shut my eyes and told him about my father and Rodya and even Donia, while the wind whipped up wilder and wilder and the clouds blotted out the sun.

It was only when the rain broke, all at once, that we leapt up from the ground and bolted to the wood for shelter, slipping and sliding in the mud all around the lake.

Under the canopy of the trees, the rain barely reached us. We stood and watched it fall, turning the lake and the hillside all to mist.

A mirror shimmered into being behind me, the library alerting me, as I'd instructed, that it was time for dinner back in the house under the mountain. I didn't want to leave Hal, but I stepped toward the mirror anyway.

From Hal's long look, he didn't want me to leave either.

"I'll see you again," I told him.

His smile was laced with sadness. "Goodbye, Echo."

"Goodbye, Hal."

I touched the mirror, and the library came into view around me. Stricken, I stepped into *The Empress's Musician* again, but back in the dripping wood, Hal was already gone.

A FEW DAYS LATER, I went out into the corridor after breakfast and found it empty. It wasn't the first time the wolf had left me on my own, of course, so I went about tending the house as usual. I'd checked the bindings on all the dangerous doors and was halfway through watering the plants in the conservatory when I spotted a woman's hat abandoned on the window seat. I picked it up, smoothing my hands over the faded ribbons, and tried it on. It fit perfectly.

I still saw evidence of the wolf's mysterious former mistress *everywhere*, though the wolf tried to distract me from noticing dropped fans and torn gowns, jewels and shoes and half-finished embroidery, scattered about in nearly every room.

Was the woman the same as the force in the wood? The powerful enchantress who had collected all the rooms of the house and bound them together? It seemed likely. But I couldn't quite reconcile the idea of her with someone who loved music, and had caused the wolf to love it, too.

Still, the mystery of the wolf was clearly wrapped up in her, and if I were to help him—as I'd determined to, no matter what he said—perhaps she was somewhere to start.

I left the conservatory, still wearing the hat.

And there was the wolf in a corridor made of flashing rubies, waiting for me.

It was too late to hide the hat, so I just fiddled with one of the ribbons, studying the wolf. "Why are you bound to the house? Where did you come from? And . . . and who *is* she?" I pointed at the hat.

The wolf let out a long sigh. His whole body seemed to sag. "Come with me. I need to tell you a story."

He brought me to the Temple of the Winds, which was empty and echoing, dust swirling up from the floor.

We paced together over to the back window, which looked out into wheeling starlight, and I sank down onto the wide sill, hugging my knees to my chest. The wolf sat opposite me, and the strange stars cast fragments of green and violet light over his white fur. "I am not of your kind, Echo Alkaev. I do not belong to your world, or your time. I am just another piece of . . . her . . . collection. But my life has been stretched past what it was ever meant to endure. At the end of the year, I will die—but I will be free. I have no wish to escape that."

I chewed on my lip, peering out into the never-ending light. It danced in my vision, sang in my ears, whispered like dew on my skin.

"Once, I had something precious. I should have held it tight, should have guarded it with my last breath, but instead I let it go. I will regret that until the end."

He let out a long breath, and I tore my gaze from the stars to look at him. Sorrow weighed heavier on him than I'd ever realized.

A little wind rushed past us. It was warm and smelled of lilies. I closed my eyes and drank it in. "You said you were going to tell me a story," I murmured.

He did. "The North Wind was despised by his brothers. He was the favorite of their mother the Moon, and his powers were stronger than theirs. He commanded death, and time, and could bend others' wills to his own."

I thought of the dark, angry force beneath the mountain. "What happened to him?"

"He traded his power for the oldest of magics."

"What is the oldest magic?"

"Love. That is what created the universe, and that is what will destroy it, in the end. Threads of old magic, binding the world together."

I watched him in the shifting light, his eyes fixed on some faraway point I couldn't see.

"The North Wind gave away his power to be with a human. That is how it began."

"How what began?"

A low growl came from the wolf's throat. "All of this," he said heavily.

I blinked back out into hurtling stars. "Then it's his fault."

"Fault? No. He held on to the thing he loved. It is more than I ever did."

"Wolf." I stretched out a hand to touch the scruff of fur on his neck, and he didn't pull away. I tugged the ribbon on the hat, thinking he hadn't quite answered my question. "What did you lose? Who did you love?"

"Nothing. No one."

But his eyes said *Everything. Someone.*

He sighed, a long huff of air.

"I wish you would let me help you."

He buried his muzzle in the crook of my arm. "My lady, you cannot help me."

But I didn't believe him.

"WHAT DO YOU KNOW ABOUT the old magic?" I asked Mokosh.

We stood in a castle's high tower that was open to the air, while dwarves sailed above us in ships that somehow flew, painting the sky with swathes of swirling light. That book world had no moon or stars; without the dwarves' brushes, the darkness would be complete.

In the castle below, a centaur-king was having a party, and the whisper and rush of cymbals and strings drifted up to us.

"Magic is in everything," said Mokosh matter-of-factly. She finished the painting she'd been working on with one last flourish of her brush—it was a view from the tower, dwarves and flying ships and all. I stood before an easel as well, but I wasn't a painter, and had given up after only a few brushstrokes, alternating watching Mokosh and the sky instead. She glowered at her canvas. "My mother would hate this."

"I think it's beautiful."

Mokosh waved my comment away. "Shall we go down and join the party?"

"I'm not much of a dancer," I confessed, trying not to think about my father and Donia's wedding, or the various village holidays I spent lurking in the background, because no one wanted to dance with a girl marked by the Devil.

"Oh, then I'll teach you! It's the easiest thing in the world.

Here." She grabbed my arms and moved me to the center of the tower, just as the white underbelly of a dwarf ship sailed overhead. It gleamed like it was made out of pearls. "All you have to do is listen to the music and move your feet, you see?"

She steered me around while I tripped over her spectacularly, until I began to learn, little by little, what to do.

"Step *back*," she said. "To the side, then forward. That's it! You're not entirely hopeless, you see?"

I let the music sink into me, and after a while the movements became more natural. High up in the tower, it seemed like everything was dancing, the flying ships and the dwarves' paintbrushes and Mokosh and I, all part of the same intricate pattern.

"Is there magic where you come from?" I asked Mokosh, when we'd grown tired of dancing and sank to the floor opposite each other. The stones beneath us hummed with music.

"Certainly there is. My mother couldn't rule without it."

"And the *old* magic," I pressed. "The magic that governs the world—do you have that kind?"

Mokosh frowned. "My mother has the most magic of anyone. Of course she has the old magic, too."

I shrugged, uncertain why that had offended her. In my mind I saw the bauble room, the spidery clock and the spinning crystals, the blood on the wolf's white fur. I knew there were answers to be found there, but I was still too afraid to seek them out. "What about enchantments?"

"Echo, why are you asking me so many questions?"

Above us, the dwarves had finished painting the sky, and their white ships were drifting slowly away into the night. "I'm trying to help a friend."

"And you think your friend might be enchanted?"

The wolf's words spun round in my head: *I do not belong to your world, or your time. I am just another piece of . . . her . . . collection.*

"I do."

Mokosh stretched out, leaning backward on the palms of her hands. Her forehead creased in concentration. "Every enchantment is as unique as a snowflake—but none are impenetrable. I'm sure there is a way to break it, if that is what you wish."

Break the enchantment, free the wolf, and then—what? Would I just stay with him in the house under the mountain forever?

In the curved wall of the tower, a mirror shimmered into being—the library calling me back. I had no idea it had grown so late. I scrambled to my feet.

Mokosh grinned at me. "What's your rush? Now that you can dance, we've a party to get to." She stood, too, and brushed the dust from her skirt.

"I'm late for dinner," I told her apologetically.

"Can't dinner wait?"

I thought about the wolf, alone in the dining room, staring mournfully at a mountain of food he didn't want to eat. "I'm afraid not. But I'll be back again soon."

Mokosh smiled. "More partners for me, then. Goodbye, Echo!"

She disappeared down the tower's spiral stair, while I stretched my hand out to the glimmering mirror.

Magic curled through me, and the dark tower melted away into the bright light of the library.

I'm sure there is a way to break it, echoed Mokosh's voice in my mind.

I'm sure there is a way.

But how was I supposed to find it?

CHAPTER FIFTEEN

I DO NOT BELONG TO YOUR *world, or your time. I am just another piece of . . . her . . . collection.*

I'm sure there is a way to break it.

I'm sure there is a way.

I paced through the rain room, where rain grew like plants in various pots, some of the water-plants tiny and hanging from arches in the ceiling, some nearly as big as the living room in my father's cottage. I stopped at each plant and poured out a little light from my bucket, which I'd collected earlier in the sunroom. The rain plants didn't make any logical sense, but they were beautiful, and I always looked forward to my visits each morning.

I paused at my favorite plant, a huge vine-y thing that twisted and moved in some invisible wind. Blossoms grew all along the vine; they were made of dewdrops and chimed like tiny cymbals when I fed them their light.

I touched one of the flowers; it was damp and cool against my finger.

I am just another piece of... her... collection.

But what *was* he? What had the wolf been before the mysterious force in the wood had brought him here, bound him here? I tapped my finger absently against the compass-watch, hanging as always about my neck, ticking down the seconds.

The first time I'd met Mokosh, she'd told me that readers project their preferred versions of themselves in the world of the books, whether they were aware of it or not. I wondered what version of himself the wolf would project, and if it would give me any hint of his secrets.

I wondered if that was why he didn't want to come reading with me.

I left the rain room, a plan unfolding in my mind that would keep me from having to return to the room behind the black door.

I FOUND THE WOLF CURLED UP and sleeping soundly on one of the garden steps, the grass pressed down beneath him and a few bright flower petals clinging to his white fur. Bees buzzed in the blossoms behind him, roses and asters and twists of orange honey-suckle. The air smelled sweet.

I almost hated to wake him. "Wolf?"

He opened one amber eye. "Do you need assistance with the house?" He'd left me on my own more often than not, lately.

I shook my head. "Not exactly. I found a room I've never seen before—I want to show it to you."

He got slowly to his feet, like he ached all the way down to his bones, then stretched, yawned. "Lead the way."

I turned from the garden, jittery with anticipation. I hoped the house remembered my instructions. "House," I said as we stepped inside, "bring us to the new room." The air trembled around us and I thought I heard a far-off breath of laughter—the house was amused.

I climbed a stair made of bare dark wood, the wolf's nails clicking behind me. Down a hall of whispering shadows and around a corner, then up another stair, this one made of snow, to a red-and-gold door I'd asked the house to invent for me.

The wolf grunted and I glanced down at him. "Wolf?"

"You are right, Echo. This *is* a new room. I thought I had seen them all."

I ignored a twinge of guilt and opened the door. There was no disguising the library now that we were inside, but I rushed to the nearest book-mirror anyway, my fingers wound tight in the wolf's scruff.

He realized what I was about, and tried to jerk away from me, growling, but he wasn't fast enough.

My hand was already brushing the surface of the glass.

Magic rushed through me.

I stood suddenly in an autumn meadow, the golden grass brittle and tall, seeds sticking to my sleeves. An ominous cloud loomed dark overhead, and the wind was sharp as needles.

I took a breath, turned.

The wolf stood there, unchanged. His back leg was crooked and scarred. There were bits of dried blood in his fur from his latest visit to the bauble room.

I reached inquisitive fingers to the left side of my face, wondering if that particular book-mirror didn't work like the others. But my skin was as smooth as the day I was born.

I had changed.

The wolf had not.

We stared at each other, the wind whipping wild between us. His sorrow was so heavy I could nearly taste it.

He didn't say anything, just looked at me for a long, long moment, his amber eyes piercing down to the darkest parts of me.

And then he turned, and vanished, and I was alone.

I sank to my knees in the grass, guilt squeezing so sharp I could hardly breathe. I had been so sure he would be different in the books, so certain his true self would be revealed.

Instead, I felt like I had betrayed him.

Hoofbeats thudded across the ground, and I lifted my head to see a rider hurtling fast toward me. As the rider drew near, I recognized Mokosh, her silver hair and voluminous split riding skirt flapping madly in all that wind.

"Echo!" she cried, pulling up in a cloud of dust and grass. "I'm so glad I found you—why do you look so miserable? There's a princess who's about to fight an evil sorceress using only the *weather*, and it's sure to be loads of fun. Coming?" She leaned down in her saddle and offered me her hand.

I couldn't face the wolf after what I'd done. Not yet.

So I took Mokosh's hand, and let her sweep me away on an adventure. But the whole time, I couldn't stop thinking about the look in the wolf's eyes. The look that said he was ashamed of me.

I DIDN'T SEE THE WOLF again until I climbed into bed that night and was about to turn down the lamp. The door creaked open and he padded in, but he didn't look at me. There was more blood in his fur than I'd ever seen before. Guilt and hurt writhed inside of me, but I blew out the lamp without saying a word. *Coward*, I told myself.

The bed sagged as the wolf climbed up; the linens rustled. I stared into darkness and listened to the beat of my heart.

Finally I said, "I shouldn't have tricked you like that. I shouldn't have pulled you into the book-mirror against your will. I'm sorry."

His breathing sounded quick and shallow from the other side of the bed. "The fault is mine, Lady Echo."

I listened to the darkness, felt the immensity of the divide between us, though we were separated by mere inches. "Why won't you let me help you?"

"Because no one can. Stop trying. Stop pretending you care about what happens to me. Stop behaving as if we are friends."

His words stung like wasps. "Then what are we?"

"I am the demon who tricked you," he spat. "You are my prisoner."

I gnawed on my lip to keep from crying. Silence swallowed me whole.

The minutes stretched on. Tears dampened my pillow. "You are my friend, you know. No matter what you say. You've been watching over me my whole life. I trust you."

The wolf made a sound halfway between a sob and a snarl. "My lady, you should not."

"But I do."

The darkness pressed in and in. We didn't say anything more. Somehow, I slept.

Deep in the night I woke to deep, muffled sobs that made the whole bed shake.

I wondered how a wolf could cry like that, and sound so very human as he did so.

CHAPTER SIXTEEN

A FTER HALF A DOZEN LESSONS, MOKOSH informed me that my dancing was so much improved, we had better put it to good use and attend a ball. "Meet me in *The Masque of Adella*!" she said merrily as her book-mirror home wavered into existence. "Tomorrow afternoon! Bring something fancy to wear—I hear there will be princes in attendance!" And then she stepped through her mirror and vanished.

I told myself I hadn't firmly decided whether or not I would join her, and yet, the next afternoon, I went directly to the library and asked the house to provide me with a selection of gowns. Three giant wardrobes appeared in a semicircle around me, filled to the brim with rustling silks and satins, sequins and jewels and embroidery. I looked through all of them, running my hands along the delicate fabrics, pulling out the occasional gown to get a better view of it in the light.

I hadn't seen the wolf since I'd forced him into the book-mirror more than a week ago—he hadn't come to give me my lesson, or appeared in the dining room. Every night he climbed into bed after I'd blown out the lamp, and every morning when I woke he was gone again. I had been tending the house on my own, wracked with guilt.

One of the gowns made my breath catch, and I slipped it off the hanger. It was pale gold and embroidered with metal thread, and had a lower-cut neckline than I was used to. The sleeves looked like puffs of confectioner's cream. It whispered tantalizingly against my arms.

I turned to the book-mirror, touched the glass.

I stepped directly into Lady Adella's dressing room, where Mokosh sat waiting for me on a red velvet chaise longue.

"Echo!" She leapt up and spun me about in a tight hug, then pulled away to examine the gold dress I'd brought. "Oh, it's stunning. Just the thing. You'll outshine Adella herself tonight!" She glanced sideways at the small army of Adella's frowning maids, and stifled a giggle behind her hand.

The maids set the three of us—Mokosh, myself, and Adella, who was a pale, dark-eyed beauty—side by side in front of a trio of large, ornate mirrors, and got to work. They slipped me into a silk chemise, which lay smooth and cool against my skin, and then a bone corset, cinching the laces just tight enough that I felt secure, like I was clothed in armor, but not so tight I couldn't breathe. After that came the gown, and it settled around me like it had been sewn in my exact measurements—which, knowing the house, I supposed was quite likely.

The maids braided my hair with gold thread and white ostrich feathers, and then hung a strand of flashing sapphires around my neck. Last of all came the masque, tied on with silk ribbons. I was resplendent in starlight, my dark hair contrasting starkly with the gold gown and white masque. I turned to Mokosh for approval.

She wore a deep violet gown sewed with opalescent shells that shifted blue or green or silver, depending on how they hit the light. There were strands of pearls in her hair, and her masque shone with silver scales.

"Beautiful!" we both exclaimed at the same time.

Mokosh laughed and grasped my hands, and we looked to Adella, to see how her toilette compared. She was dressed in the dark regal colors and masque of a peacock, but she was crying behind all the feathers and sequins.

"Her betrothal is tonight," Mokosh whispered to me, "to a man she's sworn she can never love. It's all delightfully tragic."

But I was too excited to feel terribly sorry for Lady Adella.

Mokosh and I strode down a grand hallway and then a wide, sweeping stair into the ballroom. The entire back wall was filled with huge, multipaned windows that looked out onto a snow-covered countryside. Hundreds upon hundreds of candles danced overhead in massive chandeliers, and from some hidden balcony music curled into the air, elegant and light as wildflowers in the summertime. The floor was marble inlaid with gold.

Lady Adella stepped into the ballroom just behind us, and a tall, black-coated gentleman in a blue masque bowed smartly over her hand. She took it, stiffly, and he led her out onto the dance floor.

"Over here, Echo." Mokosh tugged me away to the edge of the room, where the people who weren't yet dancing chatted and mingled, sipping wine in crystal glasses.

The music and candlelight washed over me, and I wondered what it must be like to live in a palace, to be fawned over and courted for one's beauty and riches. To not have to worry about villagers' accusing stares. My fingertips twitched to the left side of my face, whispering across the masque and the smooth, unscarred skin that only existed here, in a world that wasn't real.

A sandy-haired gentleman wearing a dragon masque came up to Mokosh, and bowed low. "Dance with me, my lady?"

Mokosh beamed at him, and took his hand. They spun away to join the other dancers, and I was left alone.

I paced toward the windows, watching as the sun sank slowly westward, red-orange shadows spilling across the snow.

"It's very beautiful, to be sure," came a voice at my ear, "but are you certain you want to dance and eat iced cakes on the eve of revolution?"

I turned to see a tall stranger dressed in dark green, his masque the shape of a white bear's face; the masque looked somehow sad, but his voice was familiar.

"Hal?"

He gave me an elegant-yet-exaggerated bow. "I thought I'd fool you for longer than that." He loosed his masque and there was his face, smooth and laughing, his blue eyes flashing in the candlelight.

"I'm very hard to fool," I told him, smiling.

"So I belatedly see." He offered me his hand and I took it, startling a little when my fingers touched his skin—it was smooth and warm; neither of us were wearing gloves. His hand curled around mine and he led me out into the midst of the dancers.

I didn't know the steps to this particular dance, but Hal taught them to me, his other hand solid and strong on the small of my back.

We danced, not quite in time with the music, and I could feel our pulses, beating together in our joined hands. Mokosh danced on the other side of the room; she'd already traded partners.

"I remember my family," said Hal then, quietly. "I wanted to tell you. I haven't always been like this. Stepping from book to book."

I held his gaze; for some reason, it made my stomach lurch.

"What do you remember about them?"

His eyes turned thoughtful. "My mother is beautiful. My father is stern. I think I have brothers and sisters. But I haven't seen them in a long, long while. I don't even know their names." His voice cracked.

I studied his face and wondered, for the first time, what he looked like in real life. What lines and scars did the book worlds smooth away from him? "I'll help you find them. If I can."

He gave me a sad smile. "I'm afraid I might have lost them a long time ago."

Mokosh whirled by in the tide of dancers, and waggled her eyebrows at how close Hal was holding me. I flushed, and was glad when the dance drew us apart again.

"Did you say we're on the brink of revolution?" I asked Hal. "I didn't pay any attention to the description plate."

He grinned. "Oh yes. I'm afraid the festivities are cut short in a shockingly gory bloodbath. I read ahead."

I laughed. "Is it soon?"

He held me a little closer, and some impulse caused me to lay my head against his chest. His arms were warm and strong. Secure.

"Not until midnight," he breathed into my hair. "We are quite safe until then."

I leaned into him, all the air in the room swallowed up in the sensation of his heart beating quiet against mine.

We danced awhile longer, then retreated into a corner where

pillows had been strewn over the floor. We sat together, sipping currant wine and nibbling the aforementioned iced cakes, which were delicious.

"Do you remember where you come from?" I leaned back against one of the pillars, brushing cake crumbs from my skirt.

He was sitting close to me, but not as close as when we were dancing.

His forehead creased in concentration. "I think my father rules a duchy."

"You're a duke, then."

"I suppose I am."

I laughed. "Am I to call you Lord Hal?"

"You may call me whatever you like." A lazy smile crinkled up the corners of his eyes. "What about you, Echo? What do you want to do when your year in the house under the mountain is over?"

Across the ballroom, stars were appearing outside the windows, gleaming points of white fire. "I want to attend the university, if I can gather the entrance fee. I want to be a doctor."

Hal's eyes fixed on mine, an intensity in his gaze that I didn't understand. "I was not like you when I was young. I didn't care for anything or anyone but myself."

His words struck a strange chord. "You can't be much older than me."

He frowned, that line pressing into his forehead again. "I think . . . I think I might be very old indeed."

I thought again of my scars, entirely erased in the worlds of the books. What would Hal think of me, if he truly saw what I was? What would I think of him?

I took his hand, smoothing my thumb across his skin. I couldn't imagine him as an old man. I didn't want to. His eyes met mine as he lifted his free hand to my face. He loosed my mask, let it fall into my lap, then grazed his thumb across my cheek. Heat poured through me. I was caught in that moment, fixed, unmovable.

"Shall we dance?" he asked me softly. "One last gavotte before midnight?"

I nodded, not trusting myself to speak.

He pulled me upright and led me back out onto the floor, his hands warm and trembling around me. I didn't notice Mokosh, openly staring at us from within her partner's arms. I didn't notice Adella, ripping off her masque and throwing herself at her betrothed's feet, begging him to loose her from their engagement.

There was only Hal, his breath in my hair, his chest close to mine.

We danced, until the ballroom shook and fire exploded into the night, and an army of men armed with bayonet-fitted rifles burst in, death flashing in their eyes.

I LEFT THE LIBRARY, STILL wearing the gold dress, my ears ringing with music and the incongruous clash of battle. The corridor outside was dim and earthen, lit only with orange torches that were beginning to detach from the walls—almost midnight. I walked quickly, instructing the house to bring me the shortest way back to the bedroom.

I rounded a few corners and it was there: the carved red door, the lantern growing a tail and floating away.

I didn't hear the wolf's step behind me, just his voice: "It suits you."

I turned to find him watching me, his head cocked to one side, and I fingered the skirt of the gown self-consciously.

"Did you have a lovely evening?"

Guilt bit sharp—I'd forgotten him again, in all the excitement. I stepped through the door and the wolf came after me, nudging it shut with his nose.

"Are you going to forgive me for pulling you into that book-mirror?" I said quietly.

"You think I have not forgiven you?"

"You don't even want to look at me."

His amber eyes peered up into mine. "The year slips away. Already I find I cannot bear it."

"Bear what, Wolf?"

"The thought of being parted from you."

"Why? I've done nothing to help you."

"You tend the house as deftly as I have ever seen. And you—and you have been a good friend."

I swallowed, thinking of his angry words in the dark. "We're friends?"

"Yes, Echo. Of course we are."

The dress weighed suddenly heavy on me, and I didn't know how to look at him. "In the books, I don't have any scars." I don't know why I said it.

The wolf watched me, his tail flicking back and forth. "Do you hate them?"

I went and knelt beside him; the gown's metal embroidery snagged on the carpet. Hesitantly, I brushed my fingertips along the top of his head. He pressed his muzzle into my hand. "I don't mind them as much, here. I'm glad . . . I'm glad they brought me to you." I realized that I meant it.

"So am I," said the wolf. "I should not be. But I am."

Impulsively, I hugged him.

I got ready for bed behind a screen in a hurry, the gold dress a puddle of silk around my ankles. I was sorry to hang it in the wardrobe, sad to bid the evening farewell.

I fell asleep with the wolf beside me, and dreamed Hal and I were still dancing.

CHAPTER SEVENTEEN

THE NEXT MORNING, THE WOLF WAS waiting for me in the corridor outside the bedroom.

I was surprised to see him and he ducked his head, clearly embarrassed. "It is no use mourning the end of the year, when it has yet to happen. I do not want to waste any more time."

So we paced round the house and tended it together like we had at the beginning. I was glad of his company—some of the more unruly rooms were hard to manage on my own. We checked bindings, spun the spiders' golden thread onto spools, collected water from the rain room and light from the sunroom.

We spent over an hour in the room with the venomous

garden—it was getting out of hand. We hacked away at the vine growing out of the well, and poured water from the rain room over the poisonous plants, which made them wither.

We were almost finished, when the floor began to shake and a resounding *boom* splintered through the air. I slipped and skidded into the well, where the black vine we'd just finished cutting back was already growing again. The wolf snatched my sleeve and dragged me away before the vine could grab me and sink its sharp tendrils in.

I scrambled to my feet. The room continued to shake, and a large crack appeared in the floor, stone grinding and dust swirling. The black vine began to scream.

"Echo!" barked the wolf. "We have to leave. *Now.*"

The shaking grew worse, the crack in the floor spread wider. We leapt across, and ran for the door.

The black vine shrieked and wailed. Just as we passed the threshold out into the hall, the room fell away into darkness.

I turned, heart thundering. There was no room anymore. Just coiling, echoing, blankness. Ragged threads hung from the door frame, like a piece of cloth had been ripped away. *Think of the house as a quilt, the rooms as patches.*

"Shut the door!" cried the wolf.

I yanked it closed.

It shuddered and began to melt into the wall. In the space of a few heartbeats, the door vanished entirely, not even a thread remaining.

"What *was* that?" I gasped.

The wolf's ears were pinned back, a growl low in his throat. "It's started. The unbinding of the house."

"What do you mean, the unbinding? It isn't even remotely close to midnight."

The wolf shook his head. "I do not mean that. This is more serious. The house is connected to me, and I am running out of time. I fear rooms will continue to be unbound, more and more as the days pass. I hope the entire house will not have unraveled by the time the year is ended."

I stared at the wall where the door had been, my pulse dull and heavy. "The entire house?"

He dipped his white head. "I hope not."

"What would have happened if we were still behind the door when the room became unbound?"

"We would have been unbound with it. Our lives. Our souls. We would have become nothing."

Horror shuddered through me. "I don't mind *that* room being gone . . . but what about the others?"

The wolf answered my unspoken question: "It could be any of the rooms. We will have to take care."

I was more shaken than I wanted to admit. Any of the rooms meant the library could be unbound next. I could lose access to Mokosh.

I could lose Hal entirely. What would happen to him if he was truly trapped in the worlds of the books, as I suspected?

What happened to a pressed flower if the book it was in was thrown into the fire?

"Is there anything we can do?" I asked the wolf.

"Be vigilant," he said. "Do not stray too far from the door." His ears flicked sideways. His eyes met mine. "And hope that the bedroom is the very last room to be unbound."

THERE HAD TO BE SOMETHING else I could do. Some kind of old magic I could invoke to save the house and the library, and the wolf and Hal, too, while I was at it. I still didn't want to set foot in the bauble room, so when the wolf excused himself for the afternoon, I went straight to the library, determined to finally find some answers.

I stepped into a book-mirror about a real historical king who was famous for his vast book collection. His library was huge, shelves stretching up to the ceiling, tall windows looking out over a shining moat. I glimpsed siege towers being erected just beyond the water, but decided to ignore them.

An ancient librarian came round one of the shelves, mumbling to himself. He had wisps of white hair and a quill pen tucked behind one ear, ink dripping down his neck. He held a crackly sheet of parchment and was peering at it with a violent frown.

"Excuse me, sir," I said politely, "Do you have any books about the old magic?"

He looked up at me and somehow managed to frown even

deeper than before. "Up there." He pointed to a balcony accessed by a winding staircase. "Though I don't know why you couldn't read the signs." He waved at a blue metal plate attached to one of the shelves, inscribed with swirly shapes that were maybe supposed to be letters but were wholly undecipherable to me.

I just thanked him and climbed the stairs.

The books were beautiful, with cracked purple or silver or indigo spines, embossed with gold and studded with gems. They smelled like roses and cinnamon. I opened one and tried to read it, but the words swam in front of my eyes and I had to put it back. A second book was the same, and a third. Disappointment squirmed inside of me.

"You know, you really ought to be better prepared."

I jumped and wheeled about to see Hal leaning nonchalantly on the railing at the top of the staircase. He exuded a kind of amused boredom, but the faint sadness in his eyes belied him. "Don't tell me you stepped into a living, breathing book to read the boring ordinary kind." He stepped past me and plucked the volume I was attempting to decipher out of my hands. He gave it a careless perusal and stuffed it back onto the shelf.

"Why can't I read these?"

"Made-up language. This library may be *based* on a real one, but it's not like the author ever visited it, let alone read every volume on the shelf. Window dressing, Echo. That's all this is. A glint of color and magic to give depth to the story."

I harrumphed, dissatisfied, and Hal grinned at me. He caught my eyes in his deep sea blue ones and I suddenly found it hard to breathe.

"But you should be better prepared," he said, returning to his original theme.

I gave him a wobbly smile. "For what?"

He tapped the hilt of the sword strapped to his side. "Battles. You made a rather poor showing during the revolution the other night."

I flushed—Hal had pushed me behind a curtain before plunging into the fray. I'd alternately watched him fight and screwed my eyes shut against the shocking amount of blood. Mokosh had already left by the time the battle was over. "I thought you said it's impossible to die in these books."

"It is, but you *can* get into some awful scrapes, and sometimes the book gets so wrapped up in itself it won't let you stop reading. Always best to have some skills under your belt."

"Is it?"

He grinned, not taking his eyes from mine. "Fortunately for you, I'm an excellent teacher."

"Hal, what *are* you talking about?"

"Fencing lessons! What do you say?"

I let my gaze drift to the spines of the magical books just behind him. I thought of the wolf and the unraveling house and the danger Hal himself was in. "Hal, I—"

"You gratefully accept? Excellent!" He grabbed my hand and started pulling me down the stairs but I resisted and he released me instantly, a guarded expression coming into his eyes.

"I've got research to do," I explained.

"I could help," he offered. "What are you researching?"

"The old magic."

"You can't research that. It either is or it isn't, you know."

"What on God's green earth does *that* mean?"

He laughed. "The old magic exists in and of itself. You can't bind it in a book. And besides, you can't actually *read* these books."

I couldn't stop my grin. "I suppose you're right. I guess a lesson or two couldn't hurt."

He gave a triumphant whoop and we ran together laughing down the stairs.

We started in the king's armory, an echoing stone chamber lined with weapons of all shapes and sizes. Hal picked out a sword for me: it was smaller than his, and fit as perfectly into my hand as if it had been made for me. He taught me how to hold it, standing behind me and wrapping my fingers around the hilt, just so, angling my arm in the correct way, running one hand down my spine and telling me to stand up straighter. My face and neck grew hot. I tried to convince myself he wasn't touching me more than was strictly necessary—I tried to convince myself I wasn't disappointed when he stopped.

He demonstrated fighting stances, explaining different ways to position my feet. He showed me how to raise and lower my blade, how to thrust and block. He told me fencing was like dancing, only I couldn't let my opponent know which steps I was following.

I mimicked his movements over and over, my arms growing

shaky with fatigue, sweat dripping into my eyes. Practicing the piano definitely used a different set of muscles.

And then, to my combined amusement and relief, the army of a rival nation burst into the armory—I recollected those siege towers I'd seen from the library—and we had to clear out in a hurry.

"Meet me in *The Thief's Field*!" Hal called as he sprinted away from me, dodging crossbow quarrels, his eyes dancing with laughter. "It's pretty boring for half the book—we should be able to get some sessions in!"

"Are you sure you can find your way?" I ducked as a bearded man with unnaturally red eyes swung a sword at my head. But Hal had already gone. "Library!" I cried, "*The Thief's Field*!"

I jumped into the mirror while it was still wavering into being; the sword whistled past my ear, the chaotic scene vanished.

A heartbeat later, I tumbled out into sunshine and grass. Hal was scrambling to his feet with a bright laugh just ahead of me, and I wondered how to break it to him that I didn't really have the energy for another lesson today. I realized I was still carrying the sword. Odd—I'd never brought an object from one book into another before.

To my relief, Hal was tired, too, and we didn't go more than a few rounds before he announced we were done for the day. After that, we sat with our backs pressed up against a wooden fence, staring down into a lush valley as the sun sank in a riot of yellow and orange. Every muscle in my body felt like it was made of jam and cream, but my heart sang with contentment.

Hal grew quiet, solemn, his earlier giddy mood wholly

evaporated. "Are you all right?" I asked him. I wished I dared take his hand.

His eyes flicked across to mine, his face painted gold in the light of the setting sun. "I'm remembering."

"What are you remembering? And why now, do you think?"

Hal turned his gaze back to the valley, drawing his knees up to his chin and wrapping his long hands around them. "You made me think. You made me wonder. I've been remembering little things. Quiet things."

I waited for him to go on.

"My mother had gold hair. She liked to sing in the snow, and her favorite food was honeyed biscuits. She always put out seeds for the birds. Watched them from the window."

The sun sank lower, fading into a cerulean twilight and a chorus of crickets. Down in the valley, campfires flared orange.

"I had six brothers and four sisters—I was the youngest of them all. I was spoiled. There were chocolates at Christmas, days skating in the winter, fireflies in the summertime."

"Do you remember what happened? Why you're trapped here?"

He shook his head.

The darkness made me bold. "Come home with me. Back to the house under the mountain. Maybe you'll remember more."

"I don't think I can, Echo."

I chewed my lip. "In the real world, my face is covered in scars. People cross themselves when they see me. My stepmother would be happier if I was dead and my brother and father would be better off without me."

"Why are you telling me this?"

I stood, something raw opening inside me. "Because I want you to know me, the *real* me. The me I am when I'm not here."

Hal rose, too, his eyes never leaving my face. Gingerly, he reached out a hand and touched my arm. The points of his fingers felt like fire. "I don't know who I am when I'm not here. I think I'm just a shadow, a wandering spirit. I'm not sure I even properly exist outside of the books."

I wanted to lean in to him, to wrap my arms around his neck and never let go. I wanted to kiss him, and the thought scared me and thrilled me all at once. But I just stood there.

He stepped closer. He slid his hand into mine. I felt the print of every finger where they touched my skin. "Thank you," he said. "For telling me."

The night was full above us, stars winking into being. "Do you imagine me very hideous now?" I whispered.

"You could never be hideous."

My heart wrenched. A shooting star streaked across the sky, and I almost couldn't bear the beauty of it.

And then a mirror shimmered before us, the library calling me home for dinner.

"Do you have to go?" Hal's voice was warm and quiet in my ear.

I would have stayed there forever, if not for the wolf. I squeezed Hal's hand. "I'll be back tomorrow."

His eyes searched mine. "Promise?"

"Promise."

I STEPPED THROUGH THE MIRROR into a dark and unfamiliar valley, not the library as I had expected. Rain fell strangely upward; flowers grew sideways. Something like clouds floated past my knees, only they had ears and tails and wore tinkling bells around their cottony necks, giving the impression they were some kind of cat-cloud hybrid.

Mokosh, suddenly beside me, gave a delighted squawk and snatched at my sleeve. "Echo! I've been looking everywhere for you. I'm so glad you stepped through my mirror. My mother has given me permission to bring you home for a few days! We can go riding and fishing—I can show you all the secret passages in the palace. We can eat sherbet and stay up late into the night and *oh* it will be just *wonderful*, what do you say?" She seized my shoulders and whirled me around, the rain plastering her silver hair to her smooth forehead while the cat-clouds purred about her ankles.

I was more than a little irritated that she had taken me away from Hal. "Mokosh, I—I can't."

She let go of me. Her whole face fell. "Why not?"

"The wolf needs me, and the house is shedding rooms, and I'm already nearly late for dinner—" That wasn't quite the whole truth, of course, but I wasn't about to tell her she'd interrupted my moment with Hal.

Mokosh waved an impatient hand. "*That's* all you're worried about? I'll just have my mother bend time for you, a little, and have you back the moment you leave."

The rain was warm on my skin and tasted sweet as candy. I hated to see her staring at me with such drooping hope. But I could still feel the prints of Hal's fingers, still see the haunted sorrow in the wolf's eyes. I shook my head. "I'm sorry, Mokosh."

She sagged in the rain, whispered a word to the sky. The outline of a mirror shimmered into being. "Just for an evening, then? An hour? I swear to you it will be like you never left. Please, Echo. You're my only friend."

The word pierced me, more powerful than Mokosh could have known. "An hour, then. But I *must* be back before midnight."

Mokosh squealed with delight and grabbed my hand, pulling me through the mirror.

We stepped out onto a wide terrace, the last glimmers of a sunset tracing lines over a glittering sea. Behind us loomed a huge white palace. Below us, endless ocean.

Far below us—there were no waves lapping against the shore.

"A floating island," I said. "It's beautiful."

"It's one of the twelve wonders of the world." Mokosh beamed. "My mother made it."

"She *made* it?"

Mokosh nodded. "When she was younger than I am now. I

haven't even half her ability. I'm hoping I grow into it."

I was too awed for words.

"I'll show you my room. Come on!"

And then she was tugging me across the terrace, through a tall green door, and into a grand hall. We traipsed up stairs and down a corridor—I felt like my whole life had narrowed to stairs and corridors—then into an airy suite, its windows flung wide.

We sat on silk cushions and drank tea as light as perfume. We nibbled seed cake sprinkled with sugared roses. Mokosh babbled on and on, about her endless lessons and the tediousness of her daily life—that's why she was always reading, she confided.

At one point, she leaned back on her elbows and fixed me with a knowing grin. "I've been meaning to reprimand you for abandoning me completely at the ball the other night, but I've decided I don't blame you. Your partner was *very* handsome. You must tell me all about it!"

I blinked at her, and traced the designs etched into my glass with one finger. I still didn't want to tell her about Hal. He was a secret I didn't want to share.

She must have seen as much in my expression. "Echo! You've been keeping delightful things from me!"

I flushed. "He's a reader, too. I've met him a few times."

"Another reader! What's his name? Where's he from?"

Starlight flashed out over the sea. I thought of fencing lessons and a rainy wood and dancing close enough to feel his heartbeat. I didn't want to be there anymore. I stood. "I'm sorry, Mokosh.

I really must get back."

She fixed me with a shrewd glance, the laughter in her face shifting to something hard, and dangerous around the edges. But then she smiled, and that sharp expression melted away. "Forgive me. I shouldn't press you to share if you aren't ready. Thank you for coming."

I relaxed, relieved that she wasn't angry. "I'll come back soon. You can show me the rest of the palace."

"I'd like that."

She hugged me, quick and tight, and then spoke a mirror into existence, right there in her bedroom.

I stepped into the library and ran right back into *The Thief's Field*, my heart in my throat.

It was still that blue-black dark of faded twilight. The sky was streaked with stars. The field danced with fireflies.

But Hal was gone.

Dejected, I returned to the library.

I popped into a half-dozen other book-mirrors, looking for him, but he wasn't anywhere to be found.

But out in the hall, the wolf was waiting for me. I was glad to see him, and impulsively dropped to my knees and wrapped my arms around his neck.

He whuff-laughed into my hair, and I knew he was glad to see me, too.

CHAPTER EIGHTEEN

I N THE WOOD BEYOND THE HOUSE, the trees had turned from green to gold. Swallows danced in the currents of the air. Bees sparked like yellow-bright embers among the waving grasses. Time was slipping away. I still didn't go back to the room behind the obsidian door, telling myself I was sure to find the answers I needed in the book-mirrors soon. I couldn't shake away my nagging fear of that room, like splinters deep under skin.

We were opening the cages of the gold dragon-birds several weeks after the venomous garden had been unbound, when it happened again.

The room started to shake. A crack splintered through the floor.

The wolf was further from the door than I was, and I lunged for him, grabbing the scruff of his neck and hauling him over the crack as the room shuddered, and fell into the void.

We tumbled together into the hallway just before the door melted into the wall, the ragged remnants of the binding shimmering for a moment in the air before also vanishing. The wolf shook himself, and growled. "That was too close. We have to be more careful."

I studied him, my hand still touching his neck. He was bound to the house—was he going to start unraveling as well? "Wolf . . . Are you really going to die, when the year is up?"

Slowly, carefully, he extricated himself from my grasp. "I will be worse than dead. I will belong wholly to *her*."

"You told me before that you welcomed death—that it would make you free."

His ears flattened back against his head. "I lied."

He stalked off down the corridor and I followed at a distance, watching as he disappeared into the bauble room. I didn't follow; whatever magic was bound behind that obsidian door made my skin crawl. And I couldn't shake away my fear of the library becoming unbound.

So I left him to his remembering.

I FOUND HAL IN AN outdoor market by the sea, where merchants were selling their wares under brightly colored awnings. Ships gleamed white on the horizon. The sun was warm; the wind was cool. He was haggling with a dark-haired young woman over a pair of daggers, while she smiled up at him under long lashes. She was very beautiful. I tried to ignore the jealousy that took root inside of me and started to sprout. I hadn't seen him in some weeks.

"Hal?"

His eyes brightened when he saw me. He paid the young woman for the daggers, and tucked his arm through mine. Together, we walked down to the shore.

"Shall we get some fencing practice in?" He laid the daggers on his coat in the sand, and rolled his shirtsleeves up to his elbows, loosing his sword from its sheath.

"Hal, will you try something for me?"

He must have heard the seriousness in my tone. He grasped my hand. "What's wrong?"

"The house is unraveling. I don't want you to be unraveled with it. Will you . . . will you *try* to come back to the library? You can stay with the wolf and me. We can figure out how to get you home."

The wind smelled of salt and fish and damp. The sea washed over the shore, crawling up to greet us.

A sudden longing sparked in his eyes. "I'll try," he said.

I let out a breath and gave him a shaky smile. "Library. I'd like to stop reading, please."

The mirror shimmered in the air between us.

"You first," I told Hal.

He stepped up to the glass, stretched out one hand to touch it. But nothing happened.

"Try again. Please."

He put both palms flat against the surface of the mirror. He stood so close his nose touched.

Nothing.

His eyes flicked to mine. "Please, Hal." I was shaking. *"Please."*

And that's when I grabbed his hand, and ran with him toward the mirror.

He hit it with a resounding *crash*, and fell onto the beach in a shower of glass fragments. Blood showed bright on his arms and his face where the shards cut him.

I knelt beside him in the sand. He gripped my shoulders.

"I'm sorry, Echo. I don't think I really exist, out there. I'm just a shadow."

"I can't accept that. You're as real as I am."

"Maybe I was, once. But I'm not anymore."

I touched a spot of blood on his cheek, brushed it away. He sighed and sagged against me.

I fought back my rising sense of helplessness. I'd thought it would work. I'd *needed* it to work. "I'll find a way to help you. To free you. We'll fix this." But I didn't know if I believed that anymore.

"I hope so."

Hal's breath was warm against my cheek, and the nearness

of him made my stomach wobble. I didn't know quite what to do with my involuntary reaction, so I stood to my feet, pulling him up with me. "In the meantime, how about another fencing lesson?"

He grinned, though a sort of haunted blankness lingered in his eyes. "I thought you would never ask."

We fenced for an hour along the beach, though I could tell his heart wasn't in it any more than mine was. We finally collapsed in the sand, watching the waves whisper up onto the shore and then fall back again.

Hal's hand found mine. I shifted closer to him.

An explosion shook the ground, and we looked back to see the market bright with flames.

Hal tightened his grip on my hand.

"What's wrong?" I asked.

"That's never happened before."

Another explosion wrenched through the earth, shaking us apart from each other. "What do you mean?"

"I mean I've read this book half a dozen times and that's never happened. The story is changing."

My chest tightened. My mind flew to the unraveling house, shedding rooms like snakeskin. "I have to go," I breathed. "I have to—Library, I want to stop reading."

"Echo, wait—"

But I was already reaching out for the mirror.

THE LIBRARY WAS SHAKING, BOOK-MIRRORS tumbling from the walls, crystals falling from the chandeliers like beautiful, deadly rain.

No. *No.*

Not the library.

Not Hal.

A crack splintered through the floor and one of the couches fell into it. Mirrors smashed onto the tiles. The library began to scream.

I leapt across the widening crack, stumbling on the other side, nearly falling in myself. My hand went automatically to the pouch at my hip, and I slipped on the thimble while loosing the needle and the spool of golden thread.

I refused to let the library become unbound.

I refused to lose Hal.

I flung myself toward the door, fingers scrabbling around the frame, and touched it with the thimble. My hand fell through the wall and I found the scarlet binding threads, slippery and smooth, frayed at the edges. Broken. I held tight.

The library shrieked. The shaking grew worse. Mirrors crashed and skidded around me, slivers of glass bouncing up to cut into my cheeks, my arms, while the crystals from the chandeliers sliced my neck or caught in my hair. The room tilted backward and I grabbed the door frame with one hand, my body dangling in empty space. With my other hand, I clung to the scarlet cords. My heart beat triple time: *Don't let go, don't let go, don't let go.*

But if I didn't let go, I wouldn't have both hands free for the binding stitch.

And if I let go, I would fall.

"Echo!"

I looked up into the hallway, where the wolf crouched, every hair standing on end. "Echo, *reach*! I will catch you!"

But I couldn't lose Hal.

I glanced behind me, into the chaos of shattered mirrors and the widening chasm that spiraled down into the void.

It was worth being unbound, for a chance to save Hal.

I let go of the door frame. I slipped the needle into the scarlet threads.

For three heartbeats, I didn't fall. For three heartbeats, I sewed the binding stitch, the needle humming in my hand.

And then the wolf's teeth clamped around my arm and he was hauling me upward, over the door frame and into the safety of the corridor.

"I wasn't finished!" I wrenched away from him, wheeling on the library.

It was still there, shaking, shuddering. But the crack didn't open any wider. The screaming stopped.

"We can still save it," I told the wolf.

He growled. "It's too dangerous."

"I'm not giving the library up. Go to the spider room. Gather all the binding thread you can." It was strange giving him orders, but he just dipped his head mutely and went off down the hall.

I brushed my hand around the door frame, willing the library to grow still. "By the old magic," I said softly, "I command you to stay."

And somehow the room quieted. Somehow, the shaking ceased.

The wolf was back the next moment, hauling a basket full of thread in his teeth. I grabbed it and hopped down into the library before he could protest.

I glanced back. "Aren't you going to help?"

He grunted but leapt down as well, careful to avoid the crack in the floor.

"We can fix this," I said, with more confidence than I felt. I tried not to look at all the book-mirrors, tried not to register the fact that most of them—if not all—were clearly broken beyond repair.

I knelt beside the crack and pushed the needle into the floor. It went in easily, the thread sighing and singing. Without any warning, I leapt across to the other side, skidding to a stop in a shower of broken glass. The wolf giving a sharp bark of alarm.

"I'm fine," I assured him.

He stayed where he was, glowering at me.

I ignored him and pushed the needle into the floor on that side, preparing to leap back across.

"Throw me the needle, Echo," said the wolf drily. "I will make the stitches over here."

That certainly sounded less exhausting than leaping across the crack over and over all the way down the room. I threw it to him.

It took hours to mend the library, hundreds of stitches on either side of the crack. When we'd finished stitching, I joined the wolf on his side, and we seized the thread together and pulled the seam shut, the whole house groaning and grinding beneath us. After that, I made more binding stitches around the door frame, and we pulled the room up to its proper level again.

There was nothing to be done about the book-mirrors.

"The house may be able to fix them," the wolf told me, following my mournful glance.

I didn't believe him, but I hoped he was right. I fought the urge to dig among the slivers of glass, piece together a book-mirror, and step through to see if Hal was all right.

The air in the hallway turned suddenly icy; the lamp grew a tail and floated down from the wall—it was nearly midnight.

"Come, Echo. We've done all we can."

The wolf caught my eye, and I sagged against him. "Thank you for helping me."

He cocked his head. "I would never have left you to do it alone."

We paced down the corridor as we had done that first night, my hand wound in the scruff of his fur, the wolf pressed up warm against my knee.

I dreamed that Hal shattered to pieces like the book-mirrors, and spun away into the darkness where I could never reach him.

CHAPTER NINETEEN

I N THE MORNING, I WENT STRAIGHT to the library. To my staggering relief, it was still there. I sewed six binding stitches around the door frame, just to be sure, and then stepped inside.

The crack in the floor was barely visible, reduced to a shimmering, silver scar. The chandeliers had re-strung themselves.

And miracle of miracles, the wolf was right—the book-mirrors had pieced themselves back together.

"Oh, *House*!" I breathed, giddy as a child. "Oh you marvelous, marvelous House."

The air hummed around me; the house was pleased at my praise.

I stepped into the nearest book-mirror without even checking the description plate, and found myself in a lighthouse, waves crashing noisily against the stone.

A staircase coiled above me like a nautilus shell, beautiful and strange; the stone steps were beginning to crumble, but the railing was freshly lacquered. There was a window at my eye level, and outside the sun sank softly into the restless sea.

The incongruous whistle of a teakettle drifted from somewhere above me, and I climbed the stair until I came into a little round room where an old man was just taking the kettle off the fire. He poured hot water into a teapot awaiting him on a low table, and looked up at me with a soft smile. "Stay for tea, my dear?"

"I'm afraid I can't—I'm looking for my friend."

"A shame." The old man settled down in front of the fire, the springs in his ancient armchair creaking in protest. "I would have had *two* visitors today."

"Found the biscuits," came a voice from the stair.

I jerked around to see Hal in the doorway, holding a biscuit tin and a bottle of brandy.

For a moment I forgot how to breathe. Then I squawked and leapt toward him, pulling him into a fierce hug before I recollected myself and let go, embarrassed.

He laughed. "Save the brandy, Echo! What's gotten into you?"

It was all I could do to keep from breaking down in the middle of the lighthouse. "I thought I'd lost you."

"You could never lose me."

But I saw in the haunted hollows under his eyes that that wasn't true.

"Let's have those biscuits, then," said the lighthouse keeper.

Hal and I joined him in front of the fire, me in another ancient chair, Hal perching on the arm. He leaned into me. Took my hand. I smoothed my thumb against his skin to assure myself he was really there.

We sipped tea and ate biscuits, while the lighthouse keeper told us in his soft voice about his life. He'd lived all alone in the lighthouse since losing his wife and child forty years ago. "But don't you feel sorry for me," he said. "I have the sea to keep me company. And sometimes the Winds sing me to sleep." Coughs wracked his thin body, and I noticed how frail he was. I regretted not reading the description plate, not knowing if this story had a happy ending.

When the sun began to set, Hal and I followed the old man to the very top of the lighthouse where windows ringed all around, freshly cleaned and sparklingly clear. Out over the sea, the last glow of the sun was visible, a line of fire across the water. It disappeared all at once, and the twilight grew swiftly dark.

The keeper lit the lamp in the center of the room. Light flared up, refracted by glass lenses that were directed out to sea. Hal and I watched as he wound the weights and adjusted the lenses, coughing all the while. Spots of blood flecked his beard. His body shook.

A storm rose over the sea. It raged for hours, lashing the lighthouse with all its fury, while the old man struggled to keep the lamps lit. Hal held me close, his arm around my waist, my arm around his. I didn't want to watch the lighthouse keeper's tragedy unfold, but I also didn't want to leave the story, for fear I wouldn't be able to find Hal again.

When dawn broke, the old man climbed down the stairs to his little bedroom for the last time.

We sat with him, Hal and I, while he was dying. I held his hand, tears streaming down my cheeks. Hal held mine.

Sorrow filled me up. I couldn't help but think of Hal, trapped in the book worlds, like the keeper was in the lighthouse. Is this how Hal would end? Dying alone, a character in a story?

When the old man was gone, Hal pulled me gently to my feet. We left the lighthouse, striding out onto the sand, the salt-drenched air fanning cold across our skin. I told him about the library, how it was nearly unbound.

"Thank you for saving it," he said. "Thank you for saving me."

I leaned my head on his shoulder. "I haven't saved you yet."

His lips moved against my hair. "Yes you have."

I think that's when I decided. If, God forbid, I couldn't find a way to help the wolf and he failed or died or was lost to the wood at the end of the year, I would stay on as caretaker of the house.

I would come and have tea with Hal every day, while the worlds of the books smoothed away any hint of age. Perhaps, with the last hint of life, I would step into the book mirrors to be with Hal forever, and we would fade together, little by little, until the library crumbled and we were lost to the whims of time, nothing more than ink between pages, turned to dust.

No matter what, I would never leave him to die alone.

THE DAYS SPUN AWAY, GRAINS of precious sand slipping through my fingers. The trees in the wood turned from gold to brown. Autumn was here in earnest; winter was not far away.

I was running out of time.

The house shed a new room every week. The bear room, the treasury, the laundry, countless others—all vanished. We lost the spider room, and I hoarded the remaining thread, using it to make a single binding stitch, every day, around the library's door frame, to keep it from going the way of the others. I selfishly wished that the bauble room would be unbound next. Something inside me pulled me to go back there, but my ever-sharpening fear of it kept me away. Fear tangled with guilt, and I continued to tell myself I was just honoring my promise to the wolf.

I went reading more and more. I wanted to spend every moment with Hal that I possibly could, and I was more determined than ever to find a way to help him—and the wolf. The answers had to be somewhere in the book-mirrors—I just hadn't found them yet.

But Hal seemed less concerned with finding answers than he was in having adventures.

He came with me when I sought out a caravan going on an epic journey to retrieve a magical object—he was so distracting I had to abandon the quest after an hour. We wound up playing pranks on the caravan for the remainder of the journey. ("The magical object wasn't bound to be anything useful," Hal assured me, avoiding my eyes when I asked if he'd remembered anything more.)

I stepped into a book about a wise man who lived on top of a remote mountain, hoping he might know something about the old magic. Just as I was saddling a quiet mare to ride up the mountain, Hal burst into the stable with a grin. "There's a dragon wreaking havoc on the kingdom!" he announced, leaping the few steps to my side and taking my hand in his own. "You know what that means!"

"What does it mean, Hal?" I asked him, laughing.

He raised our joined hands dramatically into the air. "It means, my fierce warrior, that we must go and slay the beast!"

"Hal, that's a *subplot*!" I objected, but he just tugged me into the tack room and managed to unearth a suit of armor just my size.

He was there when I attempted to help a princess defeat her sorcerous uncle from seizing the throne—Hal threw food in the sorcerer's face at a banquet, laughing himself silly as the sorcerer frowned thunderously and turned all the diners into snakes and rabbits. (This would have happened anyway, Hal assured me— he'd read ahead. Wouldn't I like to go dancing at the village festival under the stars?)

He was there when I went to visit a queen who was rumored to be an enchantress—or at the very least have an impressive library. The three of us took tea together in the garden—me the enchantress-queen, and Hal, who looked ridiculous in skin-tight trousers and a pointy cap with a feather. "I was just hanging around some outlaws," Hal explained his regalia. "Stealing from the rich, giving to the poor. That sort of thing."

"I beg your pardon!" exclaimed the queen, and we were subsequently thrown in prison, so I didn't get to ask her about her books or her enchantments.

And he came with me when I harnessed a chariot to a comet and rode it up to the Palace of the Sun, where the East and West and South Winds dwelled with their father in a great bronze house filled with light. The Winds themselves came to greet us, and they were tall and grim, with jewels bound bright on their foreheads: East, whose skin shone the same burnished bronze as his father's house; West, who gleamed gold and had a pair of wings folded against his back; South, who was a bright copper red and carried a spear made of mountains.

We dined with the Winds in a hall looking out over the world, and the colors tasted bright and the wine smelled of music.

"Where is the North Wind?" Hal asked.

East frowned. West looked stern. South, sorrowful. "His power was greater than ours," said East, "but he was a fool. He traded it away for the love of a woman."

I thought of the wolf, who had told me that same story in the temple. I wondered if the West Wind remembered healing me, after I'd been caught by the wood. But these couldn't be the same Winds, could they? This was a story, and that had been real.

"It's the oldest of magics," I said.

The three Winds turned to me, and I didn't think I imagined the shrewdness in West's eyes. "What is?"

"Love." The word burned through me, and I suddenly couldn't look at Hal.

But he stood near enough that I could feel the heat of him. "That's something you must never let go of," he said softly.

West nodded, his wings rustling in a cool current of air. "It could break the strongest curse. The bitterest of enchantments."

My heart stilled. "What did you say?"

The West Wind's eyes blazed with all the light and depth of the universe itself. He brushed his fingers across my temple. "You will understand, in time."

"If you know something—if you know how to help him—"

It was East who spoke next, the jewel bound to his forehead flashing scarlet and orange. "When you have found the oldest of magics, you must not let it go, not even for an instant. Then, and only then, will you be free. Free of all of this."

"I'm not the one who's trapped," I objected.

East just smiled, and he and his two brothers turned away from us.

"Wait," I said. "Please wait!"

But the East and South and West Winds stepped off their terrace into empty air. I blinked, and they were gone.

I turned to Hal. "I don't know what they mean. I don't know how to help you."

He looked after them, his body taut and still. "It doesn't matter, Echo."

"Of course it does!"

He seemed to shrink before me, and to my horror, tears dripped down his cheeks.

"You've remembered something else, haven't you?"

His shoulders shook.

"Hal?"

He pulled away from me, spoke a sharp word to the air and vanished from sight.

CHAPTER TWENTY

WINTER DESCENDED OUTSIDE THE HOUSE, ICE encasing the roses in the garden, frost tracing lacy patterns on the windows.

My remaining time in the house under the mountain had dwindled to a mere two weeks, and I was no closer to helping the wolf—or Hal—than I was at the beginning.

Nearly every day another room came unbound. We lost the rain room, the sunroom, the room with the snakes. Even the dining room fell into the void one evening, a mountain of food tumbling with it. I took my meals in the conservatory or the room behind the waterfall instead.

The house shrank and shrank; it seemed to hum with sorrow. I tended the remaining rooms with as much care as I knew how. The wolf rarely accompanied me—he spent more time in the bauble room than he spent out of it. One day, my guilt at last propelled me to approach the obsidian door, and I stood outside of it for a long while, battling my fear. The door seemed to whisper, to scream. I had almost worked up the courage to open it when the wolf stepped out of the room, covered in blood from nose to tail. I sucked in a breath, catching a glimpse of the sharp spinning crystals before the door shut behind him. He didn't look at me, just padded off down the hall. Terror twisted through me. I ran away from the bauble room. I didn't go back.

I practiced the piano. I went reading, searching desperately for answers that evaded me. Hal seemed to be avoiding me; Mokosh was nowhere to be found. So I took to wandering listlessly around the house. It was dying, just as the wolf was. It would take all the binding thread in the world to keep it together, and there was barely any left. I would never become its caretaker.

What, then? Why had the wolf really brought me here?

And what would I do when he was gone? What would I do when I ran out of binding thread, and the library was lost to me, too? Would I just go home?

I thought about that, examined my future like a painted egg: first, studying its colors and intricate design. Then, slowly peeling the shell away to see what lay hidden inside.

I found uncertainty. Hope. As much as I missed my father and Rodya, I had no desire to go back, to return to Donia and the villagers' derision and a lifetime of lurking in the shadows to hide my face. But all the same, I was seized with a sudden longing to see them again.

I went to the library's storeroom, took the ivory hand mirror from its cupboard. I settled with it on the floor, pricked my finger, plucked a hair, like I had done so many times at the beginning of my stay in the wolf's house. "Show me my family," I whispered.

The mirror swirled white.

And then I was looking down the street of my village, following my father as he strode up to the bookshop, his hands in his pockets, whistling.

He fished out a key and unlocked the door, then stepped inside and went about the business of opening the shop: dusting the register, drawing the curtains, sweeping the already-spotless floor.

A man came in when he was only partially finished with this ritual and requested a book, which my father found quickly. The customer laid silver in my father's hands before stepping back outside, tipping his hat as he went. This scene repeated several times, with various men and women, and my heart twinged— my father's business was successful, for the first time in years. I wondered what had changed. Maybe Donia was right—maybe my face *had* cursed him.

The mirror shifted.

I saw Donia sitting on the couch in front of the fire, her fingers flashing with needle and thread. Her belly was round and tight beneath her dress, and she hummed as she sewed. Snow clung white to the window.

And then the scene changed again. I saw Rodya receiving his tradesman's sigil from his master, saw him stride out into the street where a girl waited for him, nut-brown hair curling from under her kerchief. She had soft eyes and a shy smile, and she fingered his sigil and kissed his cheek.

Rodya laughed and laughed, and kissed the girl properly, holding her close and safe against him. He murmured quiet words into her ear: "We'll be wed before spring, if you'll still have me."

And then it was the girl's turn to laugh.

The mirror wavered a third time, and went blank.

I raised my head from the mirror and found the wolf beside me, his amber eyes very bright. "Echo, why are you crying?"

"They are so happy. Oh, Wolf, they are so happy without me." And I wrapped my arms around his white neck and sobbed into his fur.

THE WOLF AND I WENT to the garden, and settled on the step near the lily pond. The wind was cold but the sun was warm; the air smelled of honey.

I told the wolf everything I'd seen in the mirror, words tumbling out of me until I was emptied of them. I hugged my knees to my chest and wiped away the remnants of my tears.

He watched me, passive and sad, and for a while didn't say anything. Over the iron fence, the wood was heavy with snow.

"I did this to you," the wolf said at last, his voice low and more gruff than usual. "I scarred your face. I made your life into something it never should have been."

It wasn't at all what I expected. "Wolf, I've never blamed you."

"Then why do you blame yourself?"

That was something I had no answer for.

"What others see in you reflects upon them, not you. Your stepmother treated you poorly—your whole village did—but that is not your fault. It never was. It never could be."

I picked up a pebble and threw it into the lily pond, but it only made a pathetic little *plash* before disappearing beneath the surface. "I have always been powerless." I fought to keep control of my voice.

The wolf shook his white head. "Just because you have always thought that does not make it true. Do you think your brother and your father were kind to you out of pity? Or because they saw the trueness of your heart, your goodness and your worth?"

I swallowed around the lump in my throat. "What is my worth?"

"Deeper than you know."

Everything felt sharp and cold, though the sunlight poured warmth into the garden. I didn't want to think about my scars anymore. I didn't want to think about my father and Rodya, or be afraid they were happier with me gone.

"If others cannot see your true self, if they refuse to see it—that is a flaw in their own character. Not in yours."

"Have you seen my true self?"

He looked at me. "I'm beginning to."

"Have I seen your true self?"

For a long, long moment, he gave no reply. We stared at each other, while the wind blew dead leaves into the water. "In part."

"Will I ever see the whole?"

"I do not know, Echo Alkaev."

I thought of the bauble room, the clock and the curl of silver hair. The wood, the wood, the wood. Puzzle pieces, waiting for me to fit them together, if I was brave enough to try.

"Wolf, why did you really bring me here?"

His sorrow was palpable. His eyes over-bright. "Because you are the opposite of her. You are full of life and kindness. You are not brimming with malice and hate, or waiting to twist others' goodness to your own cruel purposes."

"What has she done to you? What is she going to do?"

But he shook his white head. "There is a . . . bond . . . on me. I . . . cannot . . . "

"I know."

He nuzzled my knee and I wrapped my arms around him and held him close.

We sat there like that until the sun sank and the air bit cold, then went back inside to our dinner.

I SETTLED THE NEXT MORNING on the piano bench and opened the Czajka piece I'd been working on. Outside the window, sunlight refracted off the snow, I started playing, easing into the notes after fumbling a bit in the beginning.

The music swallowed me and I lost myself for a while in the soaring melodies and fairy-bright ornamental passages. I thundered into the last passionate crescendo and let the remaining few notes whisper out into the room, wavering with sorrow before they died away.

I took a breath. Laid my hands in my lap. And looked over to see the wolf, who had padded in at some point while I was playing. He stared at me, a strange light in his eyes. "I have never heard you play it so well," he said gruffly.

I soared with pride. The wolf wasn't generous in his praise.

Light streamed in through the window; dust motes swirled. The wolf leaned his head against my knee. "I do not deserve you. Your kindness. Your goodness. Your beauty."

"Wolf, I'm not beautiful."

He lifted his head and peered straight into my eyes. "You are wrong, Echo. You are the most beautiful person I have ever seen."

Something inside of me cracked. Tears leaked from my eyes.

The wolf tugged gently on my skirt and I knelt on the floor and wrapped my arms around his neck. "Do not cry. My beautiful,

beautiful girl. Please do not cry."

I held him like the world had spun away beneath me, and I was left to dance with the stars, not mortal any longer but a creature made of moonlight and magic.

No one had ever called me beautiful before.

The room began to shake. I jerked my head up. A crack was splintering through the floor. "No! Not this room! Please not this room!"

But the wolf was already grabbing my skirt in his jaw, pulling me to the doorway.

The piano shuddered and groaned and fell into the widening crack.

"No! NO!" I dropped to my knees in the corridor, scrabbling for the needle and binding thread on my belt.

But there wasn't enough thread, and it was too late.

The room spun away into darkness. The door vanished into the wall. I beat my fists against it.

The wolf was quiet beside me, waiting until I'd grown a little calmer before he spoke. "I am sorry, Echo."

"The *piano*," I whimpered.

"You are more important than a piano," he said.

CHAPTER
TWENTY-ONE

THERE WERE ONLY FIVE ROOMS LEFT. The house under the mountain had dwindled to the garden with its waterfall cave, the bedroom, the library, the bauble room, and, for some reason, the conservatory. It almost would have seemed like a proper house, if its hallways weren't forever changing. But even those were beginning to crumble. I went looking once or twice for the Temple of the Winds. I couldn't find it, and remembered that the wolf had told me it didn't really belong to the house at all.

There were only three days left. My mind pulled at the mystery of the wolf like the frayed ends of a knot, but I was no closer to a solution than before. I sewed a binding stitch around the library's door frame with the last length of golden thread, and stepped into a book-mirror titled *The Queen's Company.*

Hal was waiting for me, lounging against the western tower with a sword strapped to his hip, my sword resting beside him.

I couldn't help but stare—I hadn't seen him in weeks.

He grinned, but there was something haunted in his eyes. He tossed me my sword. "We've work to do, Echo—can't let you get out of practice!"

I barely had time to draw the blade before he lunged at me with his own outstretched.

We fenced for a long while in the grassy space in front of the western tower. Hal didn't speak. There was a hard set to his jaw, a crease in his forehead. He fought like he was trying to escape something. Like he was trying to forget.

We caught our breath in a pavilion set up for a visiting prince, where iced wine and sweet-spicy tarts were being served. I sat cross-legged on a velvet-lined bench (how extravagant was this queen, that she could afford to line her guests' benches with velvet?), while Hal slouched in a carved ivory chair, eating sugared oranges.

"You remembered more, didn't you?"

He wouldn't look at me, his eyes shifting away to the queen and her visitor, a dark-skinned prince with silk robes so thin and white I got the idea they were made of spider webs.

I took a bite of tart. Its initial overpowering sweetness shifted strangely to strong spices burning in the back of my throat.

"What did you remember?"

Hal brushed his finger along another orange slice but didn't eat it. Sugar spilled onto his lap. He still wouldn't meet my eyes.

"Hal. Let me help you."

The earth shook with sudden thunder, and I slid off the bench to the ground. An arrow whizzed past my shoulder. It stuck quivering in the queen's sleeve, pinning her to her chair. The spider-silk prince smiled.

Hal cursed, and hauled me to my feet.

"What's wrong?"

"The story is changing again. Those two are allies. They get married and fight off an army of fire demons. They bring peace to the continent."

But as I watched, the prince drew a dagger and slit the queen's throat. Her head slumped forward, blood running down her neck and soaking her gown. Drops of red touched her tart.

Hal grabbed my hand and pulled me out of the pavilion. We ran until we'd left the castle far behind and pain made my side catch. And then Hal let go of me and I wished he hadn't. I wheeled on him. "What is going on?"

"The books don't change. They *never change*. Those are the rules. You can't break the rules."

My fingers felt colder apart from his. Behind us, the castle was burning. "Someone did."

He cursed again; his hands shook. "You need to get away from me. You need to leave."

"What?"

At last, at last, he jerked his face to mine. His eyes were hard as flint. "I'm going to hurt you, Echo. That's what I remembered. I was always going to hurt you. You have to leave while you still can."

His gaze *burned.*

I didn't move. Smoke drifted toward us, the air grew thick with it. My thoughts were tangled threads, an impossible knot. "The books are enchantments. The only way they could change is if an enchanter changed them." My eyes teared as the smoke came closer. I teased one of the threads loose. "Why is it that people who are . . . who are enchanted, can never talk about it?"

"I'm not enchanted, Echo." He practically spat the words.

"How else could you be trapped in the books?"

Danger lingered in his eyes. He caught my hand, and drew me so close I could feel his breath on my lips, see the specks of silver in his irises. Awareness of him trembled through me. I couldn't stop staring at the curve of his mouth, and I wanted badly, badly, to trace it with my own.

He put one palm on my heart. "You have to stay away from me."

"Hal."

"You have to stay away."

And then he turned, and vanished.

Something rumbled through the earth; heat pulsed toward me. A *craaaaaaaaack* fractured the stillness, fissures opening in the ground. Within them, fire raged.

A shape curled up from the fire, the outline of a woman sketched in smoke.

"He isn't honest with you." Her voice was like crackling flame tangled with the screech of an out-of-tune violin. "He hides things from you. He does not trust you." She circled me, brushing fiery fingers across my shoulders. My dress smoked but I felt no pain.

"Are you a fire demon?" I asked her.

She laughed. "That is not the right question."

"What is the right question?"

"You are wasting time. He will die without you. You know he will."

The heat grew worse, and away in the distance I heard steel ringing on steel, the clash and cries of battle. "How do I help him?" My lips cracked, the words coming out brittle and dry.

She smiled, a thin curl of smoky lips. "Find me, and I will tell you how."

"You're right *there*," I said crossly.

"May I give you a piece of advice, Echo Alkaev?"

"How do you know my name?"

The smoke-woman ignored me. "Everyone is searching for their true selves. But everyone hides their true selves from each other. Look for the truth. If you find it, you will see through the enchantment."

"But I don't—"

"Ask the right questions," the smoke-woman interrupted.

"Come find me in the place you do not wish to look." She smiled and uncoiled back into a wisp of white, melting away into the wind.

The fissure she had risen from shuddered and cracked wider. I tried to leap over it but my foot caught in a crevice and I fell and fell and fell, down into the fire.

Flame seethed all around me, scorching my hair, licking all the moisture from my skin. I tried to scream, but I couldn't breathe in the bone-scorched air, couldn't speak the words that would bring me safely back to the library.

I was burning and burning. Pain seared white behind my sightless eyes.

And then.

Release.

I GREW AWARE, SLOWLY, OF icy cold, sharp as a knife, harsh as deep winter. I forced my eyes open.

I was kneeling in a shadowy corridor that stretched forever both ahead and behind. I could breathe again. The sensation of heat was gone. I touched my arms, my hair. I was once more whole.

"You died," came a voice behind me. "In a manner of speaking."

I jerked around to see Hal, his hands in his pockets, his brows drawn tight together.

"Where are we?"

He shrugged. "The place I am when I am nowhere else. It's how I find you—light pulses around a book-mirror when you're reading it."

I rose slowly to my feet and went over to him, hesitant from our last encounter, but desperate to be near him, all the same.

Without a word, he folded me into his arms, and I lay my head on his shoulder, listening to the quiet beat of his heart until I'd grown calm again.

And then he took my hand and we paced forward.

The corridor was lined with shifting dark mirrors, shadow versions of the ones in the library. If they had description plates, I couldn't read them.

"I've been remembering." Hal's words floated to me as if from a great distance. "More and more. And there is—there is one story here that I think is mine."

I looked at him quizzically.

"Just a little further."

It felt like we walked for an eternity. The cold gnawed down to bone, and I thought longingly of my winter furs.

"Here," came Hal's far-away voice.

We had come to the very end of the corridor, where a tall mirror hung. It was less shadowy than the others. The frame was silver, engraved with trees, a metal forest marching around the glass.

We stepped into the mirror. I felt the weight of magic, heavy as a waterfall, pounding on my shoulders. I couldn't breathe.

And then I blinked and I stood with Hal in a sunny room. Windows stretched up to the ceiling. Bookshelves lined the walls. A blond-haired man with graying temples sat behind a desk, a pair of silver spectacles perched on his nose. He was alternately sipping wine and writing in a thick ledger book.

I glanced at Hal, who looked suddenly stricken, as if he'd taken a punch to the gut. He let go of my hand and stepped up to the desk, but the man didn't lift his head. Like he didn't know Hal was there.

The similarities between the two men were striking, younger and older versions of each other.

"Is he your father?" I asked Hal.

The man still didn't seem to hear us. He kept writing in his book.

"Yes." Hal's voice was tight. Choked. He reached out to touch his father, but his hand passed through nothing—his father wasn't really there.

This wasn't like the other book-mirrors. This wasn't a story, invented by a sorcerer. This was a memory.

Hal's memory.

I folded Hal's hand in mine. "Let's see what else is here."

Hal allowed himself to be drawn from the room, dazed.

A small boy ran down the corridor, clutching a wriggling orange kitten in one hand, and a blue paper pennant in the other. "Mama!" he shouted. "Mama, I found her!"

Hal froze in his tracks. "One of the kittens wandered away.

We thought a wolf had got her, but she was curled up asleep in the toy chest. She used to sleep on my shoulders. Even when she got big. I called her Lion."

We went on, down the hall and into a drawing room. A woman sat on an elegant sofa, braiding her long pale hair. A slightly older boy-Hal scowled at her feet. "But I *want* to go with Illia! I'm big enough."

"When you're older, dear one."

"I'm *twelve*."

"Papa will get you a horse, Halvarad."

"I don't want a horse. I want Illia!"

"We can't always have what we want."

Beyond the wide windows of the drawing room loomed a wood, dark and green.

There was always a wood.

I blinked, and boy-Hal and his mother were gone, the room empty.

Hal shook beside me. "Illia was my closest sister. Six years older than me. She went away to be married. I never saw her again."

"You were alone," I said softly. "For much of your childhood."

"I was always alone." He paced up to the window, and I went with him.

A blond boy on a chestnut horse thundered toward the wood. Even from this distance, I recognized Hal, not much younger than he was standing beside me.

Why was there always a wood?

His eyes were wet, staring at his other self. "The wood was forbidden. I was taught to fear it, all my life. But I couldn't resist. I went anyway."

"Hal?"

His face grew hard. He jerked away from the window. "I don't want to remember any more."

"What's wrong? What happened here?"

I glanced once more to the rider, swallowed up by the trees. "What happened *there*?"

But Hal shouted a sharp word, and the whole scene crumpled around us, melting back into the shadowy corridor.

"Leave me," he said. He fell to his knees. He dropped his head into his hands.

"Hal, tell me what's wrong."

His eyes flashed hot. His body was tight with anger. "*Leave me!*"

I obeyed.

I stepped into one of the shadow-mirrors, and the corridor faded around me.

I FOUND MYSELF IN AN ordinary book-world, standing under a tree on a hill. To my utter astonishment Mokosh was there, wearing a gauzy purple gown that matched her eyes.

"Echo! Where have you been? It's ages since I saw you last. Are you going to tell me about him this time? Your mysterious other reader?" She winked at me.

I felt like a battered toy, ready to rattle apart in the barest wind. I realized I *did* want to tell her about Hal. I needed to talk to someone, and the wolf didn't seem at all like the right choice.

So I told her everything, back in her palace room on her floating island, stars winking outside the window. She listened at first with a teasing interest, which morphed into a disapproving severity by the time I was finished. "I feel I should put you on your guard," she said. She touched my knee, her brows creased with concern. "You don't know what he wants from you."

Her tone irked me. "He doesn't want anything. He's my friend."

"Then why isn't he honest with you? How did he get trapped in the books in the first place? Maybe he's dangerous. Maybe the books are his prison."

I jerked to my feet and paced to the window, buzzing with nervous energy.

"He said he was going to hurt you. He warned you himself to stay away."

"He would never hurt me."

"Echo, you don't know that. You need to be careful."

I studied her in the starlight, her beautiful eyes and shining hair, her flawless perfection, even in her own world. I was sorry I had come.

I made an excuse and left as quickly as I could, not easy again until I was safely back in the library.

CHAPTER
TWENTY-TWO

I DIDN'T EXPECT TO SEE HAL again, not after he was so adamant I should leave him. But he was waiting in the first book-mirror I stepped into the next day, standing alone on a mountaintop, his eyes and face stricken. A cold wind tore through his hair. Below us rambled a wide green wood.

There was always a wood.

"Will you meet me in *Shadow of Stars*?" said Hal quietly. "I want to show you something."

I nodded, and he gave me a tight smile. "There's an old concert hall, abandoned during a war. I'll be waiting for you there." And then he vanished.

I commanded the library and a mirror wavered into existence. I stepped through, onto a hill under fierce stars, the shattered ruins of a war-torn city stretching into the night.

I wandered through the winding streets, stepping over rubble and dark stains I didn't care to examine very closely. A boy with a bloody rag tied around his head pointed me to the concert hall, a huge domed building near the center of the city. Somewhere not too far off I heard shouting. Weeping. A piercing scream. I shuddered and picked my way to the hall as quickly as I could. I climbed a broken stair, stepped through the splintered remains of a door.

The ceiling soared high above me, broken glass showing slivers of stars. Four tiers of balconies leaned over a wide wooden stage, like ornately dressed eavesdroppers peering through a keyhole. Hal sat at a piano in the middle of the stage, wearing ill-fitting black trousers and a loose blue shirt that pooled silk over his wrists. His feet were bare. I suddenly remembered the careless notes he'd played on the harpsichord in *The Empress's Musician*, the offhanded way he'd talked so knowledgeably about Behrend.

I walked toward the stage and settled into a seat in the very front row. Hal didn't look at me, but he must have known I was there.

He started playing, a low octave with his left hand, his right spinning out a melody that sounded like liquid stars, beautiful and impossible and haunting. The left hand slowly climbed up to meet the right, and a fascinating counterpoint emerged out of nothing, spiraling into a wall of raging chords punctuated by a low repeated note, erratic as a fading heartbeat. The music rose and fell. It was the most beautiful thing I had ever heard in my life, but the sorrow woven into every phrase was almost too much to bear.

It ended before I was ready, but not before my cheeks grew damp with tears. I blinked up at Hal, who leaned his elbows on the keys and put his head in his hands. His shoulders shook and I jerked up from my seat and scrambled onto the stage. I sat next to him on the piano bench, slid my arm around his waist. He felt heavy beside me, his grief a solid thing.

"I wanted—I wanted you to know one thing about me," he said. "One true thing. It was all I could think of to give you." His voice was raw, ragged.

Ask the right questions, whispered the smoke-woman, unbidden, in my mind. "Where did you learn to play like that?"

"I learned from my friend. She wrote that piece—it was her gift to me."

The words tore at my heart, and I tried to push away my jealousy. "What happened to her?"

"I lost her. A long time ago." He stood from the bench in one stiff motion.

"How long ago?"

He looked at me, his eyes wet. "A moment. And an eternity."

I rose and slipped over to him. "If there was a way to—to get everything back... to make everything right again . . . would you let me help you?"

"You cannot help me, Echo. You never could."

I stared at him, my pulse overloud in my ears. "Hal—"

He stepped back, his whole body trembling.

The stage began to shake beneath our feet. Stars exploded beyond the domed ceiling, the world fractured white. I got the feeling from Hal's sudden sharp breath that this wasn't supposed to happen—another change in the story.

He flashed one more look in my direction, and winked out of existence.

I turned to see Mokosh standing in the midst of the hall, a pale green dress blowing about her knees in some invisible wind.

"All he does is lie to you," she said. "Why can't you see that?"

"Why do *you* only show up after he's gone?" I snapped, unaccountably irritated with her. "Are you following me? Library, I want to stop reading."

"Echo, I'm only watching out for you—"

But I was already stepping through the mirror. The hall faded around me. Hal's music coiled fragile and tight around my heart.

I DREAMED I WAS DANCING with Hal in the glittering ballroom. Soldiers burst in with their rifles and bayonets, and they slit

Hal's throat in a sweep of jagged silver. He stared at me as he crumpled and fell. "You cannot help me, Echo," he whispered. "You never could."

And then I was kneeling in the snow and it was Rodya who lay there, red blood staining the white ground. He gasped for air and couldn't breathe and I turned and saw my father's bookshop, burning, burning. My father was trapped behind the window.

"Papa!" I screamed and ran toward him.

Then everything turned dark, and I stood in the room behind the black door. The baubles dropped from their strings, slicing me to pieces as they slid past. I pushed through the falling stars to the strange whirring clock, and there behind the glass was Hal's face, his eyes wide with horror.

I WOKE WITH A GASP to the sound of someone crying. The darkness was sharp and cold around me, and I was shaky from the grip of my dreams. But I knew, as I had not wholly known before, that it wasn't the wolf making that noise.

It couldn't be.

Fear bit sharp. I reached out to feel for the wolf in the blankets.

But my hand touched skin, my fingers brushed against a very human arm. I gasped.

The owner of the arm woke; there was a sudden frozen stillness, the sharp intake of breath.

"Don't touch me," came a hoarse, desperate whisper. "You're not supposed to touch me."

But I didn't pull away. My pulse raged, strong enough, wild enough, to make me burst apart.

I knew that voice. How could I know that voice?

"Please, Echo. Please."

I let go.

CHAPTER TWENTY-THREE

I DIDN'T MEAN TO FALL ASLEEP.

But I woke with a start early in the morning to find the other side of the bed empty, sheets mussed where he'd lain, his shirt a shapeless linen puddle just on top.

I could still feel the warmth of his arm, the smoothness of his skin, the strength beneath it.

"Wolf?" I said into the cool gray light.

But there was no answer.

I got out of bed and dressed quickly, shivering. The room was cold, the house still, like it was holding its breath, waiting to see what I would do.

I paced through a corridor made of dying roses into the conservatory, and tucked myself into a window seat hidden by a large feathery fern. I stared through the glass at the winter wood, snow tracing the black branches with white.

The year was nearly up. There was only today and tomorrow, and then time would be gone.

I had failed to help the wolf.

And yet.

The arm I'd touched.

The voice I knew.

I knew, I knew, I knew.

"*You cannot help me, Echo. You never could.*"

The wolf's words, the night I'd found him hunting in the garden. And yet Hal had spoken them, too, right after he'd played for me in the abandoned concert hall.

"*Ask the right questions,*" the smoke-woman had told me.

I picked away at the knot in my mind, pulled out the threads, examined them.

I asked myself:

Why was I not allowed to look at the wolf in the night? What would happen to him, really, when the year was ended? Who was the collector, and what did she want with him?

I leaned my forehead against the window, watched as my breath fogged up the pane.

I asked myself:

Why was Hal trapped in the books? Why were his memories bound behind glass? What had happened to him in the wood?

Why was there always a wood?

Outside, snow began to fall, turning the world into a blur of white. The wood was lost from view. I shut my eyes and let myself consider the thing I had come here to consider.

I let myself ask the question that terrified me:

What if Hal and the wolf were one and the same?

The room began to shake, a horrific *crack* splintered through the floor. I bid my fern a sad farewell, and left the conservatory just before it tumbled into the void.

"LOOK FOR THE TRUTH," THE smoke-woman had told me. *"If you find it, you will see through the enchantment."*

There was one room in the house I had never properly explored, and it was finally time to face my fear and go back there.

My feet brought me to the obsidian door, glossy and opaque as a pool of ink.

I brushed my fingers over the cold metal of the compass-watch Rodya had given me, hanging as always around my neck. It continued ticking steadily, a second heartbeat against mine. It gave me courage.

Adrenaline pounded through me as I touched the black door.

It swung open, the field of hanging crystals shimmering just beyond. I stepped inside.

The world seemed to grow very still, a hush in a snowstorm. The baubles spun on invisible threads, tiny birds and beasts, globes of pulsing fire, stars brought down to earth. They were beautiful, but they terrified me.

I walked slowly, the hanging crystals brushing across my shoulders, slicing through my dress. A few grazed the unscarred half of my face, and it troubled me so much I kept one hand cupped around my right cheek for the remainder of my walk.

The room was deeper than I remembered, the darkness only punctuated by those spinning, vicious globes. I stared up at the strings they hung on, twisted, shadowy versions of the golden binding threads. I felt lost, or rather, that I was becoming lost, my soul unwinding in the dark, erasing itself from mortal thought.

And then suddenly I reached the back of the room and found myself staring up at the strange clock. I let my hand fall from my face. It was streaked crimson.

The clock whirred and clicked, its spidery arms moving so quickly they blurred before my eyes. Each arm was attached to a thin silver thread that spun out into the room, connecting to one of the baubles and crisscrossing the other threads in a complex web before stretching up into infinite darkness. The clock face was just as before: a curl of pale hair tied with ribbon, a smear of what could only be blood. Was it . . . Hal's hair? Hal's blood?

I felt all around the clock face, looking for some way to open it, and found a silver latch halfway down one side. I lifted it, nerves buzzing with a sense of wrongness and danger.

To my surprise, an entire bottom section of the clock swung open, and I found myself staring straight into a mirror.

A book-mirror.

It was damaged, the leather frame scored with claw marks, half a dozen hairline fractures in the glass. The label was torn, the description obliterated, but I could still make out the title: *The Queen of the Wood.*

The sense of wrongness was overwhelming; everything in me recoiled.

There was always a wood.

I took a deep, shuddery breath, and touched the surface of the mirror.

The world wrenched sideways and a bone-rending cold poured through me. Stars exploded in my vision and pain crawled up my body like I was being pierced with a thousand fiery needles. If I had any breath at all I would have screamed.

Then I was standing on the border of a huge, ancient forest, and the pain and the cold were gone. Trees stretched above me into a brilliant, starry sky, and music sparked bright in my ears, a tangle of wind and moonlight and the soughing of the wood. Everything felt strong and good and steeped in magic. The very ground hummed with it. I could feel it buzzing in my fingers.

I caught a flash of movement in the corner of my eye and turned just in time to see a deer—or was it a dark-haired boy? It seemed to be both at once—running through the trees. I sprinted after him, straining to keep his heels—his hooves?—in sight. Starlight dappled across his body like bright leaves in a river.

He burst into a clearing and melted into a thousand other shifting shadows as beautiful and strange as he was. I stopped and stared, trying to make sense of the whirling scene before my eyes.

They were fairies, I think, or something like fairies: wispy creatures as tall as trees that seemed to be made of rain, or flowers; willowy spiders with mossy hair; bears with long fingers and masques instead of faces; hundreds of others harder to describe. They all danced together in the center of the clearing, a mass of strangeness and swirling color. In their midst sat a woman on a writhing throne, her hair the same shade as the moonlight. She peered through the horde of dancers straight into my eyes, and lifting one long pale hand, beckoned me closer.

I went as if drawn on a string, slipping through the fairies who laughed as they danced until I came to the woman on the throne. I knelt in the grass before her.

"I have been waiting for you, Echo Alkaev." Her voice was slow and slippery as fine-spun gold.

I knew that voice. "You are the smoke-woman," I said, lifting my face. And thinking even further back, "The thorny queen."

"I became them for a time. But they are not who I am, even as this form is not."

I studied her, her skin mottled like stone. Her eyes seemed to have no color at all. "Then who are you?"

She spread her hands wide as she smiled at me. "Who is anyone? The truth of who *you* are is not represented here. Is it, Echo?"

I flushed with shame as I reached up to touch my face, smooth on both sides only within the pages of these impossible book-mirrors. I didn't answer.

"I've been watching you. Waiting to see what you would do. Have you figured it out?"

Danger crawled along my skin. The noise of the fairies' laughter grew harsh in my ears. "Figured out what?"

She smiled again, and her eyes sparked orange as flame.

Realization wrenched through me like an earthquake. I took a step backward, the sense of danger sharpening into fear. "You. *You're* the 'she' the wolf spoke of. The one who controls the wood. The one who gathered the pieces of the house. The one who trapped him there—maybe even the one who enchanted him in the first place."

She watched me with amusement. Fire crawled hot just beneath her skin, and I felt the sudden, awful heat of her.

She was the roaring fire behind the bedroom door. The wood that had tried to devour me.

I took another step back.

"Poor scarred girl. Lost and broken and unwanted. Marked by the Devil for his pleasure alone. No thought to how to change your fate. You haven't figured it out at all. I am surprised."

"Figured out *what*?"

She lifted a finger, and flame burst bright from the tip, a tiny flare of yellow that vanished again the next moment. "How to break the enchantment."

The whole world stilled around me. My throat felt ragged and raw. Horror and hope warred within me, a lion raging against a bear. "Tell me. Tell me how to break it."

She laid her hands back in her lap. "There is one thing that you must not do, one rule you must not break. You must break it." Her eyes were dangerous, specs of blackness from the heart of the earth. Flames seeped from between her lips. "That will nullify the enchantment. That will free him."

I thought of the lamp, a spark of light in the dark. "I don't believe you."

Fire danced around the ends of her hair. "You are thinking it is too simple an answer."

Her heat bit into my skin, and I took yet another step back.

"You were looking for the truth. The truth is always simple, but that does not make it easy."

Anger burned. "Who are you? Why have you trapped him?"

"My dear, Echo." She rose from the throne, sparks raining down from her hair and searing black spots in the grass. "It is not of my doing. He chose this. He chose *me*. They always do, in the end. He came to me, in the wood. He loved me. And so I saved him. Preserved him. So he could live forever." She held out a hand, flames curling through her skin. "What about you, Echo Alkaev? Would you like to live forever?"

The fairies surged around me like a sudden ocean tide, drawing me into their swirling, tangled mass. Stars wheeled bright above my head, close enough to touch. I moved with the dancers, straining to understand the words in the fairies' voices, sweet as honey, sweet as rain. They folded over me, and I thought it would not be so bad to stay with them, forever, forever.

Heat pulsed behind me, and I turned to see the Queen of the Wood wreathed all in flame. She smiled as she stared straight into my eyes. "Make your choice, Echo Alkaev. Won't you stay with me?"

I opened my mouth to answer her, to say *Yes, let me stay*.

"No!" came a sudden voice at my ear, "No, she will not!" A hand closed around my wrist and I turned to see Hal, wild-eyed and dirty. "Run," he breathed.

He jerked me forward. For half a heartbeat I stumbled and thought I would fall, but Hal held tight to my hand, and the next moment I'd found my feet and was running with him.

We ran and ran and ran, twisting through the ranks of the dancers, fleeing from the queen of the wood. I could hear her roaring behind us, sense the heat of her unquenchable fire. She did not want to let us out.

But we broke through the last of the fairies and dashed across the border of the forest, a wide meadow stretching forever beyond. The sun shone brightly here, though it seemed pale compared to the starlight we had left behind.

I gasped for breath, still clinging to Hal, whose jaw was tight and hard. His eyes burned with fury. "What were you *thinking*?" he cried, grasping both my shoulders and shaking me, hard.

I cringed away from him and he let go, swiping one hand across his eyes and cursing vehemently.

"I'm sorry, Hal," I gasped. "I'm so sorry. Please——"

He turned back to me, his face twisting with a sadness that seemed even stronger than his anger had been. "It's not your fault, Echo. It's not your fault."

"I wanted to help you. I was only trying to——"

"I know," he said. "I know." He wrapped his arms around me and held me tight against his chest. I breathed in the scent of him: leaves and sun, wind and stars. And then he said: "I will miss you, dearest Echo, when you leave me."

I drew back to look up into his face. "I'm not going to leave you. Not ever."

"Oh, Echo," he said as if his heart were breaking. "My dear Echo." He wrapped his fingers around my chin, gently, gently.

And then he kissed me.

CHAPTER TWENTY-FOUR

Hal's lips were soft and warm, a little salty and a little wild. I wanted to sink into him but he pulled away from me, his face wracked with emotion, his eyes filled with secrets I didn't understand.

"She lies," he said. "She always lies. Whatever she told you—don't listen. Promise me."

"I promise." In that moment, I meant it.

He smoothed my cheek with his thumb. I couldn't help but wonder if he'd touch my scarred face in the real world like that.

"I miss you," I whispered, "In that other world far away."

He tilted his forehead against mine. "I am always there."

"I know." A stillness settled inside of me.

He drew back again, his fingers light on my arms. "I have to go now, Echo. I am sorry."

I bit my lip to keep from crying, but I nodded. "Thank you for—thank you for saving me."

"You are the one saving me." He sighed, and turned, and vanished.

I told the library to take me home, and stepped through the mirror that wavered into existence.

I was back in the bauble room, knife-edged crystals brushing my shoulders, blood dried and sticky on the hand I was just drawing back from the mirror.

I stood there shuddering, staring at the fractures in the glass, the shredded leather frame, the barely-legible title.

The wolf had tried to destroy it. He'd obviously failed. Maybe that was the answer: destroy the mirror, destroy the queen—whoever she was—break the curse.

"She always lies," said Hal in my head.

She'd tried to trap me. It had almost worked. Whatever hold she had over the wolf—and, I was now certain, over Hal—I was going to break it if I could.

I straightened up, ignoring the pain in my shoulders and my face and my hand. Ignoring my fear.

I could still feel Hal's hand closing around my wrist, yanking me away from the dancers and the fire. I could still feel the echo of his lips against mine.

"House," I commanded, "Bring me my sword."

It appeared in midair and I caught it by the sheath before it hit the ground: the sword Hal had given me when we first started our fencing lessons. I wrapped my hand around the hilt and drew it out. Above me the wicked baubles began to hiss and spin on their silver threads, like a gust of wind had torn suddenly through the room.

I turned to the book-mirror, feeling stronger than I ever had before. I swung my sword as hard as I could and it crashed into the mirror, the reverberation shooting up though my fingers and into my skull. But it made no mark. I tightened my grip and swung again, throwing my whole body into it.

This time the impact knocked me backward, and I landed hard on my left side. I leapt up and attacked again, hacking at the mirror with everything in me. Over my head the knife-edged crystals started shrieking like children in pain. But I didn't stop. I struck the mirror again and again, until a spider-web crack appeared in the glass. Triumph surged through me. I could do this. I *was* doing this.

And then a blur of white crashed into me, hurtling me away from the book-mirror and onto the floor in a tangle of limbs. Blinding pain seared into my shoulder. I saw teeth and eyes and spots of red. I screamed, scrabbling desperately backward.

"Wolf! Wolf, what are you doing?"

He came toward me, his body low and tight, his ears pinned back, his mouth opened wide. There was blood on his teeth.

"Wolf, it's me. It's Echo." My back hit a wall. The wolf crouched, ready to spring at me and finish what he'd started. Terror made my vision crawl white. "House! House, my sword."

It was in my hand half a breath before he leapt at me in a snarl of teeth and anger; I nicked his side, and blood dripped down his white fur.

I scrambled to my feet and started moving in the direction I thought the door must be. My hand slipped on the sword hilt and I didn't want to think about why. I gripped it as tight as I could.

The wolf recovered himself and stalked after me, snarling, blood leaking down his chest.

"Wolf, stop. Please. I don't want to hurt you."

He crouched again.

"Wolf, *please*!" I screamed.

He jumped at me and I knocked him away with the flat of my blade. I ran three more steps to the door, not even noticing the swaying, shrieking, knife-edged crystals slicing into my skin.

He leapt again, I knocked him away for a third time. I glanced back and I could see the door.

One more time the wolf snarled and sprang toward me. He collided with the blade, screaming as it bit into his chest and blood spurted red. The cut looked deep.

And then I was at the door, through the door, slamming it behind me, asking the house to lock it tight.

I shuddered and shuddered. I couldn't stop. I sobbed in the hallway because I thought I might have killed him.

I DON'T KNOW HOW LONG I sat crying outside the obsidian door, but I finally lifted my head, brushed the hair out of my eyes with my blood-streaked hand, and stood shakily to my feet. The sword lay quiet on the floor, the blood on the blade already darkening.

There was no sound from the bauble room. I opened the door the barest crack and peeked in. The wolf wasn't there, the only sign of his presence a pool of red. So much blood.

Too much.

"House," I whispered. "Bring me to the wolf." I grabbed my sword and started down the hall, the pain from my own injuries suddenly asserting itself: my shoulder, my side, my face, my hand. But none of it mattered to me.

So much blood on the floor in the bauble room.

I walked faster.

The house led me down a stair and out into the garden, where the wind bit shockingly cold. There were bloody paw prints in the snow.

I followed them, panic searing into my bones. Past the dead roses and the white stone paths winding up the steps. Past the lily pool and the hammock hidden in the willow. Through the waterfall to the hidden room beyond, where the wolf lay too still in a pool of widening crimson.

I dropped down beside him with a cry, shouting instructions at the house almost without thinking: a fire, bandages, clean water. I brushed my fingers tentatively across his fur; I could feel his heartbeat, wavering just beneath his skin. He was still alive.

The supplies appeared at my elbow even as a fire flared up in the hearth on the back wall of the cave. I dipped a clean cloth into the water and carefully worked to clean the blood away from the wolf's wounds. He had many smaller cuts on his back and his long white legs, but the wound in his chest was jagged and deep. I hadn't punctured any vital organs, or he would be dead already, but it wouldn't stop bleeding. I thought of the diagrams in my medical books, the instructions for how to close such a serious wound, and my hands went to the pouch at my hip. The needle was there, but the spool was empty.

"Bring me thread," I whispered to the house.

It appeared in my lap, strong and white. I slipped it into the binding needle, shaking so hard it took too many precious seconds to accomplish. But the moment I put the needle into the wolf's skin, my hands grew still and certain. I tugged the thread through, pulling the ragged ends of the wound together, just as, not that long ago, the wolf and I had mended the tear in the library. A lamp flared into existence just above me without my asking, the house instinctively knowing what I required.

I stitched in silence, aware of every beat of the wolf's heart, every ounce of blood that seeped onto my hands and stained my skirt as I worked.

And then it was done. I washed more blood away and spread the stitches with an ointment made of yarrow leaves. Then I bandaged it, lifting the wolf's heavy head as I passed the roll of cloth around his chest and over his shoulder several times. The bandage was thick when I'd finished.

I laid the wolf's head down and immediately started shaking again.

I made myself bandage my shoulder and my hand. I made myself get off the floor and sit in one of the armchairs in front of the fire. I asked the house to lay a blanket over the wolf; it settled around him in a soft cascade of blue.

I think I fell asleep for a while, because when I opened my eyes, the light coming through the waterfall was a deep amber orange.

The wolf was gone.

I WENT TO THE LIBRARY. I stepped into five different book-mirrors, looking for Hal. He didn't come and I wasn't surprised. Because if Hal was the wolf, he was too injured to come. The thought twisted inside of me, sharp and terrible.

At last I went to my room and crawled into bed. I blew out the lamp earlier than usual. I curled myself into a tight ball. I'd tried so hard to help him and I'd made everything worse. I'd almost been trapped by the Queen of the Wood.

And I'd nearly killed the wolf.

I felt him climb into bed beside me a long while later. My tears were dry by then and I was profoundly glad. I didn't want him to catch me crying, not after everything he had suffered.

We lay a long while in the silence and the dark, not speaking. I knew he wasn't asleep—his breathing was too quick and sharp for that.

"Echo," he said at last, his voice tight with pain. "Thank you for saving me."

I took a breath. "I didn't mean to hurt you."

"I attacked you."

The image of him lunging at me, eyes wild, teeth dripping red, would haunt me forever. "What would have happened if I had broken the mirror?"

On his side of the bed, the sheets rustled. "It would have killed me."

I cursed myself.

"Echo do you remember the day you freed me from the trap?"

My heart seized up. The blur of white. The blinding pain. Looking in the mirror for the first time at my ruined face. "Of course I do."

"I have fought the wildness every day for nearly a hundred years. But sometimes—sometimes it seizes me no matter how I resist. Like it did with the trap. Like it did today. And that—that is when I hate myself the most."

"Wolf—"

"When I hurt you." His words were choked, like he was fighting tears. "I hurt you from the moment I met you. I do not mean to, but I cannot seem to help it. I—I do not want to hurt you anymore. You should leave. Go back to your father's house. I will see you safely through the wood in the morning."

"But I promised you a year. I gave you my word."

"There is only one day left. It doesn't matter."

"I will fulfill my promise. I'm not leaving you."

I listened to him breathing, three heartbeats, four. "If you are certain."

"I'm certain."

He said nothing more.

Sleep stole slowly over me, and as I was slipping into the realm of my dreams I thought I heard the wolf's quiet voice at my ear, just a breath away. "Forgive me, Echo. For what I have done. For what I will do again."

And then, in the last few moments of consciousness, human fingers tangled in my own, and a heartbeat that was not mine beat quick and sharp in my palm.

When I woke in the morning I was once more alone in the bed, but I knew with absolute conviction that the voice and hand had not been a dream.

And it was time to prove that to myself.

CHAPTER TWENTY-FIVE

I ROSE AND DRESSED, DONNING A FUR cloak against the chill permeating the room, and skipped the breakfast the house had laid out for me. I went straight to the library.

The magic mirror was still locked in its cupboard in the back room. I took it out, settled down on the floor, and pulled out a hair and pricked my finger.

"Show me Hal."

The surface of the glass rippled and changed.

I saw the wolf in the room behind the black door, roaring and raging, ripping the glass baubles down from their strings. His cries seemed to shake the room, and his fur and his bandage were streaked with blood. Behind him the spider clock ticked, whispering and whirring, the mechanism winding down.

The mirror shifted. I saw Hal pacing a shadowy corridor, his body so faded it was nearly translucent. He dropped to his knees before the mirror that contained his memories, bowed his head into his hands. His shoulders shook as he sobbed.

The image blurred before me.

There was only one day left, and I didn't know what to do.

I PACED THROUGH THE WINTRY garden, huddled in furs, my breath a white fog before me. Panic seethed in my mind, festering like an open sore.

Hal was the wolf, the wolf was Hal, and I had less than a day to save him.

Snow clung to my eyelashes and the last of the dead roses dropped their petals to the ground like blood. God in heaven, I didn't know what to do.

"I have fought the wildness every day for nearly a hundred years," whispered the wolf's voice in my head.

I blinked and saw the clock, the gears winding down. Maybe all I had to do was wait, see the year through to the very last day without lighting the lamp. Maybe when the time was up the wolf would transform into Hal in front of my eyes and be free forever. The Queen of the Wood had said the truth was always simple.

But what if I was wrong?

Ice stung my cheeks and I pulled my hood tighter. A mouse scurried beneath a tangle of dead ivy, scrabbling for seeds in the snow. My boots crunched and the wind bit sharper, but I didn't turn back to the house.

I couldn't stop seeing him, tearing the baubles down from their strings, howling in rage. Kneeling in the shadowy corridor, weeping.

In the fairy stories, there was always a *thing* to do. A kiss to give. An object to retrieve or destroy. A magical sword. A magical mirror.

Or a lamp, perhaps?

"There is one thing you must not do," the wood queen had told me, *"one rule you must not break. You must break it. That will nullify the enchantment. That will free him."*

But Hal had said: *"She always lies."*

I trusted Hal, certainly more than I trusted the queen—but what if his enchantment forced him to say that? What if lighting the lamp *was* the way to break the curse?

I'd promised to live with the wolf for a year. I'd promised to never look at his face in the night.

Hal's face.

What if I lit the lamp and broke his curse?

What if I lit the lamp and imprisoned him further?

It was impossible to know, but I needed to know it.

What was I supposed to do?

The clock behind the black door was ticking.

Time was almost up.

I WENT BACK TO THE library, shrugging out of my cloak and sling-ing it across one of the couches. I was desperate to speak with Hal and stepped into a book-mirror at random, hoping he would come to me.

I found myself hurtled along on a sea voyage to find a lost kingdom and a mythical prince. I let the story carry me, leaning over the ship's railing and drinking in the salty air, listening to the haunting cries of the sea-wisps—strange creatures that appeared to be a cross between fire and mist. They swirled about in the sky above the ship, sparking orange or blue or rose-blush pink.

Hal didn't come.

I waited for several book-days, through raging storms and an attack by an opalescent sea-dragon. The ship landed on an island in the eye of another storm, and as the crew and I and a brave red-headed farmer's daughter stepped onto the shore, the East and West and South Winds came and drew the whole island up into the sky. They seemed younger than before, fierce and full of anger, and they didn't seem to know me.

Still no Hal. I climbed the mountain in the center of the island with the farmer's daughter, up to a crumbling old castle where the mythical prince had been imprisoned for centuries.

I half expected the prince to turn out to be Hal, but he was a wizened old man with white hair and sapphires studded into his skin. The farmer's daughter turned him young with a kiss.

I walked away from them to the edge of the island, peering down, down, down through the clouds at the sea far below.

What was I supposed to do?

Should I light the lamp?

Should I not light the lamp?

"Echo! I was hoping to see you again before your year was up."

I blinked and saw Mokosh coming toward me, riding on one of the sea-wisps, which she'd harnessed with ice and moonbeams. The wisp was the same violet color as Mokosh's eyes and had curls of fiery hair.

"Have you found out how to free him?" she asked, reining in the sea-wisp so it hovered mere inches from where I stood. "Have you decided what you're going to do?"

I thought of the clock, winding down behind the obsidian door. I thought of the lamp on the bedside table, of human fingers, tangled with mine in the dark. "I don't want to get it wrong."

The sea-wisp hummed with energy and music, and Mokosh regarded me with pity. "So you will do nothing? What about the lamp?"

I looked at her sharply, a sudden horrible suspicion darting into my mind. "Are you the Queen of the Wood?"

She shook her head. "I am not. But I know her."

"Hal says she always lies."

"He is wrong. She speaks only the truth." The wind teased a strand of Mokosh's silver hair out of its braid. It blew about her face like a tendril of spider silk. "What did she tell you to do?"

"The one thing I can't do."

"Then you have your answer. Light the lamp. Set him free."

The violet sea-wisp opened its strange mouth and started singing. I felt the light print of rain on my shoulders.

"Who *are* you?" I demanded.

Mokosh stroked the sea-wisp's neck, and her hand sunk through it. I didn't understand how she was sitting on the wisp at all. "One who cares for Hal as you do. One who would see him free."

I tried to ignore my wrench of jealousy, and failed.

"I will speak plainly to you, Echo. You are the only one who can help him. To succeed or to fail—it is in your hands. But if you fail, know this—you will regret it forever. And this time there will be no going back."

Tears pressed hard against my throat. "I can't lose him."

"Then you know what to do."

"But I *can't.*"

"Echo." Mokosh put her hands on my shoulders, and somehow the weight gave me comfort. "Don't fail him. Don't fail yourself. Only you can do this. I have faith in you."

The sea-wisp sang one last keening note.

"Do what you know you must," said Mokosh. "Farewell." And then she tugged on the sea-wisp's reins and they both swirled away into the sky.

I told the library to take me home.

CHAPTER TWENTY-SIX

I DON'T KNOW QUITE WHEN I decided. Maybe watching the wolf who was Hal destroy the room behind the obsidian door. Maybe listening to Mokosh's words to me on the floating island. Maybe even the day before, stitching up the wound in the wolf's chest I had made with my own sword.

There is one thing you must not do, one rule you must not break.

I scrubbed the tears from my face and swept out of the library. I went back to my bedroom, shut and latched the door behind me.

You must break it.

"Matches, if you please, House." They appeared on the

nightstand. I curled my fingers around the packet, and shoved it deep in my pocket.

That will nullify the enchantment.

I had to force my next request past the lump in my throat: "And oil for the lamp."

The lamp filled with oil.

That will free him.

That will free him.

My whole body was trembling when I left the room.

I SEARCHED FOR HAL ALL day, stepping into one book-mirror after another. He didn't come and didn't come and didn't come. But I kept looking. I couldn't do what I was about to do without seeing him one last time. It would steady me. Assure me I wasn't about to make a horrible mistake.

At last, when the time for dinner had slipped away and there were only a handful of hours left before midnight, he came.

He met me on a high hill overlooking a valley that danced in the light of two setting suns. He looked solemn and fair, and stepped up to me without a word. He folded my hand into his, and I felt suddenly stronger.

A faun with flowers in her hair and a silver bear wearing a rose-thorn crown held onto the cords tethering a huge hot air balloon to the earth. It was shaped like a painted egg and decorated like one, too, beautiful designs swirling blue and gold across the violet material. A basket was attached to the balloon and fire roared hot just beneath the fabric envelope.

"One last adventure, my lord Hal?"

He gave me a quick sharp smile and helped me climb into the balloon, then scrambled in after me. I looped my arm around his waist, holding him close.

The faun and the bear untied their cords and the balloon rose into the air, chasing the wind and the falling suns. The valley grew small beneath us. The sky grew large.

I wanted to say "I love you, stranger I met in a book—my white wolf. Tonight, I will free you." The words echoed in my brain and I could almost taste them. But I didn't speak, didn't let them out. I just shut my eyes and listened to the sound of Hal's breathing, warm and close at my ear.

I love you, stranger I met in a book.

We didn't speak until the suns were gone and the stars were out, globes of radiant color that spun and flashed through the darkness.

I felt small and lost and empty. I didn't want that moment to ever end.

"I will miss you, when you've gone," said Hal quietly into my hair. "More than you can imagine."

"Will I ever see you again?"

He glanced away, wordlessly folding my hand into his,

and didn't answer. He seemed older than I had ever seen him, weighed down with memory and sorrow and time.

"Hal." *Tell me the truth*, I wanted to beg him. *Please. There's so little time left.*

"I hope so. I hope——" He cut himself off and I dared to lift my free hand and touch his face, turning it once more to mine.

"Hope what?"

He swallowed, but did not pull away. His pulse beat quick and sharp in his throat beneath my fingertips. "I hope that you will not grow to hate me."

I tried not to feel like my heart was breaking. I tried not to see that his was, too. "How could you even say that?"

"Thank you for trying to save me."

And he bent his head and kissed me, soft and gentle and tangled in starlight. I kissed him back, despair unfolding inside of me, my hand wrapped around the packet of matches waiting in my pocket to free him, or destroy him, or maybe both.

THE WOLF WAS WAITING FOR me in the hall when I left the library, the print of Hal's kiss still warm on my lips. I wanted to tell him that I knew his secret, that I was going to free him.

I love you, stranger I met in a book. I love you, Wolf who once was human.

"My Lady Echo," he said, his voice slow and rough. "Will you walk with me in the garden? One last time?"

My heart pressed hard against my rib cage. There was maybe an hour left until midnight. No more. "I would be happy to."

I followed him out to the garden and we rambled quietly through it, the stars gleaming cold over our heads, me bundled once more in the fur cloak. The wolf paced beside me and I lay one hand on his shoulder, trying to give him what comfort I could.

We sat behind the waterfall for nearly half an hour, the fire warm at our backs, and my hand went frequently to my pocket, checking that the matches were still there. I pondered telling him what I was planning to do, but what would that accomplish? There was a bond laid on him—he couldn't talk about "her" in the house. And what if my attempt to tell him nullified everything? Or worse, what if he grew wild again and tried to stop me? No. It was better if he didn't know.

"I will miss you, Echo Alkaev," said the wolf, gruff and sad. "More than you can imagine. I am sorry. For everything."

Tears swam before my eyes. "You won't have to miss me, Wolf. I'm not going to let you go. Do you hear me? I'm not going to let you go."

But he sighed and laid his head on my knee.

It was almost midnight. I wondered what would happen if we both stayed in the room behind the waterfall. If that would be enough to break the curse.

But the wolf rose wearily to his feet. "It is time, my lady."

I nodded, and asked the house to bring us to the bedroom. A door appeared in the back of the cave, and we walked through it into the corridor just outside of my room.

It was strange, getting ready for bed for the last time. I dressed behind the screen, fumbling to transfer the matches from my skirt to the pocket in my nightgown. Snow fell soft outside the patch of window. I sent the screen away and crawled into bed. I blew out the lamp.

I heard the wolf crawl up beside me, his breaths uneven and quick, matching my heartbeat.

Did he know what I was planning to do? Would he stop me if he did?

"Good night, Wolf," I whispered into the darkness.

"Good night, Echo," he said.

CHAPTER TWENTY-SEVEN

I LISTENED TO HIM BREATHE BESIDE me, quieting my own breaths, trying to quiet my heart. The compass-watch ticked away the minutes against my breastbone and I waited, the packet of matches pressing sharp against my palm.

His breathing evened out, after a long, long while. I felt sure he was asleep, but still I waited, doubting my resolve.

At last, when the night was half spent and I couldn't wait any longer, I reached quietly for the lamp on the bedside table.

I freed a match from the packet, and struck it. There was a flare of light and a smell of sulphur, and I lit the lamp with trembling hands, then shook the match out.

My heart was a tumult in my ears. I could barely breathe.

But I turned in the bed, and lifted the lamp to illuminate who lay beside me.

A little cry escaped my lips, and the hand holding the lamp shook.

It *was* Hal, lying there. He slept deeply, his face pressed into the pillow, his eyes shut tight. He looked different than he had in the books, lines in his face and threads of silver in his hair, but he was the most beautiful thing I had ever seen.

I wanted to set down the lamp, crawl into his arms and fall asleep with my head tucked under his chin. But I didn't, just watched him, the lamp quivering in my hand.

Hal shifted in his sleep, and the movement startled me. The lamp wavered, and, shining like a spot of amber, a drop of oil spilled onto his cheek.

For half an instant, nothing happened, and then Hal jerked awake, a cry of pain on his lips. His eyes roved wild around the room, and fixed in horror on my face.

"Echo," he gasped, his voice high and hoarse. "Echo, what have you done?"

The room began to shake.

I dropped the lamp.

CHAPTER TWENTY-EIGHT

F LAMES LEAPT UP FROM THE FALLEN lamp. The house shook. The *world* shook.

"Listen to me," said Hal. "Listen to me. She's coming, Echo. She's coming to take me and you must leave this place. As fast as you can, do you hear me? Run. Run through the wood to your father's house and don't look back."

He put his hands on my shoulders and I stared at him, shaking as violently as the house. "Hal, I thought—Hal—"

"Promise me. Echo, you have to promise me you'll run, that you won't try and find me. Not this time."

The flames crawled higher, casting wild shadows on Hal's

face. Fear seared through me. "But what about you?" I cried over the noise of the house. "I wanted to save you!"

"You have."

He clung to me as the house wheeled roaring around us, and then all at once a spot of snow touched my cheek and a coldness deep as death crept into my bones.

Hal released me. The house was gone—we stood in the snow below a high hill, the lamp somehow still beside us, spitting flames into the dark.

And then I realized we weren't alone. Enormous black wolves were coming toward us, their eyes glowing red, their teeth flashing sharp in the firelight. Foam dripped from their mouths.

Hal's eyes met mine. He stood in the snow in only his shirtsleeves, shuddering with cold.

I had chosen wrong.

I had betrayed him.

"The Wolf Queen has claimed me." His words sounded hollow, his voice not quite his own. "She enchanted me."

I whispered, "And if I hadn't lit the lamp?"

"I would have been free, but Echo, that doesn't matter—"

"Where is she taking you? How can I save you?"

The wolves drew closer. They wore silver collars around their necks, and their cruel muzzles were studded with jewels that glittered in the light from the burning lamp.

"Hal, *please*. Where is she taking you?"

Pain stretched across his forehead, snowflakes catching on his eyelashes. "She rules in a place where the mountain meets the sky, and the trees are hung with stars."

"What does that *mean*?"

The wolves drew closer.

"Echo, you have to run. You have to run far from here!"

"Hal!" I grabbed his sleeve.

But two of the wolves seized Hal's arms in their huge jaws. They ripped him away from me.

"HAL!"

He looked into my face, his eyes wet. "North, ever north. But Echo don't come after me. Promise me you won't. This isn't what you think, and I couldn't bear it if—"

I blinked and he was gone, no trace of him or the wolves but the lamp burning bright, oil seeping like blood into the snow.

CHAPTER TWENTY-NINE

S O I LOST HIM TO THE snow and the ice and the wolves. I lost him to the wind and the dark. I lost him to a flare of lamplight and a spot of oil.

I lost him, and it was all my fault.

I dropped to my knees, screaming his name into the dark. Shame raged inside of me.

He was gone, he was gone, he was gone.

I wept as I knelt in the snow, the cold and damp creeping through my thin nightgown and soaking me to the bone. My tears turned to ice.

But no amount of regret could erase what I had done, could bring him back to me.

I lifted my shuddering head and stood, my legs so stiff and cramped with cold I barely managed it. I was an aching, wretched void, my heart a bird flown from its cage, my soul a wisp of smoke evaporated on the wind.

Some distant part of me knew I would freeze to death before the morning came if I didn't do something. Numbly, I rescued the lamp from the ground. The flames had burnt out but there was a tiny bit of oil left, and matches still in my pocket. That distant, thinking part of me understood I'd need both.

The snow fell thicker; huge wet flakes settled heavy on my shoulders. The thinking part of me scanned my surroundings for shelter, and spotted a little cave miraculously dug into the side of the hill. I wondered if the house was somehow still looking out for me.

I slogged through the snow in my soaked stocking feet, forcing myself to hold onto to the lamp even though I wanted to smash it against the rocks.

I ducked into the miraculous cave and my heart seized up. It was the room from behind the waterfall, or what was left of it. The armchairs where the wolf and I had sat so often were smashed beyond repair, the little side table tilted over between them. There was a broken tea set, scattered cake crumbs. The fireplace, thick with ashes. Ragged edges of bandages, a jar of salve. A bloodstain on the floor, where the wolf had lain while I stitched his wound closed.

I couldn't bear it, but the thinking part of me broke the end table, used the pieces to build a fire.

I stared into the flames without seeing them. All I saw was Hal, sleeping beside me, the spot of oil burning his cheek. I saw him jerk awake and realize what I'd done.

Saw him standing in the snow in his shirtsleeves, his eyes dark with terror.

Saw the wolves pull him away.

He was gone, he was gone, he was gone.

I had no more tears, but still I wept, dry and ragged into the flames.

And I swore by my father, by my scars, by God in heaven, that I would find him, that I would atone for my mistake and free him from the hell I'd sent him to.

Ever north. Where the mountain meets the sky and the trees are hung with stars.

I would find him, even if I spent my whole life searching.

I DREAMED OF A WOOD: a clearing under cold starlight, an arching hall made of twining trees, open to the sky.

The Wolf Queen was waiting for me, on a throne made of thorns.

She was extremely tall, with long silver-white hair that flowed down around her shoulders and pooled in her lap. Her hands were furred with silver, her fingers ended in claws that had been sharpened and ornamented with jewels. Her face was too angular to be human, her lips unnaturally pale. Gray lupine ears showed through her silver hair.

Her eyes were pure fire.

She rose from the throne and came toward me, the grass flattening under her feet as she walked. She touched my face with one clawed hand. "What will you do, Echo Alkaev?"

Even in my dream, I felt the bite of her claws. "I will find him. I will free him. And I will destroy you."

She laughed. "You are wrong three times over. But come, if you can. I think I shall enjoy it."

And then she released me.

The dream changed.

Hal lay on his side in an underground hollow, his wrists and ankles bound with roots. Blood stained his white shirt. Ragged sobs wrenched his whole body.

"Hal!" I screamed. But I was frozen in place. I couldn't go to him.

And he couldn't hear me.

He wept and wept.

Somewhere above, the Wolf Queen was laughing.

I WOKE TO FIND MYSELF half-buried—snow had drifted into the cavern while I slept. I shoved free, numb with panic, hating myself for falling asleep.

The house had one more offering: a fur cloak in the snow just outside of the cave. All I had left to my name was my mother's emerald ring, and the compass-watch from Rodya, ticking steadily against my heart.

I shrugged into the cloak, opened the compass.

I went north, to where the stories always said the wild things lived, where the folktales came from and still magic in the mountaintops.

I passed through open fields of snow and scatterings of forest, climbed up and over a jagged mountain range. I stopped at the first village I could find and bartered away the cloak for supplies, asking everyone I met if they had heard of the Wolf Queen, or a place where the mountain met the sky and the trees were hung with stars.

No one had. They all stared at my scarred face and whispered about devils and passed me hurriedly by.

Every night, I dreamed of the Wolf Queen. Sometimes she spoke to me, and sometimes she did not. But she always, always laughed. And there was always Hal, standing in the snow in his shirtsleeves, or sobbing in the dark, blood staining the ground.

Winter deepened as I journeyed further north.

I happened on a reindeer caught fast in a briar bush. The

wind whipped icy down from the distant mountains, and I almost left the beast to her fate, but something pricked my heart and I stopped to help her. I wrestled her free from the brambles and we sheltered together underneath an outcropping of rock as the storm raged fierce and cold around us.

After that the reindeer traveled with me, sharing in my feasts and in my famines, too. Her antlers were velvet and she made her own heat and could sniff out the barest traces of lichen under the snow. Her company eased my heart a little, at least during waking hours.

The weeks dragged on.

I heard no word of the Wolf Queen, no hint of the place ever north. Despair numbed me. Dreams haunted me.

And then I met a reindeer herder in a snowstorm. He shared stew with me from an iron pot hanging over his fire, lent me furs to wrap around my shoulders. I scooped the stew into my mouth with such haste I burnt my tongue, but I didn't care—I hadn't eaten anything in two days.

"There's a storyteller who comes sometimes to the village on the mountain," the herder told me. "He spins tales of wonder and horror, stories no one has ever heard before. If anyone knows of your Wolf Queen, it'll be him."

And so I crossed the valley and climbed the mountain to the ancient village on its ridge.

I came to find the storyteller.

I came to find you.

PART TWO

CHAPTER THIRTY

STEAM CURLS UP FROM THE SPOUT of the teapot that sits on the soft-polished table between us. Through the narrow window to my right I can look down the mountain into a sea of fog and snow-capped peaks, but instead I study the man sitting across from me. He's past forty—neither as old nor as young as I imagined in the day and a half it took the reindeer and me to climb the mountain. He has black hair with a few threads of silver, weathered brown skin, and a neatly trimmed beard. His eyes are like bits of dark glass, staring beyond me as he ponders the impossible story I've just told him.

It's taken three days, the telling. I'm running out of coins to pay for tea and meals in this tiny mountaintop café. The owner, a wrinkled old woman with shrewd eyes, tried to throw us out the first night when she had to close up shop, but I sold her the reindeer and she let us stay.

My voice is hoarse from all this talking, no matter how much tea stirred with honey I've drunk.

I watch my companion, his brown fingers—each bearing a brass ring—wrapped about his tea mug. When I first started telling him my story he asked a few questions, but after that he just listened. I feel exhausted, oppressed by the weight of my own words.

"Well?" I say, when the minutes stretch on and he doesn't offer any commentary on my mad tale.

He adjusts his glass gaze to my face. "It is very strange," he muses. "I seem to remember hearing that story once before."

"You can't have. You are the first soul—the only soul—I've told it to."

He peers intently at me for half a moment and then gives an absent smile. "Just a dream then, I suppose."

I'm not sure why he thinks that matters—I don't even care if he believes me, or if he ever could.

"Can you help me? The herder down the mountain swore if anyone on God's earth could tell me about the Wolf Queen . . . it would be you."

The storyteller nods, a regal dip of his chin. "I know of the Wolf Queen."

My head feels like it's fracturing into a thousand pieces but I force myself to focus, listening with every ounce of my being. "What do you know of her?"

"Old stories. Whispers. Fragments of tales."

His voice is deep and rich, with a singer's cadence. I lean forward without meaning to, my tea forgotten. "Who is she?" I ask him.

He leans toward me, too, his elbows pressed hard into the table, his rings clinking against the tea mug. He lowers his voice. "Some say she's a witch, an enchantress of terrible power. A shape-shifter, a fairy, a demon from hell."

"But who do you think she is?"

He doesn't reply for the space of too many heartbeats. He pours himself more tea, drizzling it with honey. A gust of wind blows snow against the window glass, and it seems to be tangled with a high, eerie laugh.

I grip my own mug tighter and try not to hear it.

"To make a bargain with the Queen of the Wood is akin to making a deal with the Devil," says the storyteller. "The price is the same. She steals your life from you. Your heart. Your years. Your soul. Yet when she traps you in her domain you *beg* her to bargain with you."

"Why?" I whisper.

"Because you want your freedom, no matter the cost. She has many names in many stories: the Fairy Queen, the Godmother, the Devil's Daughter, the Witch of the Wood. Only in the oldest of tales is she called the Wolf Queen. I did not think anyone knew her by that name anymore.

"She is powerful and ancient. She manipulates the words of the poor fools who bargain with her, so that they can never pay her what they owe. She takes, and does not give back. If your Hal has been taken by her, made a deal with her—" The storyteller shakes his head, and raises his dark eyes to my face. "I do not know that you could free him, save by making a deal with her yourself. And even then, she would seek to keep you both."

Fear curls through me and I shudder in my coat. The little old woman who runs the café comes out of the back and lays a tray of sliced ham and biscuits on our table. I don't reach for the food, waiting for the storyteller to go on.

"The Wolf Queen has ruined emperors and kings, brought mighty warriors to their knees, stolen the power of gods and spirits. She turns the world to her will, and her will alone. If she wished to rule every continent on the earth she could do it, but thank God she is content to dwell in her own domain."

"If I was to seek her out," I say, looking carefully at the tray of ham and biscuits, "would you know where to find her?"

He taps his fingers on his tea mug. "She has the power to step into any corner of the world, but she hides her realm from those who seek it."

"But you know where to look." It's a guess, a hope, a prayer.

He nods, slowly. "Your wolf said 'ever north,' and that's a start. There have been only a few expeditions north of this village, and of the few that have gone, even fewer have returned. It could be that in the wild north lies a place where the mountain meets the sky and the trees are hung with stars—the Wolf Queen's domain. Or it could be what most people say."

"And what's that?"

The storyteller blinks at me. "A wasteland."

I stare thoughtfully into the dregs of my tea, long since gone cold. Ice rattles against the window. "Why is she called the Wolf Queen?"

"The oldest stories say she was there at the beginning of the world, a wolf imbued with intelligence and human thought, that she saw the creation of mankind and wished to be like them. So she sold her soul to the Devil in exchange for human form."

"Wolves don't have souls," I say, then think of Hal and flush.

He shrugs a little, reaching for a slice of ham. "Other stories say she was the first woman, but she loved the Devil more than God, and so was cursed to a half-life. A bargain with the Devil earned her the power to do as she wished, but she was never counted amongst the line of man. Still others say that the Devil created her, the first in a line of powerful creatures formed to plague the children of men.

"But no matter how it happened, she once had a wolf's form, and she commands the beasts, and so is the Wolf Queen."

"She turned Hal into a wolf."

"So it seems."

I consider my next words carefully, tracing the scratches in the table with one finger. "It's my fault she has him in her power again. If I hadn't lit the lamp—" I swallow down the sudden taste of bile "—if my life is the only thing that might save him, I don't hesitate to give it. Only . . . "

"Only?" says the storyteller.

Once more I meet his eyes, and see in their depths that he already knows what I'm going to ask him.

"Only I need a guide to take me into the wild north. To follow the stories and find the Wolf Queen. To try and save him, if I can."

"And you would ask that of me, a storyteller?"

"You are not a mere storyteller. Your face is weathered, your hands rough with work—you have traveled far, I think."

He smiles a little sadly. "You see deeply, Echo Alkaev. I have traveled all my life, farther than you know. I collect stories but I'm a trader, too. Stories alone don't fill the bellies of my wife and my daughter."

I bow my head, understanding his meaning and feeling a twist of guilt for keeping him here so long. But he's my best chance—my only chance—at finding Hal, and I'm not ready to give up. "I can pay you with this, for now." I tug off my mother's emerald ring. "I will compensate you further upon our return.

But I can offer you something even more rare than gold."

He studies the ring but doesn't take it. "What is more rare than gold?"

I take another chance: "A story. My story. About a girl with a scarred face, and a white wolf who becomes a man at night, and an evil queen in an enchanted wood. The story is yours, to do with it what you will. But it will have more meaning if you come with me and find out the ending."

"I do not want your mother's ring. It is too precious to give."

"And the story?" I prod him.

His brows draw close together. "Come and see my wife. Tell her your tale, and we will see what she thinks—if I should come with you, or if I should not. Is that agreeable?"

It's more than I hoped for. "Yes."

I pay the old woman who runs the café the remainder of my few precious coins, and as I turn to go, she grasps my wrist, pulls me back to her.

Her grip is shockingly tight. Fire flickers in her eyes, and her face creases in rage. "It will go poorly for you." Her voice is not her own; it's guttural, harsh. "If you go with him, it will go poorly for you, and worse for your white wolf. Turn back, while you still can."

I wrench away from her, heart pounding. Her nails leave long, painful scratches on my arm. "You can't stop me. You don't scare me."

She sneers. "Fool." And then her eyes grow clear again. She gives me a strange look, as if wondering why I'm still standing there, seeing as I've already paid.

If the storyteller noticed our exchange, he gives no sign. Shaking, I pull my coat close, and he leads me out into the snow.

WE WALK PARTWAY DOWN THE mountain, the world whirling and white all around us. Despite the encounter in the café, hope gnaws like a lion at my heart. I focus on the form of the storyteller, tall and strong in front of me, breaking a path through the snow so it will be easier for me to follow. The powder squeaks under my boots, and my nose starts to run. The cold is sharp, and the wind has teeth. Laughter whispers past my ears and I wonder if the storyteller can hear it, too, or if somehow the Wolf Queen is toying with me.

Before half an hour has passed, the storyteller slogs his way toward what looks like a snow-covered hill. As we draw nearer, I realize it's a reindeer-skin tent, smoke swirling up from the hole in the center and disappearing into the sky.

The storyteller lifts the flap and ducks a little to step in. I follow, shaking the snow from my hair.

It's warm in the tent, which feels much larger on the inside. Wooden slats like whale bones form the frame—reindeer skin is stretched tight over it. There's an iron stove in the center of the room, with a chimney pipe disappearing into the roof. The floor is wood, and there are bundles of furs about the edges, with an expensive-looking rug on one side. There's a bookshelf, too, and a low table laid with tea things. A woman sits by one wall, rocking a baby in a cradle suspended from the ceiling by a sturdy length of braided leather cords.

The woman looks up at our approach and smiles at the storyteller, her whole face coming alive. There is laughter on her lips, contentment in her dark eyes. The storyteller crosses the room to her, kneels down and kisses her soft on the mouth. I stand awkwardly in the doorway, every instinct telling me to flee.

I cannot ask him to lead me north. I cannot ask him to leave his wife and child and head into the unknown.

But then the storyteller looks back at me with a smile and beckons me over.

I come, reluctant, and the woman pats the fur laid out beside her. I sit, my toes and fingers tingling in the welcome warmth of this quiet house.

"This is Echo Alkaev," says the storyteller. "She has told me a story and asked for my help, promising the story itself as payment."

The wife lifts her eyebrows and gives a brief nod. "What is the story, dear lamb?"

I tell her, in snatches and starts, a much condensed version of the tale I spun for three days in the café. Weariness presses down on me; my tongue feels thick and slow.

The wife gives me soup in a stone mug and I drink it all,

warmth flooding down into my stomach. Without quite realizing it, I allow her to coax me to one wall of the hut, where I lie down on a bed of furs and close my eyes. Just for a moment, I think, and then I will hear her answer.

Sleep claims me.

When I wake I hear voices on the other side of the hut, and I open my eyes to see the storyteller and his wife sitting close together, cradling the baby between them. My heart aches, and I think again that I cannot possibly ask him to come with me. I will tell him that and slip out alone into the snow . . .

I dream of Mokosh, drinking tea in her palace room. I sit beside her. Her silver hair shines and she looks familiar to me, in a way I can't quite pinpoint.

"You really should turn back now," she says, pouring a cup of tea for me as well. "There's no need to involve the storyteller and his family. You can't undo what is already done—how do you know Hal is even still alive?"

I don't drink the tea, just stare into it. "I can feel it."

"Feelings are all very well, Echo, but look where they've gotten you."

"You're the one who told me to light the lamp!"

She shrugs. "Perhaps you shouldn't have listened to me."

"I'm not giving up. I'm going to find him. I'm going to free him from the Wolf Queen."

Her violet eyes look very seriously into mine. "How do you

know he even wants to be free?"

The dream shifts, and I see Hal kneeling in the midst of the Wolf Queen's court, bound in thorns. She smiles as she places a gold crown on his head, and hauls him upward. "Not long now, my prince. Not long until this will all be over."

But there is blood on his shoulders. And his eyes—his eyes are empty.

When I wake a second time, the wife is making tea and stirring a pot of bubbling liquid on the stove. The storyteller isn't here.

She looks to me with a smile. "Good morning, Echo," she says. "I am glad you slept so well."

I shudder, still caught in the grip of my dreams. "Where is—"

"Ivan? He's gone to fetch supplies."

My brain feels sluggish. "What supplies?"

Her smile saddens a little. "For your journey, love."

This jerks me fully awake. Mokosh was right about one thing. "But he can't! I changed my mind—I'm not asking it of him anymore. He should stay here. With you and the baby."

She stirs the pot and shakes her head. "Once, long ago, Ivan gave up everything he was to save me. I understand why you must do the same for your Hal."

I stand from the furs and come to join her at the stove. Porridge bubbles in the pot, thick and sweet.

"There is one magic older than the Wolf Queen's, a magic not even she can defeat."

"Love," I say quietly.

"Yes, dear one. It was there when the world was created, and it will stand when the world is remade. If you love something you will not give it up, not for anything. It belongs to you, it is part of you. If you grab hold of it and never let it go—no one can take it from you. Not even the Wolf Queen."

Her words are like the ones the wolf said to me, but deeper, somehow. They make me feel fragile and strong, a globe made of glass.

"I will miss Ivan, of course, but he will come back to me. He always does. It's written in the stars, you know." The baby stirs in her cradle. "Will you fetch her for me?"

I step over to the cradle and peer in. The baby stares up at me, smiling, her cheeks plump and brown, her eyes fierce and dark, just like her father's. I scoop the child up gently into my arms, hoping my scarred face doesn't scare her. But she just laughs and tugs at my hair. She feels heavy in my arms—soft, warm. My throat constricts as I think of Donia's tight belly, a brother or sister I might never meet. I think of Rodya and his new wife, I wonder if they will have a child soon. I don't ponder a child for myself. There is too much ahead of me to even wish for one. But I somehow don't want to ever put this baby down.

Ivan comes back just then, a huge pack over his shoulder, his breath fogging in front of him.

I feel guilty, holding his child, but he smiles and steps over to fondle the baby's tiny cheek. "I see you've met Satu." Then, to his wife, "I've everything we need."

She smiles at him. "Lay the table, will you, my greatheart? Breakfast is almost ready."

So Ivan sets the table and I keep holding Satu, while her mother spoons porridge into earthenware bowls and then pours us all tea.

We sit down and the wife takes Satu, settling her in her lap. Before I can say anything about retracting my request, Ivan lays out a map, weighing it down with his teacup, and begins explaining our route.

"We'll leave the village here," he says, pointing, "and follow the northeast track down the mountain. From there we should be able to head due north. I've enough supplies to last us three weeks, which ought to get us to a frozen lake or river. We can do some ice fishing."

Satu almost dunks her whole face in the porridge and the wife laughs as she scoots the bowl out of her reach just in time. Ivan laughs, too, and I can't help but smile.

"There will be glaciers," Ivan continues, "frozen streams, wide expanses of tundra. No forests for shelter."

Ivan sounds more knowledgeable than I'd hoped for. I swallow, studying the map. It ends not very far north of the mountain village. "How long . . . " I glance up at Ivan, the question plain in my face.

"Two months, three. It's hard to know."

"And if it's longer than three months?"

He looks determined, but his wife bows her head over the baby, and once more my heart constricts. "We will go until we cannot continue. We will know when we come to it."

"I can't ask you to do this. I can't ask you to leave for so long."

"Isidor and Satu will be well taken care of." Ivan moves one hand to his wife's shoulder. "Provisions are laid by, there is money enough."

"But you know I can't pay you."

"You promised me the story. That is enough."

Isidor looks up at me. Her eyes gleam with moisture, but the same determination lines her face as does Ivan's. "You must find your wolf. You must find your Hal and bring him home again."

I have to fight to keep back the tears. I am suddenly, terribly afraid that the Wolf Queen will bring harm to Isidor and Satu, to punish Ivan for helping me.

But their minds are made up. And without Ivan, I know I won't get much farther. I need him to get to Hal. So I push my fear, and my guilt, down.

After breakfast, we prepare for our journey.

Ivan has bought new boots for me, a reindeer-skin coat with a hood lined with fur, wool socks, and men's trousers—also made of reindeer-skin. Isidor *tsk*s when he pulls out the trousers, but Ivan just laughs at her. "She isn't going to a ball, my lovely, a gown wouldn't do."

He has snowshoes for the both of us, packs stuffed with food and furs, matches and a tinderbox for when the matches run out. There's also a tent, folded and bound tight, that he'll strap to one of the ponies. He's acquired two, both sturdy, stocky beasts: one is black and the other gray.

Isidor helps me dress in one corner, when Ivan has gone out to ready the ponies. The trousers and shirt hang loose on my frame, grown thin from my weeks of traveling, but I belt them tight. The coat is quite warm, and I don't button it closed yet.

She gives me a kerchief for my hair: it's blue, and embroidered with exquisite gold firebirds. I tie it at the nape of my neck, then sit down to pull on socks and boots. When I've finished, I yank the emerald off my finger and hold it out to her. "I want you to have it. Take it as surety that I will send Ivan back to you."

She shakes her head, closes my hand back around the ring. "I do not need it, little lamb. Ivan always comes back. It will be luck for your journey."

"Isidor, please take it."

But then Ivan comes back in, trailing snow, and the moment is lost. "We are ready," he says.

"Thank you for everything," I tell Isidor.

She pulls me into a hug and kisses my head, and I have a sudden longing for my father. "Godspeed on your journey."

I kiss Satu and then step out of the tent, leaving Ivan and

Isidor to say their farewells in private.

He comes out a few minutes later with Isidor hovering by the entrance to their home, the baby held fast in her arms.

Ivan claps me on the shoulder, and I follow him to where the ponies wait, laden with our packs. I button my coat. The sky is heavy but it's not snowing yet. Still, the wind bites sharp. I climb up onto the black pony and close my fingers around his reins.

Ivan lifts his hand in farewell, then nudges his pony off down the road.

I glance back once at Isidor and Satu, and have to quickly look away. I pray to God that Ivan will come home again, safe and soon. And that the Wolf Queen will not harm them while he is gone.

CHAPTER THIRTY-ONE

THE FIRST DAY IS MOSTLY JUST riding, winding down and down the mountain, then crossing a wide expanse of snowy fields. The clouds break away late in the afternoon, and on the distant horizon a high mountain range stretches into the sky.

Ivan is a quiet traveling companion, but even though I can't shake away the guilt of forcing him to leave Isidor and Satu, I'm glad to have him.

It doesn't snow that first day, and the heat of the pony radiates through my legs and up my spine so I stay quite warm, though my nose tingles in the sharp air. I'm glad for the mittens, keeping my fingers from frostbite.

We walk awhile, to give the ponies some relief, leading them behind us in the white crust of yesterday's snow. The sky ahead begins to redden, and Ivan calls back to me that we should make camp for the night.

We have made it almost to the shadow of the mountain range, and Ivan unfolds the tent from its bundle. I help him set it up, holding the poles while he adjusts the skins and drives stakes into the hard ground. Then he makes a fire, a little away from the tent, and I unpack salted meat, traveler's bread, and tea.

The fire crackles red, warming our faces as we sit and eat in companionable silence. The ponies eat nosebags of grain. I feel weary and anxious, but glad I am finally on my way to Hal, on my way to atone for my mistake.

"It won't be as easy, from here." Ivan sips tea from a tin cup. "It is a long, hard road. I want to be sure you are ready to face it. I would not speak so in front of Isidor, but no mortal who has traveled more than a day or two north of the village has ever returned. Are you certain you want to walk this road?"

I don't even have to shut my eyes to see Hal standing in the snow, his face tight with terror. "I am certain."

Ivan doesn't ask me again.

We sleep in the tent, on either side of the center pole. I wear my coat, and burrow beneath the other furs. I dream of Hal sobbing in the dark, of Mokosh with a crown in her hair. Of a forest of thorns, growing up around the reindeer tent, trapping

Satu and Isidor inside. The Wolf Queen laughs. "I told you to turn back, but you did not listen."

Hal marries Mokosh in the wood. They sit together on silver thrones, and the trees bend to their will.

But his eyes are empty.

WE REACH THE MOUNTAINS, AND climb them. The trails we blaze through rocks and ice and snow are too steep for the ponies to navigate with us on their backs. So we lead them, Ivan first with his pony, me after with mine. The wind bites sharp, spitting ice into our faces, and it's only the climb that keeps me warm.

Ivan sings as he ascends the mountain, and snatches of his music come back to me with the ice on the wind. It's a beautiful melody, haunting and sad, and I wonder that he has the breath to spare for it. I don't want him to ever stop—it drowns out the sound of the Wolf Queen's ever-present laughter.

We camp at the top of the peak in a little half-cave formed of jumbled rocks. There is enough space to light a fire, the smoke curling through a crack at the top, and we do not have to set up our tent.

The ponies graze outside, nosing bits of scrub out from under the snow. I unpack today's rations while Ivan hangs a kettle over the fire for tea. It is only our second evening, but already there is a rhythm to it: the kettle starts to boil as I lay out salted meat on tin plates; Ivan puts another log on the fire and then settles across from me. I hand him his food and he chews, thoughtfully, as if he's in another world.

"There is another story-thread about the Wolf Queen that perhaps you ought to hear," says Ivan.

I'm chewing on my own meat, and I nod for him to tell me.

His voice takes on the cadence of a song, like his melody climbing the mountain today. "In the Wolf Queen's court time passes differently. There are many tales of men and women coming into the Queen's realm, spending what they think is an evening there, and returning to the outside world to find a hundred years have passed. Their families are dead and gone. Everything they knew crumbled away into dust. Once you enter, Echo, even if you can save both of you and be free of that place—it could cost you everything."

His words make my eyes sting, but I tell myself it's just the smoke from the fire.

My mind crowds with images of my father in his shop, Rodya bent over his work table, Donia with her swollen belly, laughing in the firelight. But there's Hal, too, fast asleep in the bed, running with me down the hill, plunging into battle at the ball. Standing in the snow as the wolves close in, staring at me, stricken, because of what I'd done.

I turn away so Ivan can't see that I'm crying.

When I sleep, I dream of my father. His face sags with

wrinkles. Spidery veins show blue behind papery skin. He settles at the roots of a huge old tree and slowly turns to dust. The wind blows him away. There is nothing left.

And then the Wolf Queen is there, blood dripping from her teeth. "This is what you wish for. This is what you seek—your father's death, your family's hurt. Turn back. I will not warn you again."

I am raw with aching. "I'm coming to save Hal. You can't stop me."

"The way is long and treacherous. You will be sorry."

"But still I will come."

She hisses at me. I am left to watch Hal, sitting on his silver throne. Vines grow up, twist around him. They cover all his body, twine into his mouth and nose and ears. They leave only his eyes, blue as the sky and just as empty, staring forever into nothing.

I know he is already dead.

In the morning, we scatter the ashes of our fire and start down the mountain.

Still no snow, but the trail is even more treacherous winding down. I slip on loose gravel and bits of ice and scree more than once. I tear a hole in my jacket, but Ivan says he's packed a sewing kit, so I'll be able to stitch it shut. The ponies stumble, too, but somehow they keep their footing. Ivan sings again, his voice rich and thick as honey, banishing the Wolf Queen's laughter to the back of my mind.

At the bottom of the mountain lies a giant, wild forest, snow heavy on the boughs of the trees. Ivan is surprised to find it here but grateful, too, for our stock of wood already dwindles.

Night is falling fast as we erect our tent in the shadow of the trees, and then all at once a third day is gone, and we've eaten our dinner and crawled to our separate furs. I'm afraid to sleep—I don't want to dream. The forest makes strange noises, creaks and snaps and whistles. Wolves howl in the distance, and I'm seized with a wild hope. Could we be closer to the Wolf Queen than Ivan has imagined?

But I hear his voice from the other side of the tent: "It's just the wind, lass, filling the gaps. Sleep now."

And at last I do.

THE BLIZZARD STARTS IN THE morning, and it doesn't stop. We travel through the forest for two days, sheltered somewhat by the giant trees, their branches catching the brunt of the snow.

Misfortune dogs us. The first day, a branch snaps without warning and comes crashing down. I leap out of the way in time, but Ivan is knocked flat on his back, pinned underneath it. His face creases with pain. The branch is too heavy for me to drag off of him, so I dig desperately in the snow and the dirt, until I've made a big enough gap for him to squirm free. Ivan doesn't say as much, but I think he's broken one or more of his ribs.

The second day, I catch my foot in an unseen hole under the snow and wrench my ankle. I gasp, collapsing to the ground, just as a huge brown bear comes thundering through the trees and takes a vicious swipe at Ivan's side. The ponies rear and scream. The wind shrieks with laughter.

But Ivan stands calm. He reaches out a hand to touch the bear. "You are far from home, my friend. It is winter. Go. Sleep. Wake in the springtime no more of hers."

To my astonishment, the bear bows its head and lumbers away.

Ivan soothes the ponies next, then sags down beside me. Red leaks from jagged tears in his coat drip out onto the snow. "She's watching us."

The Wolf Queen's voice coils through me: *The way is long and treacherous. You will be sorry.*

Fear seizes me. "You don't think we should turn back?"

"No. But we must be more careful."

I stitch up Ivan's side and he wraps my ankle, and we hobble onward.

I'm not sorry to leave the wood behind.

Ivan speaks less and less as the days spin on, but I don't mind his silence. I have little breath for conversation anyway, trudging after him and his pony through the endless snow. We don't ride the ponies anymore—we've laden them with bundles of firewood, and they have enough to carry without us. Their progress would be even slower with our added weight.

The land stretches out before us in an endless frozen tundra, the eternal white broken only by the occasional low scrub poking through the snow. We walk and walk and walk, for hours every day, and stop just before nightfall to make our camp. We only put up the tent if it's snowing—it is too much effort, otherwise. I fall asleep on one side of the fire, bundled up in furs, and Ivan on the other. Dreams haunt me. We wake always to a world of blurry whiteness.

I lose count of the days, after a while. There is nothing but the weariness of walking, the weight of my pack, the tired fog of the ponies' breath and Ivan's singing. He sings more than he talks, his music constant, tangled with the icy wind.

The tundra stretches on and on. Our rations and firewood dwindle; there is no more tea at night, just snow melted in a pot over the fire.

"We may have to eat the ponies," says Ivan one evening, as we sit chewing on tiny scraps of meat. "If it comes to it."

I don't want to eat the ponies, but I know he's right. There's hardly any food for us, and less for them, and our faithful pack beasts are more likely to die of starvation than not before we reach our destination.

"We may not," Ivan assures me, seeing my stricken expression. "I was just thinking aloud."

I nod over my mug of melted snow.

"Two weeks," he adds. "Since we left Isidor and Satu."

"It feels like an age."

Ivan smiles. "Or three."

It's the most we've spoken since our first couple of nights, and the sound of his speech comforts me.

"Have you heard the tale of the Four Winds?" His voice catches up the thread of a story.

"Part of it," I answer, thinking of the wolf's words to me in the temple, of visiting the Palace of the Sun in the books with Hal. "But I want to hear it all."

"They were brothers, the only children of the Sun and the Moon. East was the eldest, and he favored his father the Sun, with bronze skin and hair the color of fire. He was a hunter, and roamed far and wide slaying terrifying beasts and winning great renown.

"West and South were the second and third born, and they too favored the Sun, though not with such magnificence as East. They were always quarreling, trying to outdo each other with feats of strength so that they might rise in their father's eyes to the status of East. But North was the youngest, and favored his mother the Moon, with eyes like stars and hair of silver and skin pale as snow. He was lonely, for his brothers scarcely regarded him, and when they did take notice, mocked him for his quiet voice and meek spirit, which they mistook for weakness.

"But North had within him great power: to stop time, to still hearts, to turn warmth to coldness and light to dark. He could have killed his brothers if he chose, but he didn't. Instead he allied himself with the Wolf Queen."

I peer at Ivan across the fire. That wasn't quite what the wolf and the Winds in the book-mirror had told me. "Allied himself?"

His voice picks up an odd note. "She tricked him. Stole his power for her own. It's why she can bend time to her will."

My heart tugs and I shut my eyes and see Hal. "I thought the North Wind traded his power for the love of a woman."

"That is why he went to the Wolf Queen in the first place."

I think of the gatekeeper in the wolf's house, all malice and power. "Do you know what became of them?"

Ivan's eyes glint orange in the light of the fire. "The stories do not say."

In the morning, the landscape begins, at long, long last, to change. Glaciers jut out of the ground, jagged formations of ice skewering the sky. We wander into a maze of them and have to wend our way through, our snowshoes leaving crisscrossed patterns behind us. The wind whistles between the splintered walls of ice, ringing loud with the Wolf Queen's laughter, and the weary ponies droop their heads and drag their hooves.

"There must be a body of water," says Ivan ahead of me. "Somewhere near."

The glaciers stretch on and on, growing larger and more magnificent as we walk. They soar over our heads, sending ice-blue shadows across the snow. Hunger gnaws tight in my belly.

All day we wander through the ice maze, no end in sight. When we make camp, we shelter beneath one of the glaciers and eat the last of our food.

Ivan builds a fire. "The North Wind himself would be hard pressed to go any farther," he says. He seems to be making a joke, but I don't understand and he doesn't explain.

I am weary and sick of heart, and Ivan can sense it. He tells me a nonsensical story about an old lady and a magical spoon, and I fall into my dreams with a smile on my lips.

The next day, Ivan kills the ponies.

CHAPTER THIRTY-TWO

THE FIELD OF GLACIERS LEADS US to the edge of a frozen lake, so vast it might as well be the ocean. But Ivan is equipped with small spikes to attach to the bottoms of our boots so we'll have purchase over the ice.

I cried about the ponies—Ivan did, too, and he wasn't ashamed. "They served us well, lass. Now they help us one last time. But I am sorry they must end this way."

We start off across the lake, the spikes on our boots digging into the ice, crunching with every step. It hasn't snowed for days, but the sky is hazy and little sunlight shows through. The cold bites deep, and yet I see beauty spread out all around, and it humbles me.

The ice is strong and impossibly thick, surface cracks splintering out like the threads of some giant spiderweb. We hear it shifting sometimes, great thundering groans as, far beneath our feet, it cracks or moves or shudders.

"The ice is singing to us," says Ivan, and he lets the ice sing instead of him.

I grow used to it after a while and it ceases to frighten me, the ancient music of this strange scarred land.

The ice seems endless. We camp on the frozen lake as the sun slips to its rest behind the clouds, and I can see nothing but ice in every direction. The clouds are knitting tighter, the wind whipping wild.

Ivan studies the sky. "Storm coming."

We put up the tent.

The ice is thick enough to build a fire on top of so we do, Ivan using a few scraps of our precious wood to roast strips of meat in the coals. We eat, and I try not to remember that the meat is pony.

It's then that I notice the absence of the compass-watch's steady ticking. I peer at it in the firelight—the clock has stopped once more, but the compass, when I check it, still points steadily north.

We shelter in the tent as the snow starts. The wind slams hard against the canvas, seeking, seeking, seeking to get in, to rip us away from the lake and fling us into the sky. The Wolf Queen's voice echoes all around, a shrieking, eerie song. I shudder where I lie.

Ivan hears it, too. "The land feels her power. She wields winter like a sword—it should not have as strong a grip here as it does."

"Do you think Hal is still alive?" I whisper. I can't shake away the image of his dead eyes.

"If he wasn't, she wouldn't bother with us."

I hold on to those words, try to take the comfort in them.

Sleep is a long time coming, but at last it finds me.

I dream again of the hall in the wood, and the stars burning fierce above it. Mokosh paces, her silver hair bound in tight braids. She's dressed as if for battle, in plates of leather armor, with knives strapped across her back. The Wolf Queen watches her, passive, amused. I realize with a jolt why it isn't strange for Mokosh to be there: the similarities between her and the Wolf Queen are striking, startling, in a way only parent and child could be. I wonder how I didn't see it before.

"What worries you, my daughter?" asks the Queen.

Mokosh keeps pacing, restless, uneasy. "You underestimate her, Mother. She is coming. She will not stop, and you should take care."

The Wolf Queen laughs. "You are just afraid she will see your face—your real face, and revile you."

Mokosh snarls, drawing one of her knives. But the Wolf Queen gives a flick of her clawed hand and the knife falls to the ground.

"Time grows short. I fear you will not honor your promise."

"Peace, Mokosh. You shall have your reward before two moons' ending, and another besides: a Wolf Prince, for the daughter of the Wolf Queen."

But Mokosh isn't convinced. "The girl is stronger than you know. She has the power to defeat you."

The Wolf Queen smiles, her teeth curling white past silver lips. "Let me worry about the girl."

Hal is chained in the dark, clawing at his skin, screaming. Nettles grow up from the ground, piercing every part of him. "Why did you look?" he sobs. "Echo, why did you have to look?"

When I wake, a lamp is burning. It's morning, but our tent is buried in snow. Ivan catches my eye. "We'll have to dig ourselves out."

It takes hours, and we rip the tent in the process. We'll need to stitch it up before we can use it again.

We're already weary before we even start for the day.

It's hard going. Ice seeps under my collar and I can barely see for the wind blearing my vision. Ivan helps me tie a scarf around my mouth and nose, almost up to my eyes, and that helps a little.

The ice seems angry, shifting and groaning and thundering all around us. It no longer sounds like music. Ivan walks quickly; I can see the tension in his shoulders, and his fear scares me more than my own. The Wolf Queen's reach is long, and if we fall through the ice, there will be no saving us.

On and on we go, leaning into the wind as the snow skitters across the surface of the frozen lake. Sometimes the wind sweeps the ice clean, and I can see once more the strong webbed cracks spidering out in all directions.

We come, sometime in the mid-afternoon, to a place on the lake where lumps of ice lie in furrows like a farmer's field. They shine beneath the snow a brilliant, impossible turquoise. I stop to examine them and Ivan stops, too. My breath catches in my throat. "Beautiful."

"Jewels from the North Wind's crown," says Ivan. "Lost when he traded his power away." His face grows tight beneath the shadow of his furred hood. "There are many stories that tell of the jeweled ice of the north. A man once sold his soul to take a bit back south with him, only to find on his arrival home that it had melted away. That very night his soul was required of him."

I try to shrug away my uneasiness.

"Some say the Wolf Queen's magic was born in the ice."

An ear-shattering *crack* resounds across the frozen lake and the ground splinters apart beneath our feet. My heart jolts, and my hand goes unconsciously to my hip, reaching for the pouch and the binding threads that aren't there. Ivan is jerked away from me.

"IVAN!" I lunge after him as he skids into a riven in the ice. Black water tugs him under but I plunge my hand in up to the armpit and my fingers close around his. I pull, I strain, I scream, and he's fighting, too, desperate to break the surface of the water.

At last he does, gasping for air. I reach for his pick, mercifully left above ground, and dig it deep into the ice. I wrap my other hand tight around Ivan's arm, and *pull*.

It feels like my arm is being ripped from my body, but I don't let go. For one terrifying moment I think I've lost him, but then he's scrambling back onto the ice, gasping for breath. His body shakes with violent cold—if I don't get him warm, pulling him from the water will have been in vain, and the Wolf Queen will have won.

I tug Ivan as far as I can away from the gash in the lake, back onto solid ice, and scramble about for the last of our firewood, scattered from Ivan's pack.

His skin is turning gray, he's mumbling to himself, rocking back and forth, shuddering. I strike flint against tinder and coax a fire onto the wood, shoving Ivan as close to it as I can. I make him strip off his outer layer of furs, which are soaked through, and wrap him in our sleeping furs. The day is already waning, and I can tell by the clouds more snow is on the way. We're nearly out of wood. More laughter shrieks with the wind over the ice. It would take very little for the Wolf Queen to kill us now.

I scramble for the sewing kit from my pack and do a hasty job of repairing the tent, thinking once more of the golden needle and thimble, lost somewhere in the ruins of the house under the mountain. Ivan starts to look less gray and breathes more easily. Already the fire burns low.

The sun begins to set, and I scatter the ashes of the fire to conserve what wood we can, then set up the tent. We crawl inside. I make Ivan tell me stories until I'm certain he is warm again; only then do I let him lie back on his furs.

Ivan sleeps, murmuring and shifting where he lies, and I stare at the canvas above, terrified to fall asleep lest the Wolf Queen cause another crack to open wide and swallow us whole. Hal would never know that I had tried to come and save him.

So I lie awake, listening to every sound outside the tent, certain I hear howling that doesn't belong to the wind.

The howling sharpens, drawing near. I jerk upright. Wolves, coming fast over the ice.

"Ivan!" I reach across the tent floor to grab his shoulder. "Ivan!"

The next moment something hits the sides of the tent and bursts through my hasty stitching job. There's a flash of eyes in the dark, angry snarling, the scent of wet fur and fresh blood.

"Ivan!" I scream.

He wakes with a gasp, wrestling to extricate himself from the furs. His hand closes about the ice pick, while I reach for the knife at my belt. The tent pole could be a makeshift sword, if I can reach it in time.

The tent rips apart even further, and moonlight floods in, reflecting off the surface of the ice. Wolves circle us, foam dripping from their bone-white teeth. Their fur is a mottled black and red and gray; their yellow eyes are sharp with rage, with death. Silver collars and flashing gems in their muzzles mark them as soldiers of the Wolf Queen. She's sent them to finish us off.

Ivan gives me an almost imperceptible nod, and I rip my knife from its sheath and plunge it into the wolf nearest me. It yelps and goes limp and I tear the blade from its body and turn my attention to the next.

The storyteller wields his pick, and the acrid scent of blood grows stronger.

I stab another wolf, and find my moment to wrench the tent pole out of its socket. Canvas collapses on us and Ivan and I fight free, out onto the ice, where more wolves are waiting.

They attack in a blur of teeth and eyes, and all at once I'm back in the bauble room, raising my sword against my white wolf—against Hal. I see the blood burst bright against his fur.

Pain comes roaring through my shoulder, and I'm jerked back to the present, crying out and stabbing at the wolf who has bitten me. But he evades my makeshift sword and I'm left nearly crippled with pain. Ivan is suddenly beside me, tugging me up, waving his pick like a scythe to any wolf that gets close.

"RUN!" Ivan roars in my ear, and we do, skidding and sliding across the ice, for we've left our spiked boots in the tent.

The wolves lend chase, yelping angrily, and somewhere in my pain-bleared mind I realize the direction Ivan is leading us.

It's both closer and wider than I think. In the space of mere heartbeats we reach the crack in the ice, and Ivan squeezes my hand and I catch my breath and throw all my strength into leaping across. I reach the other side and fall, landing painfully on one knee, then look back to see the wolves on the far side, snarling with hatred.

Ivan tugs me to my feet. "They loathe the water, but they'll find a way around. We have to go. Now."

I take a shaky breath and we run as best as we can on the slick surface, helping each other up when we fall, urging one another on and on.

Behind us, the wolves' howls tangle up with the wind, and I glance back to see their numbers have somehow swelled—a dozen or more are coming fast across the ice, their black coats stark in the moonlight.

A sheer wall of ice rises suddenly before us, a cavern tunneling into it. We've come, at long last, to the end of the frozen lake.

Ivan pulls me into the cave. Cool, dank darkness swallows us, but I have no illusion of safety.

"What are we going to do?" I gasp.

His eyes track the rapidly approaching wolves, his mouth set and grim. "Get behind me."

"Ivan—"

"Stay back." He crouches down, his body filling up the opening of the cavern. But he has no weapon, having dropped his pick somewhere on the ice.

The wolves hurtle closer.

Ivan starts singing, a haunting melody filled with words I do not know. They slip through the air like my binding needle, shimmering with power.

The ground begins to shake. Ivan's song grows louder.

The wolves leap toward us. Huge chunks of ice cascade down on top of them, sealing the mouth of the cave and plunging us into utter darkness. The wolves howl and shriek; I can hear them, digging.

Fear paralyzes me. "We're trapped."

"No, we're not. These are the ice caves. We just have to find a path through them. Come on."

We stumble together into the blackness. I try not to hear the sound of the wolves' continued digging; I try not to give in to the horror of the dark. Ivan is solid beside me. Certain.

"Do you still have that tent pole?" he asks.

I hand him my makeshift sword and he snaps it in two, singing a fragment of his earlier song. Flame sparks out of nothing, catching each half of the wooden pole. He gives me one and keeps the other for himself, a smile touching his lips.

I peer at Ivan strangely but he avoids my gaze. For the first time in our weeks-long journey, I realize there is more to him than meets the eye.

We walk quickly, my ears straining always to hear sound of the wolves' pursuit behind us. The cavern is immense, sprawling out in an impossible maze of interconnected caves, all of them beautiful, as if carved by a fairy artist with a magical knife. Strange ice formations overarch our heads like the meringue peaks that top Donia's pies. Ice runs constant beneath our feet, and I wonder if it is ever warm enough to melt into a raging river. Magic shivers in every fiber of the caverns; I sense it all around me.

I sense it in Ivan, too. He walks before me, holding his torch high, and I almost feel like we're dancing in the strange shadows his light casts. I begin to imagine we *are* shadows, that we died in the ice last night and are journeying to the afterlife.

"Are these caverns natural?" I ask him, to distract myself from the howls echoing distantly behind us.

He casts a glance back at me. "The North Wind made them."

"Why?"

His eyes look deep and dark, and suddenly very ancient. "To keep the Wolf Queen's court guarded from the world outside. We are close now, Echo. Very close."

The howling grows louder, and I don't think I imagine the sound of claws clacking against the ice. I droop with weariness, and Ivan touches my arm. "Stop and rest awhile. I will stand watch."

"But the wolves—"

"I will stand watch," he repeats.

I am far too tired to argue with him further, so I lay my head down on my coat, and slip into dark dreams.

Mokosh watches me from the wood, sipping tea from a

chipped china cup. Her face is drawn and sad. "Time is almost up, Echo. My mother will prevail, and your journey will be for nothing. You should not have come."

"Why are you doing this?" I whisper. "I thought you were my friend."

"I *am* your friend, Echo. I didn't mean to be. But I grew fond of our adventures together—I grew fond of you. That's why I'm trying to warn you. I cannot cross my mother. I made a deal with her, to watch you, to make sure you didn't get too close to the truth. You have to turn back. It is the only way."

"I'm coming to get Hal."

"You can't free him. He made a deal with the Queen of the Wood. Nothing can break that."

Coldness sears through me. "The old magic can."

The dream shifts. The Wolf Queen's laughter pours through the dark, and Hal stands suddenly before me in a shaft of moonlight. But it is not the Hal I know. His mouth twists with cruelty. He draws a dagger and slices into my face. Blood pours hot. Pain burns. But understanding runs deep.

I know how to free him.

When I wake, Ivan is holding his torch high, the flames dancing violet and white and blue. Beyond the reach of the light a dozen pairs of eyes gleam orange—the wolves, crouching in the shadows, watching us. Waiting.

"Ivan," I gasp.

"I will not let them harm us."

"But how——"

He speaks a sharp, unfamiliar word, and a gust of strong wind comes whistling through the cave. The wolves yelp and whine, shrinking back from him.

"What *are* you?" I whisper.

His hand tightens around the torch. "It seems I am a man with a little magic left. We'll have to run. Can you?"

"Yes."

He gives me one sharp nod.

I take a breath.

He hurls the torch behind us; it explodes in a shower of fire and we break into a run, dashing headlong into darkness. The wolves scream, and the awful stench of burning fur rises strong on the air. Ivan whistles three long notes. Light sparks in the air ahead of us, illuminating our way. Our feet slap hard against the frozen ground.

I don't dare glance back—I don't need to. Claws dig into the ice and teeth snap just behind my heels.

Ivan grabs my arm and we run faster, gaining ground from our pursuers as ice rains down around our heads.

My lungs scream for air. My feet stumble and slide—if not for Ivan, I would fall and be devoured.

All at once we burst out of the ice caves into open air. Stars burn bright and cold above; the whole sky glows an eerie, shifting green.

Ivan gives a shout, clapping his hands together, and a strong wind comes gusting past me. The caves shake, huge pieces of ice and earth breaking off, tumbling down, just as the wolves leap through the opening after us.

The wind whirls round Ivan; he gathers it up, holds it in his hands. He stares at it for a moment with a kind of wild joy, and then a hardness comes into his face and he hurls it at the wolves. They're knocked backward into the cave, and with one downward jerk of his hands, Ivan pulls the entire cavern down on them in a roar of rock and ice.

He turns toward me, a fierce power shining in his eyes.

I gape at him.

He smiles, nods past me. "Look where we are, Echo."

I turn to see a mountain soaring straight up into the sky. It's thick with pine trees, and stars glimmer amidst their branches like jewels.

I stare and stare. "Where the mountain meets the sky," I whisper.

"And the trees are hung with stars," says Ivan soft beside me.

I look into his weathered face, and my heart seizes as I realize something. "You're not coming with me."

"I have been to the Wolf Queen's court before. I cannot go back—the deal I made with her will be null if I appear again before her throne."

Somehow, this doesn't surprise me. Once more I see the ancientness in his eyes. "What deal did you make with her?"

"I, too, loved a woman. I traded my power to the Wolf Queen in exchange for humanity. Mortality."

"*You* are the North Wind."

He smiles a little sadly. "I am. Or was, long ago, before my deal with the Wolf Queen bound me in a human body and stranded Isidor and I both in a time that was not our own. But it seems the Queen did not take all my power, or else it creeps back to me, so close to her as we are now. I chose to please myself. I chose love. But in doing so I gave her greater capacity for evil than she possessed before. I have wanted to help you since you first told me your story. So you might defeat her, and undo what I set in motion long ago."

I think of Isidor and Satu. I think of Hal. I would have done the same in Ivan's place.

"I will wait for you at the base of the mountain for three weeks, and if you do not return by then, I must leave you to your fate, and go and find my Isidor and Satu again."

I nod, my vision blearing.

"I cannot go with you, but I will not leave you powerless. Call upon the Winds if you need them, Echo Alkaev. Call upon my brothers: East and West and South. I have done my part in atoning for my mistake by bringing you here. They can help you now."

I feel the truth in his words, a breath of air coiling gently past my cheek. "Thank you."

"You are very welcome, my dear girl." He tilts his head sideways and gives me a sudden quirk of a smile. "I'm glad you liked them."

"Liked what?"

"The books. The library."

I gape. "*You* made the library?"

Laughter sparks in his eyes. "I enchanted the books when I was the North Wind long ago. I was lonely in the Palace of the Moon, and I collected the stories of men and made them into something more. I put them all in a marvelous library, and there I lived out a thousand lives never meant for me. I brought Isidor there in the old days, before I traded my powers away. The Wolf Queen must have found the library when she stole my power. I thought it was lost forever."

"You have always been a storyteller."

He laughs softly. "I suppose I have."

I sober, gripped by a strong sense of urgency. "Take my story back with you. Give it a happy ending."

He smiles, and reaches out one brown finger to graze my cheek. "I will give it the happiest of all endings, Echo who braved the North. God and grace and all good cheer go with you."

I hug him tight. "Farewell, North Wind."

He bows to me, very low, as if I am a queen.

And then I turn and start up the mountain, alone.

CHAPTER
THIRTY-THREE

T HE WIND IS WARM ON THE mountain, the scent of earth and dew and leaves strong and sweet. But there is a darkness, too, some acrid tang of fear or death that makes me shudder as I climb.

Morning awakes glimmer by glimmer around me. The cold slips away and I discard my coat, laying it over a rock to retrieve upon my return, if there is one. I try not to think about that, or the fact that the North Wind will only wait three weeks. And then I think how odd it is that I have journeyed so far with a Wind and not found it strange.

The trail is steep and makes my breath come in sharp gasps,

but the path is clear: a dirt track winding ever upward, lined on both sides by stately, ancient pines. Sunlight glints through the boughs, but after a while the branches grow thick and close over my head, and the light is blocked out. I am the only thing that stirs on the wooded path, or anywhere near it—no birds in the trees, no animals in the underbrush. After a time, there isn't even the barest breath of wind. With every step I take I feel the trees watching me, listening, wary of my presence but not alarmed.

She knows, I think, fear pulsing sharp. *The Wolf Queen knows I'm coming.*

I have climbed for a little more than an hour when the path spills unexpectedly over a ridge and comes to an end. The wood spreads out before me, more wild and ancient than the trees observing my ascent. But here there are neat stone paths, twisting away among the forest, and bright red flowers peering over the stones that smell of honey and fire. A glitter of light sparks on a tree branch, and then it winks out and my eyes are drawn to another tree, another glitter. The sparks are everywhere, blinking on and off amongst the pine boughs, and I wonder if *this* is what Hal meant by the trees being hung with stars.

I step into the ancient forest, pulling the compass-watch out from under my shirt. The hands of the clock are now spinning madly, as are the compass needles. This place clearly cannot be understood by Rodya's careful mechanism.

I choose one of the stone paths that seems to wind gradually upward, and my felted shoes make almost no noise as I walk. Shadows flash past me. The red flowers nod and wave, though there is still no wind, and I get the distinct feeling that the glints in the trees are laughing at me.

Two shadows jerk across my path from either side: a pair of wolves who stand as high as my chest, growling and barring my way. Both have dark gray brindled fur and the Wolf Queen's silver collars. My hand closes once more around the compass-watch, seeking comfort in its familiar shape.

"Let me pass." My voice is overloud in the unnatural stillness of the wood.

The wolves clamp their jaws down on my arms and drag me forward, astonishingly fast. I stumble trying to keep up with them. The wood passes in a blur; the chatter of the tree sparks grows louder. I wish my hands were free so I could clap them over my ears and block out the noise.

As the wolves pull me deeper into the forest, the pines become tangled with other trees, elms and oaks and aspens, until the pines disappear altogether. The ground rises steadily upward, and it grows increasingly more difficult to catch my breath. The light dims as if we're approaching night, though I know it can't be more than an hour or two past dawn—can it? The glints in the trees illuminate our way.

We come to a break in the wood, step into the clearing I know so well from my dream. Starlight burns cold overhead, and the unnatural hush redoubles. Here is the hall of twining trees: the Wolf Queen's court.

The wolf guards drag me on, across the clearing to a door in the hall.

Two other wolves stand guard here, their eyes flashing as my guards bark at them in their strange language.

The new guards step aside, pulling the door open with a creak and snap of twigs, and simultaneously my arms are released and I feel teeth at my back, propelling me forward. Pain makes my head spin. There's a blur of light. Silent dark shapes sit on one end of the clearing, and the scent of honey and fire is stronger than before. There's a thin, eerie music. Starlight.

I'm forced onward, and my vision clears. Beyond the trees the moon is rising, a huge disc of white silver.

"Hello, Echo," says a voice at my ear.

I look up into a large pair of violet eyes that I know very well, even though I've never seen them set in this face.

"Mokosh," I whisper. I can't help but stare. She's very like her mother, the same furred hands and moon-silver hair, but her head is almost entirely lupine, those eyes her only human feature. She wears a gold breastplate and wrist guards over a thin gown the same color as her hair; two pale, human feet peek out from underneath it. There's a sword at her hip. "I will escort her from here," she growls at the guards. And then to me: "It's time you met my mother."

She strides forward and I stumble after her.

The dark shapes on the edge of the clearing focus into a maze of thrones, occupied by cold figures I realize with horror are people, or what used to be people. We pace through them, and it takes everything I have to keep from being sick. All of them are dead, heads tilted forward or to the side, vines coiling tight around them, eyes staring vacantly into nothingness. Some are little more than brittle bones, some just dust in scraps of cloth. There are hundreds of them, both young and old, men and women. Every one has a crown on their head.

This is Hal's fate, and mine, if I fail.

Mokosh doesn't even glance their way.

Beyond the sea of thrones is a group of—I can only call them children. They run on two legs and some have human feet and hands and faces, but the rest of them is wolf: ears and snouts, flashing teeth and flagging tails. I get the feeling they're Mokosh's siblings. They run back and forth, howling and laughing, carrying a long vine between them that bursts with those red flowers. They weave the vine around themselves as they run, and the vine looks to have a life all its own, an evil, vicious snake.

Mokosh growls as we approach, and suddenly we're caught in the midst of their frantic, teeming ranks. They coil the vine tight around us, the red flowers catching at my sleeves and my ankles, hidden barbs stinging like wasps.

"Get off!" Mokosh barks. "Wretches, get *off*!" She pushes

them away, none too gently, and they yip and whine and let us pass, shedding flowers like red snow in their wake. Tension pulls tight between Mokosh's shoulders.

I forget how to breathe.

Ten paces in front of us stand three more thrones. Two of them are empty.

But on the third throne, a circlet of gold pressed onto his hair, sits Hal.

The sight of him pierces through me, as cold and sharp as the wind over the frozen lake. He is worn and thin and filthy. There are bruises on his face and a small, angry scar on his right cheek, like—

Like the burn from a spot of oil.

He is chained to the throne, a silver band around his throat, matching manacles on his wrists and ankles. He doesn't speak. He doesn't even look at me.

I am sorrow and rage and hope. My fire burns brighter than the Wolf Queen behind my bedroom door.

I found him.

And now I will save him.

CHAPTER
THIRTY-FOUR

S o, Echo Alkaev. You have found your way to my wood." The
Wolf Queen's voice resonates behind me, clear and cold and
brittle as ice.

She sweeps past me and Mokosh to settle on the central throne
and I let my eyes follow her. This throne is the largest, made of twining vines and tree branches, more of those red flowers blooming
bright from its edges. She looks the same as she did in my dreams,
silver hair and clawed hands, angular face and lupine ears. She looks
more human than her daughter, but Mokosh is more beautiful.

I look her square in the eye, and hold fiercely to my fire. "I
have come to free Hal."

She regards me with a cool indifference, and the scent of the red flowers growing from her throne burns strong. It's cloying, too sweet. It chokes me. "Free him? He dwells willingly in my court, according to the terms of our agreement."

"Is that why you've bound him where he sits?"

I don't take my eyes from the Wolf Queen's—I don't dare—but I can feel Hal watching me, and it gives me strength.

"He will be more than willing when his time is fulfilled, and that is soon now. Quite soon. I am surprised you have gotten here before it expired."

"I came on the back of the North Wind."

"If that were true you would have gotten here faster." She taps her clawed fingers against the arms of her throne. "But I fear your journey has been in vain. I cannot release him, and even if I could I would not. You are human. Frail. You have nothing to offer me."

Mokosh grunts, throwing me one swift, piercing glance, before going to sit on the third throne, tension in every line of her body. For the first time, I wonder what deal she made with her mother, what she could possibly want so badly she would barter her life away to get it.

Everything within me yearns to look at Hal, but I fix my gaze on the Queen. "What are his terms? What are the rules you have bound him under?"

"What do you know of *terms* and *rules* but what *I* have told you?" She stands from her throne and strides over to Hal. He trembles as she approaches him, and bile rises acrid in my throat.

"I have much to thank you for." The Queen brushes one claw across the scar on Hal's cheek. He flinches back from her, but the silver band keeps him from moving very far. "I thought you would take him from me. But now he is here, forever. He will marry my daughter and become immortal. As I am." She smiles, and I try not to shudder at the sight of her jagged teeth.

I dare a glance at Mokosh. "What did she promise you? What deal did you make?"

But Mokosh doesn't answer, and I turn back to the Queen. I fight to keep the shake from my voice. "I won't let you have him. I won't let you damn him forever."

"Won't *let* me?" She draws her hand away from Hal's cheek. "What do you even know about this *boy* before you?"

"His name is Hal, and you cursed him. To take the form of a wolf by day while his human self was trapped in the books and to resume his own shape by night."

"Echo."

Hal's voice comes, ragged and hoarse, and I turn toward him like my heart is drawn on a string.

The Queen strikes him across the face and his head jerks back against the silver band. A line of blood appears on his neck—the band is knife sharp.

The Queen straightens, any pretense of a smile fled far from her face, and hatred coils tight inside me.

"His name is Halvarad Perun Svarog Wintar, youngest son of the Duke of Wintar who lived, oh—four centuries back, or so. Halvarad was the curious son. The beautiful son." She brushes her human-wolf hand across his shoulders and he shuts his eyes, his skin blanching paler than before. "He found me in the wood. Came to me every night. Loved me dearly. He wished me to come home with him, to meet his father, to declare me as his prospective bride."

I stare at Hal, willing him to please, please open his eyes. I can bear anything, even the Wolf Queen's awful story, if he will just look at me.

"And so I showed to him my true form: half wolf and half human, imbued with greater power than any human this world or any other has ever possessed. He was not afraid." She smiles, wrapping her clawed fingers about Hal's throat. He sits perfectly still, but I can see a muscle jumping in his jaw. "He wanted to be like me, one of my own kind, but he said his father would not understand such a transformation. And so we struck a deal: for him to be partly with me in the wood, and partly at home with his father. A hundred-year trial: a wolf by day and a man by night."

"You tricked him," says Mokosh quietly from her throne. "You always trick them. It isn't the deal he thought he'd struck."

"I didn't know we even made a deal at all," whispers Hal, from inside the Wolf Queen's grasp. "And the hundred years were not a hundred—three centuries spun away in your wood the night you cursed me. My father was already dead before my curse had even started—"

"Fool!" barks the Queen. She releases him, leaving five spots of blood on his neck where her sharpened nails cut him. She stalks angrily away.

I don't follow, just watch her, waiting for the rest of her story.

"As soon as the deal was struck he seemed unhappy with the arrangement." The Queen stands calm again, resting one hand on the side of her throne. The red flowers stir and whisper at her presence, dipping their heads in reverence. "And so I offered him a way out of his promise: a human girl must live with him for a year without glimpsing his human face in the night. Fulfill this requirement, and he would be free of me. If not, the century would spin on, and he would belong wholly to me at the end of it."

Hal shudders in his bonds, a bruise purpling on his cheek where the Wolf Queen struck him.

"And so you see, Echo Alkaev, the way out was yours to give him, or not, and you failed to uphold your end of the bargain."

Anger roils inside me, a wave against a ship, deep water under ice. "I refuse to accept that."

"Refuse to accept what?" The Queen plucks a flower from her throne and drinks deep of its nectar before she shreds it with her claws and lets the ragged remains fall to the ground. "That you betrayed him? That your journey was entirely in vain?"

"No."

One silver eyebrow arcs upward. "What then?"

"I refuse to accept there is no other way to free him."

She brushes her fingers against another flower, but does not pick it. Instead, she strides over to where I stand, coming so close I can feel the heat burning in her eyes, and smell the blood on her breath.

"I can help with these, you know," she says, so quietly I'm not sure I hear her correctly. She grazes her claws down the scars on the left side of my face, gentle enough that she doesn't cut me, but I can still feel the cold points of her nails.

"I can make them vanish. I can make you beautiful."

I stare straight into her fire-eyes. "My scars don't control me anymore. I don't need to get rid of them to be beautiful."

"Don't *control* you anymore? This from the girl who prayed to God every night since she was seven years old to make her pretty again? This from the girl who bought a jar of cream worth more than a shipment of books from the city, then buried it in the back garden when she found it had no effect on her? Don't control you anymore *indeed*."

The rage is burning me up from the inside. My eyes snag on Mokosh, and suddenly I *know* what deal she made with her mother. "You want to be entirely human. That's what she promised you."

Mokosh ducks her head, ashamed. "You don't know what it's like, Echo. To be a monster, to revile your very existence, to not belong wholly to one world."

"Oh Mokosh. I wish you would have told me. Of course I know."

"But how could you?" she whispers. "You are so beautiful."

My heart tears. "It may not even be in her power. You know you can't trust her. Why would she make you wholly human when she hasn't done the same for herself?"

"She doesn't need to be human. She commands all the magic of the world."

A strange wind breathes through the clearing, stirring through my hair and smelling of ice. "Not all of it."

The Queen has been listening to our exchange with a kind of bemused scorn. "Are you quite done?"

I turn back to her, my voice clear and strong. "I am here to free Hal, and I'm not leaving without him. I invoke the old magic."

The Queen releases a breath and steps back from me, like I've slapped her. "The old magic?" she echoes uneasily.

"I told you, Mother," says Mokosh. "I told you she has the power to defeat you."

The Queen doesn't even acknowledge her. I dare a glance at Hal. His eyes are shut and his lips are moving as if in silent, desperate prayer.

Words pour through me.

The wolf's, in the Temple of the Winds: *Once, I had something precious. I should have held it tight, should have guarded it with my last breath, but instead I let it go.*

The East Wind's, in the book mirror: *When you have found the oldest of magics, you must not let it go, not even for an instant.*

And Isidor's, in Ivan's tent: *If you love something you will not give it up, not for anything. It belongs to you, it is part of you. If you grab hold of it and never let it go—no one can take it from you. Not even the Wolf Queen.*

"The old magic is stronger than you," I say. "It has the power to break your curse. *I* have the power to break your curse. Now. Tell me. How long until his hundred years is fulfilled?"

She doesn't answer, her expression cold, aloof. And yet I can feel her anger.

"How long?"

"Three days," says Mokosh, rigid on her throne. "His hundred years are fulfilled in three days."

"Careful, daughter," growls the Queen. "You overstep yourself."

Mokosh says nothing more.

"I want to make you a deal," I say.

The Wolf Queen turns to me, silver brows raised, and Mokosh is instantly forgotten. "What deal?"

"Give Hal to me for the remainder of his century, and I will hold onto him. I won't let go even for an instant, no matter what you do, no matter how you try to take him from me. I will hold back your curse. And when the three days are over and his hundred years are fulfilled—he won't belong to you anymore."

"He will belong to you, I suppose," the Wolf Queen scoffs.

I look at Mokosh, who crouches miserably on her throne, and I am sick that the Queen thinks I would want to own anyone. "He will belong to himself. The old magic—the first magic— will free him."

She considers me. "And if you fail, girl-child?"

I stare her down, hold my head high. "I have set my terms. You set yours."

She smiles, deep and dangerous. "If you fail, you both will belong to me, and be bound to my court for all of time."

"Echo, no."

I look over at Hal. Tears slide down his cheeks. He throws himself against his knife-sharp bonds, struggling and swearing as he tries to get free. Blood seeps into the hollow of his neck, pours down his arms. "Don't bargain with her! She'll trick you. With her it is always a trick. You have to run. You have to go now, and don't look back! I'll not have you trapped here, too. I couldn't bear it. Please, Echo. Please go."

"You hear how he pleads with you," says the Queen. "But time slips away. Choose now, what you will do."

"I'm sorry, Hal, but I'm not leaving here without you."

He sags where he sits, his whole body shuddering. "Please, Echo. Please."

But I turn once more to the Wolf Queen. "I invoke the old magic. I accept your terms."

CHAPTER THIRTY-FIVE

"RELEASE THE BOY, MOKOSH," SAYS THE Wolf Queen, without a sideways glance at her daughter.

"Release him yourself. I will not be your pet. You do not own me."

In one swift movement, the Queen sweeps to Mokosh's throne, and grabs her daughter's muzzle with one clawed hand. "I *do* own you, just as I owned your father, just as I own your filthy half-siblings. You will do as I say."

Mokosh's ears are pinned back flat against her head. "You don't have any intention of keeping your promise to me, do you?"

The Queen digs her claws in deeper, making Mokosh flinch.

"You could never be anything more than a hideous creature in a beautiful dress."

Mokosh jerks away, the Wolf Queen's claws tearing at her face. Blood grazes her silver fur. "I should have known better than to make a deal with you. "

The Queen smiles, her white teeth curving up over her lips, and touches Mokosh's wound with one finger. "Now do as I command. Release the boy."

Mokosh growls, but obeys, stepping down from her throne and over to Hal's. She frees his neck first, loosing the band with a metallic *click*, then his wrists, his ankles. She steps back, her furred hands balled into fists. She's trembling. "I'm sorry, Echo." Her voice is so quiet I barely hear her. "Save him. If you can." And then she slinks back to her throne, bows her head into her hands. Her shoulders shake.

"Well?" says the Wolf Queen. "Stand, boy. Meet your fate."

Hal takes a ragged breath and tries to stand, but his legs fold underneath him and he collapses to the ground. I am beside him in an instant, my arms around him, hoisting him back to his feet. I wonder how long he has sat bound to the Wolf Queen's throne.

His eyes meet mine. The scar on his cheek from the spot of oil looks raw, ugly, as if still freshly made, though it is months old. "Please, Echo. Please don't do this. Don't let her trap you. Leave me. Save yourself. *Please*."

"I am here to save *you*," I tell him fiercely, "and I'm not leaving till I've done it."

"But I'm not worth saving. Echo, you still don't understand—"

"Come to the center of my circle," thunders the Wolf Queen.

I lead Hal the few steps to where she's pointing; he leans heavily on my shoulders. He feels fragile beneath my touch—brittle, impossibly old. And if what he and the Wolf Queen have said is true, he *is* old, more than four hundred years. "Echo, *please*!" Tears drip down his cheeks.

The moon is looking full into the Wolf Queen's court. I have the feeling that it's truly watching us, interested in the choices we make amidst the dust and the trees.

Hal faces me, standing a little straighter, a little grimmer than before.

I take both of his hands in mine; they're cold, but they feel strong. "For the next three days, I'm holding on to you, Halvarad Wintar. And then you will be free."

"What magic is stronger than hers?"

"The magic that made the world." My voice cracks on the next word: "Love."

He smooths his thumb across my cheek and smiles at me, the sad, hopeless smile of a man who has lost everything. He's accepting my choice. "Thank you for coming to save me. My dear Lady Echo."

"I'm just glad it's not too late, Lord Wolf."

He smiles again, and this time it's a true smile.

From my peripheral, I see the Wolf Queen pacing toward us, and I have the sudden realization that this is not going to be as simple as holding Hal's hands for three days. The Wolf Queen is bent on destroying us both—if she didn't think it an impossible task, she wouldn't have accepted my challenge.

"Don't let go," says Hal.

"Never." I tighten my grip around his fingers.

And then the Wolf Queen raises her hands to the sky and begins to speak to the moon, a liquid, chanting language that seethes with fire and reminds me of the North Wind's stories.

Hal begins to scream and shake, his eyes rolling back in his head. I slide one hand up his arm, my fingers digging through his thin shirtsleeve. He screams as if he's being tortured with hot irons, and suddenly he's burning, flames bursting raw from his skin, engulfing both of us.

And now I'm screaming, too. We both sink to our knees as the fire rages round. I can feel it eating away at my flesh, I can smell the stink of it. My hair catches fire and I am burning, burning, and yet I am not consumed. Hal weeps, ragged, rough, and anger cuts through my pain.

"You can't kill us!" I cry out. "You don't have the power!"

The fire burns and burns. I am in agony and Hal is worse. He shudders and shakes in my arms. His flesh chars black. His screams fill up the world, and mine are tangled with them.

But I don't let him go. I cradle him in my arms, rebuking the fire and cursing the Wolf Queen. The flames slide away from me, but not from him. My pain evaporates. His does not.

He burns and burns and burns, but does not die. I think he will burn forever, or turn all to ash and blow away on the wind. I will not be able to hold him then. He will be lost to me.

I cling to him tighter than before. He screams and screams and weeps into my hair.

The fire abates, so slowly I don't realize it's happening until it's suddenly gone, leaving Hal cracked and feverish in my arms. But he isn't burnt to nothing, isn't scarred beyond recognition. His screams fade to whimpers, and he's trembling and human and somehow still whole.

"An illusion." I wipe the tears from his eyes even as my own well up. "Only an illusion. Like the ones in our book-mirrors."

He shudders and shudders. "It isn't the worst she can do—" But his words are cut off in another cry of pain.

His body convulses. His bones crack and his skin tears apart and he transforms into a giant serpent, sinuous and black. He writhes and shrieks and I hold on, hold on, though his scales are sword-sharp and they slice into my hands. Hot, slippery blood runs down my arms. I dig my fingers under his scales, deeper and deeper, down into his flesh. I won't let him go.

He strikes without warning, fangs biting deep into my shoulder, and violent, white-hot pain sears through me. I'm screaming again, the world white around me, but somewhere in the haze of agony I remember what I am, and what he is.

I screw my eyes shut. I don't let go.

I feel him begin to change beneath me, and I open my eyes to see him growing larger and larger and larger, until I find my hands wrapped around the claw of a giant monster, with the shoulders and horns of an ox, the body of a lion, the feet of an eagle. His eyes glow fire red, and in one hand he wields a whip made of stars. He reeks of death and I am sick with fear.

The monster looks at me and laughs as he tries to shake me off his claw. But I wrap my whole body around his foot, tucking my head down between his claws, my feet cinched tight around his ankle joint. He cracks the whip and the tail hits the back of my head; excruciating light explodes in my vision. The fire and the pain tunnels into my mind, deeper and deeper, driving me mad.

But under the agony pulses a single, desperate thought: *don't let go, don't let go, don't let go.*

The fire fades a little, and I open my eyes to see Hal again, kneeling on the forest floor, weeping and raging in his anguish. My hand is curled about his wrist. He lifts his face to mine, and there's hatred in his eyes.

"What do you want with me?" he demands. "She-witch. Devil's daughter. Beast of the pit!"

The words cut deep but I fight hard against them. "I'm not leaving you. No matter what you say to me, I'm not leaving you."

"Did you think I wanted you to come and *rescue* me in this foolish way? I was glad to escape you, escape that dreary house and your horrid company. To return here, to the Queen and her daughter who alone truly care for me. You are worthless. Wretched. Ugly. I cannot stand to look at you."

Something cracks deep inside. It hurts. It hurts. It hurts *so much*. "How can you be so cruel?"

He tips his head back and laughs, laughs and laughs, and I think I hate him, but I feel the pulse of his heart beneath the skin at his wrist and I remember—

This is not Hal. This is *her*.

And I don't let go.

Then he's screaming as his bones once more break apart and feathers burst sharp from his skin.

He transforms into a great black carrion bird, and his talons pierce the skin beneath my collar bone, driving like a knife to the heart. I shriek in pain as he beats his wide wings and hurtles us both into the sky. His claws tear through me and I scrabble desperately to hang onto his leg as the world spirals away below us.

He flies, up and up and up, toward a tall white cliff where the moon shows its silver face just beyond.

He dashes me against the rock and pain explodes in my shoulders, my back, my legs. I hear a sharp *snap*, and a scream tears out of me. The agony is all-encompassing, filling the world.

But a thread of my being remains inside, a small voice

whispering *don't let go, don't let go, don't let go.*

And I obey.

Then suddenly we're back in the wood again, crouching together on the forest floor, and the pain is gone. Rain falls, somewhere far away. Or no—close; I feel it sweet on my skin.

"Echo—" gasps Hal.

But the Wolf Queen isn't finished yet. Once more his body breaks apart and he transforms into a huge white mass before my eyes: a giant arctic bear, with claws as long as my hand and teeth bigger than the stalactites in the ice cave.

He opens his mouth and roars, swiping at me with his free paw—I'm clinging desperately to his other one. Hal's claws rake deep into my back, and wetness leaks from the raw lines of fire in my skin. I sob for breath. The rain around us now is sharp as needles.

And I can still hear the Wolf Queen's song-spell, tangled in the wind.

Everything in me screams to let go, to end the pain, to be free of it. Everything but that tiny thread that remembers.

I hold on to him, as his claws tear into my flesh, as he lowers his great head and sinks his teeth into my shoulder.

I weep and weep. I can't stop the cries of pain ripping out of me.

But I listen to that quiet thread.

And I don't let go.

Hal changes, again and again and again.

He's a dragon, a demon, a fish with slicing scales. He's a

scorpion, a spider, a creature made of wind that bites like glass and tears raging at my skin. The creatures blur all together into a haze of anguish and torment and pain. Blood blears my eyes. I long for release.

But still my heart beats within me: *don't let go, don't let go, don't let go.*

And somehow I am strong enough to hold on to him.

And then he shifts into a form I know very well: the great white wolf.

I gasp as he crouches there, growling at me, my hand tight around his back left leg. I can feel his scars, the marks left by the wolf trap I tried so hard to free him from.

I breathe hard, desperate, afraid.

He twists and leaps at me, and I'm barely able to keep hold of him as his teeth sink into my arm.

The pain cuts down to the bone and a cry rips out of me. My throat is raw from screaming. My mind is numb with pain.

"Hal. Hal, please stop." This form hurts more than all the others.

Or so I think—until he shifts into my father.

I'm so startled to see Peter Alkaev staring at me in the wood that I almost do let go, right then, but I stop myself just in time. I'm holding his hand, something I haven't done with my real father since I was a very young child. It feels strange.

"I know you're Hal," I say aloud, more for my own benefit than the Queen's latest creation's.

My father smiles at me. There's flour dusted in his beard, and he smells like cinnamon. "You know I care nothing for you, child. Even before you ruined your face, you killed my darling wife, and resigned me to an existence of misery. If not for you, I would never have lost money at the shop. It was your curse that did it. That made everyone hate us. That made crops fail and rains come out of season. You are devil-touched. I should have left you in a snowbank. You would have frozen to death, and I would have been rid of you."

His words cut deep, though I know, I *know* they are the Queen's words, not my father's. He does not attack me as the creatures did, but still I feel pain—every pulse.

"We have stopped mentioning you at home," he continues. "We did it the moment you went away. Peace came into our lives again. I cannot believe how you fooled us into keeping you all those years. Donia saw the truth, but I wouldn't listen. Now we don't need you. Rodya is married. Something that could never have happened to you. And Donia is with child and I thank God every day I never have to see you again."

"Stop!" I cry, beating at his chest with my free hand. "Stop! I know it isn't you."

He grins, his eyes flickering red. "Why do you ask me to stop? Because you know I speak the truth and you are too water-willed to hear it? Foolish child. You are nothing. You have always been nothing, and that is what you will be forever."

"Stop it, stop it, stop it!" I scream at him.

He just laughs and laughs, and I know it is the Wolf Queen's laughter, but I still can't bear it.

And then suddenly he is Hal again, and his mouth presses soft and warm against mine and he's wrapping his arms around my shoulders and clinging to me as I'm clinging to him.

I sob into his chest and his tears fall into my hair and I can't bear it.

"Echo, Echo, Echo," he whispers. "I'm sorry, I'm so sorry."

I sag against him, still shuddering and scared. There's tension in his arms; it isn't over yet.

I hear the Wolf Queen's step and look up at her. She stands cool and silver in the moonlit wood, and I realize the sudden silence is the absence of her spell-song. I regard her in exhaustion and fear, my arms still locked around Hal.

"You have done tolerably well so far." Her tone is aloof. "But I don't think you know everything." She's holding another of the red flowers from her throne, and she strokes its petals thought-fully. It trembles in her hands, and I have the feeling that, to her, I am nothing more than another flower, for her to toy with as long as it amuses her, then discard when she grows tired of the temporary diversion. "Does she, Hal?"

He turns his head to look at her, and I feel again his own fragility, the weight of the curse stretching him too far, too long. "I don't know what you mean, your majesty," he answers softly.

But I can sense he's lying.

"Don't you?" The Queen's lips turn up in a momentary, humorless smile. "Well, let me remind you of the terms of your enchantment. The terms that she agreed to, when she came to live in your house for a year. What really happened when she broke those terms." The Wolf Queen steps slowly around us, her skirt sweeping the forest floor behind her as she walks. I have the sudden idea that she fashioned it from ice and snow, with wind for thread. "I think you should tell her."

Hal sits a little back from me. I can feel his heartbeat echoing in our joined palms. He doesn't speak.

The Queen keeps circling us. "Let me rephrase. Tell her, Halvarad. Tell her exactly what you made her agree to. Tell her what would have happened if she didn't light that lamp. *Tell her.*"

He doesn't look at me, just stares at the ground and shudders like he's breaking to pieces.

"TELL HER!" thunders the Queen.

I can feel the shiver of magic pass between them. She's using the enchantment to command him. He cannot help but obey.

"And look at her, when you do," she adds.

His chin jerks up, against his will. His eyes are wet. The scar from the spot of oil is stark against his pale skin. "Echo." His words sound strangled, torn from his lips. "If—if you would have waited. If you wouldn't have lit the lamp—"

The Wolf Queen is laughing, and begins picking up the

threads of her spell-song once more. I sense its rising power.

"You would have been free," I say. "I know. Instead I doomed you to come back here. Back to her."

He nods, tears leaking down his cheeks. "It's true, yes, it's true. But Echo, all the things I told you. About being a caretaker for the house. About seeing your family again—" He wants to look away but he can't, and his whole body trembles with his resistance to the spell. "If you hadn't lit that lamp, I would have been free. But—but she would have taken you instead. That was the deal. The only way to break my curse. Your life for mine. That was what I asked of you. That is what you agreed to, though you didn't know it."

CHAPTER THIRTY-SIX

HAL'S PULSE BEATS BENEATH MY FINGERTIPS: erratic, unstable. His eyes still meet mine, but I glance away. I can't bear it. My breath is ragged and wild in my chest, my whole body sears with the pain of everything I've endured. I can't bear it. Can't bear it.

"He never wanted you," hisses the Queen. "He never loved you. He was just trying to save his own worthless skin."

"No."

"Tell her!" the Queen commands.

Hal's wretched voice, torn from his lips without his consent: "It's true. I'm sorry, Echo. I'm so sorry—but it's true."

I stare at my hand, wrapped around his wrist. I am collapsing inward, falling through a jagged crack in the ice, dark water closing over my head and sealing me into oblivion. In the service of the Queen there will be peace. Forgetfulness. When I belong to her, body and soul, I won't remember him—won't remember this.

I am outside myself as I watch my fingers loosen their hold. They move so slowly, too slowly, as if my own body rebels against me.

"Echo," breathes Hal, "Echo, *no*." And he jerks himself close to me, his leg grazing my foot as he grabs my head with both his hands, fingertips piercing into my skull. "Let her see." He says it like a prayer. "Let her remember."

Light explodes behind my eyes and pain bursts inside of me. I fracture into a thousand different pieces, spin out and out and out, beyond sight and sound and breath. But not beyond feeling. Not beyond pain. Somewhere I think I'm screaming.

An image unfolds in the nothingness around me: a woman lying in bed in a square room, a fire burning on a hearth, two men standing over her. One is my father, much younger than I've ever seen him. He's tall and thin; there is no silver in his beard. He's crying.

The woman in the bed isn't moving. There's a baby cradled in her dead arms, a baby with blue eyes and dark hair and smooth, perfect skin.

The other man eases the baby from the woman and hands her—hands *me*—to my father. *"I shall call you Echo,"* he whispers, *"because you have the echo of your mother's strong heart. No one can ever take that from you."*

The image melts away like honey in hot tea and another uncurls to take its place: A dark-haired girl playing in a fort built of books in her father's shop, laughing as a pile of them collapses on top of her. A dark-haired boy pulls her free and spins her in a circle before setting her firmly on her feet again. *"Best put them back before Papa gets here!"*

The girl and boy scramble to collect the books, slotting them expertly onto the shelves as though they've done this many times before.

Confusion swells hot and sharp inside of me. This girl is me, but not me. I remember this, and yet I *can't.* Because this me is nine years old, and the skin on her face is as smooth and clear as the day she was born.

Impossible.

The strange, cruel not-memory fades into another: the me-who-can't-be-me is several years older, sharing lunch with a crowd of children at school. She's laughing and happy. She has *friends.* No one is throwing stones at her. No one is cursing her as the spawn of the Devil or crossing themselves.

I'm breaking. This can't be. And yet some part of me remembers it—the taste of the sunlight on my skin, the easy friendship of a girl called Sara, the sense of belonging strong enough to banish a lifetime of loneliness.

I don't understand. *Make it stop!* I try to scream, but I'm caught fast in the sticky unwinding of my life as it should have been—as it could have been.

I watch as the other me grows up. She still laughs with Rodya and holds Papa dear, but her world is larger than the bookshop. She visits the city with her friend Sara. She goes to a dance in the village. She blushes as boys ask her to dance. She wiles away hours practicing the piano, pouring her soul into Czjaka and Behrend. She dreams of studying music at the university, of filling all the world with song.

My father introduces other-me to Donia, who doesn't seem to disapprove of my existence any less for the absence of the scars. Her hatred oozes from her like muck from a bog. My father shows me the cottage in the woods. We work on it together, fix it up just as I remember, only the carpet in front of the fire is blue—wasn't it red?

I watch as my father marries Donia in the new chapel, as Rodya gives me the compass-watch for my birthday. I fall asleep with it pressed up against my chest, the steady ticking following me into my dreams like it had never been broken.

Debt finds us in this version of my life just as it did in the other: Donia demanding more than we could afford, my father obliging her because he is capable of greater kindness and sacrifice than she could ever comprehend. He leaves for the city to sell his rare books and maps.

He's missing for half a year.

I watch the other me find him in the snowy wood, hear the wolf asking her to stay with him. No, not asking. Demanding. Or he'd kill her father and her brother. He'd kill her, too. I can taste other-me's fear, hot and sharp and filled with despair. But she agrees to the wolf's terms, to save her family.

I watch as the other me goes with the wolf to the house. She swears not to light the lamp, and spends the whole first night awake, staring into the darkness, afraid to shut her eyes lest the wolf devour her in her sleep.

The strange half-memories fly thicker now: beautiful-me grows to trust the wolf, even admire him. She explores the book-mirrors and falls in love with Hal. Mokosh convinces her to light the lamp, and Hal is taken by the Wolf Queen's soldiers.

Shame courses through me as I watch myself kneel in the snow, vowing to save Hal and undo my mistake.

My long journey passes in a blink. I meet Ivan and Isidor. I travel the northern wilds and discover Ivan is the North Wind. I climb the mountain to the Wolf Queen's court and invoke the old magic to try and save Hal.

I hold on to him as he writhes and twists beneath me. I am stubborn and proud. I am fiercely certain there is nothing the Wolf Queen can do or say to shake me from my purpose.

But I am wrong.

He lied to you.

He never loved you.

He never wanted you.

He was just trying to save his own worthless skin.

He never wanted you.

He never wanted you.

Heartbreak and betrayal twist across beautiful-me's face. Despair weighs in her eyes. She is broken.

She lets go of Hal.

NO! I want to scream.

But it's too late.

The Wolf Queen laughs and drags Hal away from the other me. Bonds of silver close around my wrists.

"Do not let her take you, too," says Hal, staring into the other-me's face, *"Please. Please, Echo. I can't lose you. Not like this."*

And the other me lifts her head, the Wolf Queen's laughter ringing in her ears. She looks grim. Determined. Whatever Hal had done, it was at the Queen's command—he doesn't deserve to end decaying on her throne—and neither does she. She refuses. She screams into the sky, over and over and over, and I know the words like the own beats of my heart: *"I call upon the Winds! South and East and West! Come to my aid!"*

They come in a wheeling fire, spinning and raging. Heat sparks on my skin, smoke stings my eyes. They resolve into three forms that look something like men, though they are taller and stronger and *brighter* than men should be: East blazing like the sun, West with his gold wings furled wide, South with his spear made of mountains, all with jewels flashing white from their foreheads.

The other me can feel the Wolf Queen's bonds tightening around her, but she's not giving in, not yet.

"Please," she begs the Winds, *"Take up the threads of the North Wind's power. Harness time and turn it back. Let me try again to save Hal. Let me have another chance."*

"Daughter, you do not know what it is you ask," says the East Wind. *"It is no little thing."*

"Please. I will do anything. Give up anything. Just let me try again to save him."

"Would you give up your memory?" says the South Wind.

"Yes."

"Would you give up your life? Yourself?" says the West Wind.

"I would give anything."

The words echo in my mind, glinting like embers on my tongue. I know the taste of them, know the feel of them leaving my lips. Because I said them, in another time and another life, in this very spot. In this very moment. I begged the Winds to turn back time, and they did. The other me, the beautiful me—she *is* me, or was. The first me. Before the Winds sent me back to try again.

"You won't remember," warns the East Wind. *"You won't be able to warn yourself. You could go through all of this and still die. Still lose him. Nothing might change."*

The other me—the first me—lifts her chin, unafraid. *"It doesn't matter. I have to try."*

The Winds look solemn. *"So be it."*

"No, Echo!" cries Hal. *"You don't know what might happen, you don't know—"*

The first me grabs Hal's hand and shuts her eyes. *"Find me,"* she whispers, *"And this time I swear I'll save you."*

"Echo—"

But the world breaks apart and his voice is swallowed in the spinning fragments of lost memory.

CHAPTER THIRTY-SEVEN

I AM EVERYWHERE AND NOWHERE AT once. I am pain and heat and light. I am sorrow. I am joy.

It hurts. It hurts so much.

The Winds are here, wherever I am: East with a shining sword, South with his spear, West with a spinning wheel. There is a fourth power here, too, an unharnessed, teeming energy. I can't see it, but I can *feel* it.

I know it is the North Wind, or what's left of his magic: a current of time and death and loneliness; a torrent of story, as strong as the world itself.

The three Winds gather it up, East and South coiling it around their sword and spear, West channeling it into the spinning wheel. He winds it up, winds and winds and winds, and the sadness and pain pull out of me. I can breathe again. I couldn't before.

I am in a cold square room. Pricks of light hurt my eyes, and in the center sits a man at a desk, writing in a book. Life pours out of his pen, magic and laughter.

I pace toward him and he lifts his head.

I know him: his fierce dark eyes, his kind brown face. It is Ivan, the storyteller—the North Wind who once was. He smiles at me, lifts his pen from the book. Silver ink drips on the page. "What would you wish of me, Echo Alkaev?"

The light sharpens; it's coming from the doorway on the other end of the room: there East and South stand watch, fierce and strong, spear and sword raised high.

I touch the left side of my face; it is smooth and soft and for some reason that troubles me. I dreamed once it was rough with scars.

"Send me back. Send me back so I can try again. Send me back so I can save him."

"Dearest girl." The North Wind smiles. He beckons me close and draws a mark on my cheek with his silver pen. It feels soft, like a gentle kiss. "You already have."

And I straighten to see the West Wind beside me, his golden wings spread wide. "Come, Echo. We have very far to fly." He helps me onto his back and I wrap my arms around his neck, my feet holding tight beneath his wings.

He carries me to the door, and his brothers East and South pull it open wide.

Beyond is . . .

I do not know.

Starlight.

Emptiness.

I am flying in the dark on the West Wind's back, riding through the tides of time itself. On and on and on we fly, and I feel myself unwinding, the threads of my life falling to pieces, caught up on the spinning wheel.

I forget who I am and why I'm here and where we are going. I only know I am safe, with the West Wind's wings beneath me, that all will be well.

I am lost in a sea of stars.

I am wandering, wandering.

But still I can feel the pulse of my heart, and it says *don't let go*.

We fly toward a very great light, and my eyes tear at the brightness.

And then I am falling, spiraling down and down and down.

But I am not afraid.

Don't let go, says my heart.

Don't let go.

DARKNESS, LIGHT, AIR. I AM helpless and small. Someone is weeping. I'm cradled in warm arms.

I sleep and sleep.

Papa is singing to me. I like to hear the sound of his voice. I reach up tiny hands and tug on the ends of his beard.

I grow. Old enough to be told the story of my name. Old enough to wonder what it might be like to have a mother. Old enough to know my father is the kindest man who ever lived.

I remember, I remember what I shouldn't be able to:

I have lived my life twice over.

And twice over I have failed.

Somewhere outside of myself I can feel Hal's fingers, pressing into my temples.

I open my eyes.

HAL STARES AT ME, HIS hands still tight against my head. His face is streaked with tears and my own cheeks are damp. Pain pulses through me, but it is duller than before. I take a ragged breath, then another and another. "I failed you," I whisper. "I failed you *twice*. They sent me back. Hal, the Winds sent me back to try again and I *failed*."

He rubs his thumb across my scarred cheek. "No you didn't."

"Hal, I let go."

He shakes his head. "No you didn't."

And I glance down and see my left hand still curled tight around his ankle.

CHAPTER THIRTY-EIGHT

HAL CRADLES ME AGAINST HIS CHEST, gently, like he's uncertain if I want him to touch me. I'm shaking so hard I feel like I might burst apart. I try to focus on Hal, his heartbeat strong beneath my ear, his breath on my cheek, his cold fingers tangled in mine. I don't understand what he's done, or what I've done. I don't know how to reconcile the two versions of my life, pages of a book glued together, impossible to tell what words belong to which page. But I know that it's real. I know that it happened.

And I am not the only one who is living out this story for the second time.

I lift my head to see the Wolf Queen looming over us, angry

and brittle as starlight, as ice. "If the girl-child had known everything you have made her endure twice over, she would have never come. Clever of you, Halvarad, not to tell her."

I hate that she has the power to make me doubt him even now, to make me want to pull away. But I don't. I hold tight to his hand, and strength pulses between us.

"You are wrong." Hal's eyes blaze with fury, his face is flushed and the mark on his cheek from the spot of oil seems nearly healed.

How long have we been here, holding on to one another? There seems to be a change in the wind, blowing down through the top of this woodland hall. I can feel it, I think: the cords of his enchantment falling away from him, the Queen's hold evaporating like smoke.

"Echo would have come to save me anyway. That is who she is: she gives of herself to the people around her. Gives and gives and gives. Because at the heart of it, in *her* heart, there is compassion and strength, goodness and knowledge and truth. She would have come all this way, to stand up to you, to break me free from your spell—she would do it all *twice*, even though I don't deserve it, not then and not now. That is what burns in Echo's soul. That is why she's still holding on to me now." His voice cracks and he turns his eyes to mine, tears sliding down his face. "I was so afraid, so afraid to go back to her. But I was glad when you lit the lamp, when I woke and saw you leaning over me. I was glad, because it meant you would be free. And then I remembered—

I remembered that you'd done this all before, and I couldn't bear it. I couldn't *bear*—"

"Hal, it's over. Can't you feel it? Your century is fulfilled. You're free."

He sucks in a deep, shuddering breath, and lifts his head once more to the Queen. Her hatred seethes toward us, a tangible thing. But she doesn't take up the threads of her spell-song. She just stands there, staring at us.

"Isn't he?" I demand. "I've fulfilled your terms. He's free. We both are."

"You fools," spits the Wolf Queen. "I do not require an enchantment to destroy you."

Then she shouts a harsh word at the sky and the world explodes in rock and fire.

I leap to my feet and yank Hal up after me, holding on to his hand with all the strength remaining in my body. The earth cracks in two beneath our feet and fire rages below, molten lava leaping up to consume us. I throw myself across the crack and Hal jumps with me; we run, hand in hand. Mountains explode around us, rocks and ash and fire raining down. The noise deafens me, and all sound narrows to a ringing in my ears.

We run, choked for breath. Ever the earth is rearranging itself underneath, seeking to shake us apart but we don't let it, our fingers locked hard together. Another mountain bursts ahead, and lava rushes toward us from every direction.

"Jump!" shouts Hal, and we narrowly leap over a new crack.

The lava oozes toward us; I can smell the sulphur, taste the heat. It will make short work of us—there is no escaping this.

"Up here!" Hal cries.

A rock juts up through the river of fire and Hal scrambles to the top with me awkwardly hanging on to his heel. He leans down to grasp my arm and pulls me up after him.

All around, the world shudders and shakes. Lava licks at the base of our rock but doesn't reach us. Even so, the heat singes my hair, sucks up the moisture in my skin. Soon there will be none left, and I will crack like the ground and fracture like the mountains. This is the full weight of the Wolf Queen's power, her true nature. I can't help but think that she is neither wolf nor woman but something else entirely, a creature born of fire and malice and hate.

Hal and I huddle together, his arm tight around my shoulders.

"I'm sorry," he says into my ear, and somehow amidst all this horror of heat, I can still feel the warmth of his breath on my face. "I did this to you. I did this to you twice. I forced you to make promises you didn't understand. I forced you to come here. I even—I even scarred your face."

I open my eyes to peer at him through the haze of smoke and ash and I'm filled with a profound sense of release. "It's all right, Halvarad Wintar. It's over now. I chose this. I chose *you*. I will always choose you."

He lifts his hand to my face, traces the scars with his fingers.

Gently, so gently. "Has anyone ever told you how beautiful you are?"

I thought all the moisture had been siphoned from me but I'm wrong. A single tear slides down my cheek.

And then I'm leaning into him, pressing my lips against his. Kissing Hal, who was twice a wolf, in the middle of a dying world. He pulls me close and kisses me back. A brittle wind whirls around us, tangling our hair together, my dark and his light. Ash falls like snow.

The lava creeps higher. The earth shakes.

And then Hal draws back from me, tightens his grip on my hand, pulls me to my feet. He raises our joined hands to the ragged, bleary sky. "Do you see this, Wolf Queen? Do you see? You are defeated! Your curse is undone, your rule over me ceases. She has broken it! The century is fulfilled and *Echo has broken your curse.* Do you hear me? DO YOU HEAR ME?"

"There's no need to shout."

Suddenly the Wolf Queen is beside us, floating in the air just above the tumbling lava. Her features seem sharper in the raging light, but no wind stirs through her silver hair.

"Well, then?" Hal's eyes are hard as flint.

"You have won," she snaps. "Your stupid girl has prevailed."

He smiles. "Then we are free."

"Of the enchantment, perhaps. But not of me."

She circles us, as she did in the wood.

Hatred and fear and anger gnaw inside of me, and I still don't let go of Hal. "Where are we?" I demand.

She doesn't smile, just stares at me as she passes, around and around our rock, walking on nothing, her feet making no sound. "I am the Queen of many realms, many worlds. This is one of them. I was born here. Not the daughter of the Devil as so many have guessed. Just the daughter of another world. But I did not choose to stay."

Her words are punctuated by yet another eruption, barely fifty paces away. Hal and I fall to our knees, choking on ash. The Wolf Queen regards us without pity. "You have displeased me. You have robbed me. You have brought my enchantment to naught and turned my own daughter against me. And so I shall leave you here. And you shall die."

Hal struggles to stand amidst the trembling of the world, and he pulls me up beside him. We are one, united and strong against her. "That," he says, "was not part of our agreement."

"You don't make the rules. No one does but me."

"THAT WAS NOT PART OF OUR AGREEMENT!"

I can hardly breathe. My skin cracks, the heat creeps up to my hairline. We have minutes left. Maybe only seconds.

"I care not," says the Wolf Queen.

There comes a sudden silence, and then the next second a roaring, like a storm over the sea, and a rushing of wind.

It whirls around all three of us, lifting us from the rock, away from the grasping fingers of the lava, away from the heat and the fire and the certainty of death. I think I catch a glimpse of gold wings.

The Wolf Queen is screaming.

All I can feel is my heartbeat and Hal's, still together, caught fast between our palms.

The world seems to shift, blurring before my eyes and then sharpening again. But now the fire is gone, and we are back in the Wolf Queen's court, and she is flat on her back, staring up at three figures looming over her, her face wracked with terror.

The East and South and West Winds blaze with cold fire, and the East Wind presses his sword against the Wolf Queen's throat.

"You have broken the laws of the old magic, daughter of another world. You have twisted it to your own uses, you have made a deal and failed to honor it."

The Queen is ragged and small before the might of the Winds. "Please! Please let me be. I didn't know."

The South Wind shifts his spear. *"You knew very well. You have known always what you do, every second you have been on this world. There is no innocence in your heart. And so there shall be no mercy for you."*

She weeps bitterly on the forest floor, and somehow in spite of everything she's done to hurt Hal, to hurt *me*, I feel a twist of pity.

The West Wind spreads his wings, and takes the spinning wheel from his back. *"And so we take your power from you, and so your throne is broken."*

"No. Please. *Please*."

It's the last word she ever utters.

A chaos of wind and fire whirl round her, and the East Wind and the South Wind uncurl her magic with their spear and their sword. The West Wind catches it on his spinning wheel, and winds it into shifting, shadowy silver. I think of the threads in the bauble room, the twisted echo of the binding magic.

Her screams pierce through me and I can't bear it. Hal wraps himself around me, presses my head against his chest. But I can still hear her screaming.

And then suddenly, she stops.

I lift my head.

The Wolf Queen's hall has vanished, along with the sea of people on their dead thrones. We stand in a quiet patch of forest overshadowed with stars.

In the Wolf Queen's place crouches a small silver wolf. She has the blank eyes of a beast; no comprehension burns behind them. She bares her teeth, frightened, and snarls at us. The Winds watch, silent and grim, as the creature who was once the Wolf Queen dashes off into the wood, the flag of her tail vanishing quickly amongst the trees. I pity her, but at the same time I know the Winds' mercy. She will not remember what she was. She will never know all she lost. Her evil will not haunt her in the dark of every night.

The Winds each turn to me, and bow, the West Wind last of

all. I remember how it felt to ride on his back with his golden wings beating strong underneath me, returning me to the beginning of my life, giving me another chance.

"Thank you," I whisper.

The West Wind smiles.

And then he looks past me to where Mokosh still sits on her throne, weeping, as though unaware of everything that has happened. The West Wind goes to her, wraps her in his strong arms.

"Where will you take her?" I ask.

"Somewhere safe. Somewhere she can find healing, apart from her mother's cruelty."

My heart twists. "Take care of her."

"I will take the very best care, dear one."

And then he spreads his wings, and he and his brothers are gone.

It's only then, as Hal and I turn to stare at each other, soft and weary and blinking away ash that is no longer falling, that I let go of his hand.

CHAPTER
THIRTY-NINE

IT FEELS LIKE THE WORLD GETS a little smaller when I let Hal go. He looks away from me and a soft wind stirs through the dappled leaves scattered on the forest floor.

I don't know what to say, I don't know what to do. The truth of what Hal told me sinks in, and the Wolf Queen's words eat into my mind. *He never wanted you. He never loved you. He was just trying to save his own worthless skin.*

I am hollowed out. I have saved him, but now what?

Hal speaks first, though he's careful not to look at me: "Do you know the way down the mountain?"

"Yes."

The gold circlet has vanished from his head; he's wearing only a ragged shirt and dirty trousers, and I see again the threads of silver glinting in his hair.

I'd thought the journey and the rescuing would be the hard part, but it's not. It's this. I don't know the man standing just paces away from me, looking old and young at once. We went through hell twice together, but now there is nothing to say. The Wolf Queen had a hold of him, was manipulating him for so long—is there anything of himself actually left?

"We had better go," says Hal. "The Wolf Queen's magic may yet linger."

My heart jolts. What if every second we stay here a year spins away down below us? What if any hope of seeing my father again is already gone?

"That is—" Hal's eyes flick up to mine. "That is if I can come with you. I . . . I don't wish to presume—"

"Of course you're coming," I snap.

He nods.

I stride away from the Wolf Queen's bower, and Hal follows. His gait is uneven, his left leg dragging a little behind him as he walks, and I think of that day long ago when I failed to free him from that trap, of the scars we both will always bear. I am broken forever in two. How can I still want to love him, knowing what he did, even if he did it because of the Queen? How can I forgive him?

I want to. But I don't know how.

If you hadn't lit that lamp, I would have been free. But—but she would have taken you instead. That was the deal. The only way to break my curse. Your life for mine.

The wood is quiet as we walk, but not like before. There are birds singing in the trees, a flash of a deer's white tail, a squirrel nibbling a nut on a fallen oak.

The red flowers are gone. In their place grow tangles of honeysuckle and peonies and twists of wild roses, and they make the wood smell sweet. A track still winds between the trees, but it's no longer paved with stones. I think it must be a deer path.

The ground slopes gradually downward as I follow the path, and Hal comes at my heels. Part of me wants to tell him to walk beside me, but the other part, the part that's raw with hurt, can't quite bear it. We saved each other, but I'm not sure that's enough.

We walk in silence. Leaves fall softly all around us. The trees shift to the stately, ancient pines I remember from my ascent, and suddenly we're at the edge of the mountain. The path I followed up here winds back down to the plain. I wonder if Ivan is there, waiting for me. He must be—he was just in his Wind form, breaking the Queen's power. And yet somehow I already know he'll be gone.

Our climb down takes about an hour, maybe less, and the whole time Hal says nothing to me, and I say nothing to Hal. An awful numbness creeps into my heart. What if we can't get past what happened on the mountain? Hal's confession. The Wolf Queen's truth. The scars that run deeper than the lines in my face.

We reach the bottom before I'm ready: there's no camp, no Ivan, no sign that anyone has ever been here before. Somehow I knew it would be this way.

Blood pounds in my ears and I try to fight the panic. "Please not a hundred. Please, God, not a hundred."

"Echo?" Hal lays a hand on my shoulder and I look up to meet his glance.

I don't shake him off, but I don't pull him close, either. "Ivan was supposed to meet me here. To wait for me. He's a storyteller I hired as a guide, only he's actually the North Wind, or used to be, and his brothers are the ones who helped us, back . . . there." I wave vaguely up the mountain. "He promised he'd wait for me three weeks."

"Then that's all we know. Three weeks have passed. That doesn't mean a century."

I don't know how Hal can be so calm, but I nod, my throat constricting. "He would have left me something. A note. A sign."

We search the ground by the path, lifting rocks and digging through bushes. The landscape is overgrown by tangles of briars and underbrush, and I'm ready to give in to despair when Hal finds it: a notch carved into the side of the mountain, an oilskin-wrapped package wedged inside.

Hal hands it to me mutely, and I sit down with my back to

the rock and unwrap the oilskin. A book stares up at me, the title *Echo North* stamped in gold on the cover. For a moment all I can do is stare.

Hal stands nearby, watchful but not prying, and somehow his presence bolsters me enough to open the book to the title page: *Echo North: the story of a girl and a monster and how her love saved them both, as told by Ivan Enlil.*

Ivan did it, then. He took me at my word, adopted my story as his own, gave it an ending. I didn't expect it to end like this, though: printed words on cream pages.

My heart pounds dully in my throat as I skim through the book, passing my eyes down the pages, reading snatches of my life told in Ivan's lyrical prose. It's much more fantastic than what I actually lived: book-Echo is scarred in a fierce battle with her stepmother, who is also the enchantress responsible for cursing Hal. The enchantress is a Troll Queen and Hal's a bear, and book-Echo literally rides on the backs of all four Winds to get to the Troll Queen's fortress.

I read the ending Ivan wrote for me, all the while feeling Hal's quiet gaze fixed on my face: book-Echo climbs up to the Troll Queen's fortress, where she finds Hal chained in a high tower. To free him, Echo must complete three impossible tasks. First, to sew a blanket without needle or thread. Second, to make love fit in a box. Third, to clean Hal's shirt from where the oil dripped, without using soap or water. Echo completes the tasks, with the help of magical creatures she met on her journey. The Queen goes into a rage, but book-Echo chains her in the tower in Hal's place, and hummingbirds and the giants and the Winds pull the tower to the ground. Book-Hal, a prince, takes book-Echo to his kingdom and they are married and live happily ever after.

I glance up at Hal, who's still watching me, his face blank, his manner reserved. I swallow around the lump in my throat and lower my eyes back to the book. I turn the last page and find what I've been waiting for: a letter addressed to me on two sheets of crisp paper folded in half.

I open the letter, trying to calm my raging heart.

Dear Echo,

I waited for you the three weeks we agreed on—to be truthful, I waited four. But time runs differently in the Wolf Queen's domain, and I know that you are most likely well, that you might be there even still, locked with her in combat, freeing your white wolf from her spell. I am sorry I had to leave you, but so it was.

Isidor and Satu are well. Satu has grown tall and brown and merry, and her favorite stories are the ones I tell of you. It is she who demanded I write them down, print them in a book. And I did, with a few liberties I hope you will forgive. The book has made me enough profit to buy a proper house and fine gowns for Isidor. It is a funny thing for a Wind to worry about providing for his family, but it is so, and it is you who has made it possible.

I wrote you an ending, as you wished me to, but Satu has never been easy with what really happened on the mountain. So this year, for her tenth birthday, we have made the journey back here, to see if you had yet come down. But there was still no sign of you, and after a week of waiting, I finally convinced Satu that we must return home again. She swears she will come every year or two, and one day climb the mountain herself, to rescue you if she is able. I am very loathe to lose her, also, to the Wolf Queen, so you will understand my reluctance ever to let her do so.

I hope that when you do, one day, come down from the mountain (and I do not doubt that it will happen), I am still living, and you find us, and tell Satu the real ending to your story.

Many blessings to you, child. And may the Winds be with you always.

Ivan

I read the letter twice, then fold it up again and tuck it back into the book. Hal paces over to me, his eyes fixed on mine.

"It's been ten years. Ten years since I climbed the mountain, maybe more."

He nods, and I stare at him as the world blurs before me. Hal takes my hand. "Then it's past time we got you home," he tells me gently.

THE BEGINNING OF OUR JOURNEY home is much like my travels with Ivan, minus the singing and without so much ice. The hard grip of winter has eased from the land with the Wolf Queen's defeat, and there is life everywhere we go: deer on the plain, foxes in the caves, badgers and rabbits and pheasants amidst the scrub and rocks.

Hal and I don't lack for food. We hunt, we eat, we walk. But that's all we do. We speak very little beyond the necessities of making and breaking camp, and we sleep on opposite sides of the fire every night. I miss him, I crave his company. He's here and yet not here, close by but unreachable.

We emerge from caves no longer encrusted in ice to find that the frozen lake Ivan and I spent so long trudging across has melted. We're left with the unenviable task of walking around it for untold miles, and decide to camp early. We'll face the extended trek in the morning.

We eat fresh-caught fish roasted over a fire as the sun sinks slowly in the west. I watch Hal eat around the bones and spit them out amongst our coals, and all at once I'm thrown back to the garden, watching the wolf tear into his rabbit. The memory makes my heart ache. Hal glances up to see me watching him.

"Tell me your story," I say without meaning to.

He fixes his gaze on the fire. "I was the youngest of eleven, six brothers and four sisters older than me. I was partially forgotten but mostly just spoiled and I did as I pleased, always. If I wanted a hound, I was given a hound. If I wanted to ride my father's warhorse, I rode my father's warhorse. I was closest with my next-oldest sister, Illia, who liked sunshine and reading and telling me that I oughtn't always be so selfish."

I see Hal as he was in his memory book: small and sorrowful, begging his mother to let him go and see his sister. "I'm so sorry."

He shakes his head. "They're all gone now. It hardly matters."

He reaches for another log to feed the flames. "I was seventeen when I first went into the wood. I was restless, bored. My brothers were given commissions in the army. My sisters were married or sent to learn music and manners on far-off estates. My parents had no use for me, and I had very little use for myself. So I went to explore the forbidden forest, mostly to spite my father. I met—I met *her* there, and . . . well, you know the rest."

"Not from you."

He shifts in his place across from me, bending his knees up under his chin and looking for all the world like a gangly, overgrown boy. I can see the scars on his left ankle, tight and shiny in the firelight. "She was kind to me. I thought she was just a girl my age. She spun wild stories about caring for her mother deep in the wood, and she fascinated me."

I try to ignore the stab of jealousy. "What then?"

"I went to see her every day. I abandoned everything else, even fencing lessons, which had been the last thing I loved. We met in secret for six months, and then she showed me what I thought was the truth about her: she was a shapeshifter, unjustly banished into the wood. God help me, Echo, but I fancied myself in love with her, and we schemed—we schemed ways to be together."

My throat hurts but I just nod, staring at my fingers twisting tight in my lap. This time I feel his eyes on my face, but I don't lift my own to meet them.

"I agreed to a bargain with the Wolf Queen without even knowing I did. I was a fool. One night in her cursed court and her true nature came clear, but it was already too late. Her enchantment had taken hold, and when I ran from the wood in my wolf form—" Hal draws a ragged breath. "The world had turned long outside her domain. My brothers and sisters, mother and father—they had been dead already many years. But it didn't count toward my century. No. I must feel every day of my hundred years. Unless I agreed to marry—at first the Queen herself, then in later years her daughter—agreed to become her creature forever, damned to even worse than the half-life I was already living.

"So I shut myself in her enchanted house, and felt every hour, every second of my life spinning away from me. By day, I was torn in two, my human self trapped in the worlds of the books, not remembering my true nature, while my wolf form raged, because I could not be free of her. Sometimes I couldn't stand it any longer and went roaming, breaking through the wood she bound around me, searching for some spark of hope. And then I found you."

My eyes jerk up of their own accord and I stare at Hal across the fire. "Did you ever remember? That we had done it all before?"

"My book self didn't, until the end. But every night, when the magic grew thin and I shed my wolf form, I remembered everything I'd done to you—everything I was still doing to you—and everything you sacrificed to free me. Twice. And sometimes I looked at you and I knew you from before and it broke my heart. Because, in the end, no matter what happened—I would destroy you. I already had." His voice catches. "I tricked you. Trapped you. I am as despicable as the Wolf Queen, more. Because I hurt the one I loved. I hurt *you*, and then I did it again." He bows his head into his hands and his shoulders shake. He's crying, and I can't bear it.

I slip around to his side of the fire and settle next to him, wrapping my arm about his shoulders. He leans into me for a moment, then turns to look up at me, his face twisted into a tangle of emotions I can't quite understand.

He wipes his eyes and I slip my hand into his and he doesn't pull away.

"Can you forgive me, Echo? I haven't dared to ask you since the Queen was destroyed because I knew I couldn't bear it if you reviled me. But now—now I just need to know. Can you forgive me?"

My throat constricts. I hold tight to his fingers, the heat from the fire pulsing in my skin. "Yes. Oh, Hal, yes. But it *hurts*. It hurts so much."

"I know." He lifts his free hand to cradle my chin in his palm, gently. "I betrayed you. I meant for you to be trapped with the Wolf Queen. I wished for it, because it meant I would be free.

Every word she made me tell you was true and I did it to you twice. You didn't have those scars. The first time—the first time you tried to save me, you didn't have those scars. You didn't—"

"Hal."

He takes a sharp breath.

"It wasn't you. It was her. She trapped you, manipulated you, made you into a wild creature. It wasn't you. I know myself, like I never did before. I'm proud of who I am. Even proud of my scars. They're part of me—I wouldn't wish them away."

"Not even for that other life you could have had?" He smooths the left side of my face with his thumb.

"That other life didn't have you in it. Not as you should be. Free from her. "

He looks stricken, and drops his hand. "I can never atone for what I've done. I can never deserve you."

"It isn't about deserving, Hal. It never was." I long to pull him close. I *ache* for him. "The old magic is stronger than guilt or betrayal. Stronger than everything she did to you, and to me. It's stronger than time."

"Is it . . . is it strong enough to mend us?" His eyes pierce through me.

I touch his face where the oil burned him, where a tiny half-moon scar shows white against his skin. "Yes." My throat catches. "It is. It is."

And then I'm wrapping my arms around him, hugging him

close, breathing him in. He clings to me. His heart beats against mine, strong, steady. "I love you, Hal."

His lips move against my hair. "I love you, Echo."

I pull my face to his and kiss him as the lake laps quietly at the shore and the moon peeks silver over the horizon. His mouth is warm on mine, his fingers smooth against my jaw. He tastes like springtime, like promises. A seed of contentment curls sweet in my belly. I let it sprout.

I lay on his chest as we talk, long into the night. We stare up at the stars. Peace steals over us. Healing.

"Hal," I say, just before the fragrant wind lulls us at last to sleep. "Who was your musical friend? The one who gave you that piece you played for me in the concert hall?"

He smiles, and pulls me closer. "Echo, it was you. The first you. You taught me how to play in the books."

Laughter bubbles out. "It was me!"

He kisses my cheek. "It was always you."

I sigh against him.

We fall asleep.

ƐPILOGUƐ

THE TREES ARE DRIPPING SCARLET AND orange and amber leaves onto the cobbled streets of the village; smoke curls up from the shops and the houses. It's a brilliant day, if a little cold. I walk with Hal over the stones, my heart quick in my chest, my fingers tangled in his.

He squeezes my hand. "Don't worry."

I slip my other hand into the pocket of my deep blue woolen skirt, one of many things we bought with the money Ivan gave us for the journey home, and twist my fingers where Hal can't see.

I am glad we stopped to visit Ivan. He lives in a neat wooden house now, with a pen for goats and a room for writing. He's older and happier and a little more rotund. Isidor is smiling and stately as a queen at his elbow, Satu bouncing and lively and always laughing. It was good to see them—but my heart urged me on. Hal saw, and understood. We only stayed two nights.

Ten years spun away while Hal and I were on the Wolf Queen's mountain, and it's been nearly twelve now since I last saw my father. We stride up the last little ways to his bookshop. My stomach churns.

"Don't worry," says Hal again, and wraps his arm around my shoulders.

I'm glad to have him here, solid and warm beside me. His presence gives me strength.

And then we've reached the shop, and we're stepping through the door, listening to the chime of the bell overhead that heralds our arrival. We stop just inside, standing together by the window. I drink in the scents of my childhood: ink and paper, leather and dust and oil.

My father is with a customer, standing behind the counter wrapping a bundle of books in brown paper as I've seen him do so many times before. He's the same, and yet not the same: his hair has turned snow white, his face is creased with wrinkles. But he's alive. He's here. I haven't lost him entirely to the passage of time.

"May I help you?" comes a bright voice.

I jerk my attention to a young girl who must have slipped out of the back room while I was staring at my father. She's maybe eleven, and wears her hair in two brown braids draped over either shoulder, her blue and gold embroidered kerchief tied neatly behind her neck.

I stare at her, anything I'd prepared to say vanished entirely from my mind.

"We're here to see Peter Alkaev," supplies Hal.

"If you're looking for a book, I know them all," says the girl. "Well, *almost.*"

Tears prick behind my eyes. "Are you his daughter?"

She smiles, and sticks out her hand. "I'm Inna."

The customer steps past us with his package of books, walking through the door and out into the street.

"He can see you now," says Inna, evidently not minding that I'm too shocked to shake her hand. She trots toward the counter. "Papa! There're visitors to see you!"

Hal squeezes my hand once more, and we follow Inna, my heart beating so hard I can barely breathe.

My father has ducked down behind the counter, securing the customer's payment in our battered cash box. "With you in a moment!" he calls cheerily.

"They're not after books, Papa," Inna explains. "Just you."

He pops up again, smiling at his second daughter, my . . . sister . . . and then his eyes pass to me and he sees me, really *sees* me. His face blanches white. "Echo?" he says, hesitant, as though he hardly dares to speak the word.

I nod, tears rushing to overwhelm me. "It's me, Papa."

"Echo!" he cries. I'm vaguely aware of Inna's round-eyed shock as my father comes around the counter. In another moment I'm wrapped in his embrace and we're crying on one another's shoulders and I can taste my joy—sunlight and honey and sharp winter wind.

"Echo," he says, over and over again. "Echo." He weeps into my hair.

It's only then, when my father lifts his tear-stained face, that he registers I've brought someone with me, though he's forestalled from inquiring by Inna's overflowing amazement. "Inna. This is . . . "

Before he can finish, Inna has flung her arms around my neck, laughing. "I knew you would come back! I knew you would, one day!"

And now I'm laughing, too. I feel a fierce connection to her already. She lets me go and my hand finds Hal's. I can't stop smiling—I feel the happiness will make me burst. Once more, he squeezes my fingers.

"Hal, this is my father. And—and my sister. Inna, Papa . . . " I swallow, glancing from Hal to my father and Inna, then back again. "This is my white wolf."

I TELL THEM MY STORY in the room above the bookshop, where a fire licks quietly at the grate and steam curls from chipped tea mugs. Rodya is there, with his wife and two half-grown boys, who seem to very much like pulling Inna's hair. Donia isn't there. Donia hasn't been there for several years now. Rodya tells me she tried to sue Papa for his money (he has grown more than solvent again), but the solicitors would have none of it. So she packed her bags and left in the night without a word. The divorce papers arrived by courier several months later. But let's not focus on that right now, Rodya says—today is about me and my homecoming.

So I tell them everything, with Hal beside me, holding my hand and filling in the gaps if I leave anything out. Inna keeps the tea coming, and partway through the story Rodya's wife, Ara, serves us stew and bread with honey.

When I finish, the night is half spent. Rodya's boys have fallen asleep by the fire, and he and Ara watch them, smiling. Inna is snuggled up close to my father, and I lean my head on Hal's shoulder, listening to his heartbeat, the rise and fall of his breath. My heart is full to overflowing. I never thought I would have so much family as I do.

"What now?" asks my father, breaking the silence. He lifts his eyes to mine, and I am thankful beyond words that a century didn't pass us by on the mountain. Ten years is too much, yet it's a blessing. I ache for Hal—he will never have such a happy reunion.

He squeezes my hand as if reading my mind. "We are going to the university. It's been a while since Echo was accepted, but they might still have her application filed away."

My father smiles and I laugh and kiss Hal's cheek. "I'm going to be a doctor," I say.

"And I've got four centuries of history to catch up on," Hal adds. "I'll find some sort of occupation in the meantime."

"But we'll visit as often as we can, and when—and when I *am* a doctor, we want to live here, in the village. Not waste any more time." My throat cracks.

"Oh, my dear girl," says my father quietly, "I think your time has been very well spent."

Tears slip once more down my cheeks, and Hal nudges me toward my father. I go, sinking to a seat beside him. He hugs me close, careful not to disturb Inna, who has fallen asleep on his other shoulder.

I glance across at Hal. He smiles at me, and gives a little nod.

"There's one other thing, Papa."

I think he knows—there's laughter sparking in his eyes. "What is it, greatheart?"

I draw my right hand out of my skirt pocket and show him the ring on my fourth finger, three interlocking bands of yellow, rose, and white gold.

My father smiles and kisses my forehead. "Congratulations, my dear girl."

And then I'm laughing, and Inna wakes up and demands to know what she missed and I tell her all about how Hal and I were married on a mountaintop with the North Wind and his family standing witness.

It's only later, when Hal and I crawl into the tiny bed in my old room that we have a moment to talk just the two of us. My father sold the house after Donia left and the room is Inna's now, but she insisted on sleeping on the couch. I tuck myself under Hal's chin and he wraps his arms around me and pulls me close.

"Thank you for saving me," Hal whispers into my hair.

"I never wished to do anything else."

"Thank you, all the same."

Sleep creeps in at the edges of my mind, but I don't let it claim me, not yet. "I love you, Halvarad Wintar."

"And I love you, Echo Alkaev."

I nestle even tighter against him. "Hal?"

"What is it, my love?" he mumbles, his words slurred with sleep.

"Don't ever let me go."

"Not ever." He hugs me fiercely. "Not ever."

He kisses my hair, and our hearts beat as one, and I fall asleep to the sound of his gentle breathing.

AUTHOR'S NOTE

*E*AST OF THE SUN, *W*EST OF the Moon, is a Norwegian fairytale that has its roots in the myth of *Cupid and Psyche*, as does *Beauty and the Beast*—all contain elements of a girl going to live with a monster in a magical castle. In the original *East of the Sun*, the wolf is a white bear, and he's been enchanted by a Troll Queen who lives in a place that's east of the sun, west of the moon. The girl embarks on an impossible journey to find him, enlisting the help of all the winds on her way—the North Wind is the one who takes her to the Troll Queen's castle.

For Echo's story, I have also borrowed a big element from the Scottish ballad *Tam Lin*, in which a brave girl frees an enchanted man from the Fairy Queen by holding on to him while he is transformed into all kinds of hideous monsters.

The setting for *Echo North* was inspired by nineteenth-century Siberian Russia, and the landscapes Echo travels through in the latter part of the book are real, including the frozen lake, which is based on Lake Baikal, the turquoise ice, and the ice caves. The reindeer skin tent that Ivan and his family live in is real, too.

Behrend and Czjaka, the composers that the wolf introduces Echo to, are Bach and Chopin, very thinly disguised, and Hal's quip about Behrend/Bach and the harpsichord is true.

I hope I have done justice to Echo's story and the source materials I've drawn from—any inaccuracies or misrepresentations are, of course, my own.

ACKNOWLEDGMENTS

I AM A HUGE LOVER OF fairytales and am so honored to add a retelling of my own to the many, many wonderful ones that have come before me. This book wouldn't exist without Robin McKinley's *Beauty*, which I discovered at the library when I was eleven or twelve (it's the first book I remember ever making me cry). I'm indebted to Edith Pattou's beautiful and captivating *East*, which introduced me to *East of the Sun, West of the Moon*, and to Diana Wynne Jones's mesmerizing *Fire and Hemlock*, a retelling of *Tam Lin*.

Huge thanks to my wonderful wizardly agent, Sarah Davies, for her insight and tenacity.

To my editor, Lauren Knowles, for her wisdom, encouragement, and brainstorming sessions, and for loving Echo's story as much as I do.

To the whole team at Page Street, for making my lifelong dream come true a second time!

To my critique partners, Jen Fulmer and Laura Weymouth—I couldn't function without you! (Special thanks to Jen for the idea to describe the house as a quilt—you're a genius.)

Thanks to Jenny Downer for her astute comments, for keeping me company while I write/edit, and for that marvelous teapot—I'm still in awe.

Thanks to Hanna Hutchinson for reading an early draft— can't wait for our future joint book tour!

Thanks to Sharon Lovell for introducing me to Chopin all those years ago, and to my piano students, past and present—you guys are the best.

I couldn't have finished my edits for *Echo* without my wonderful army of babysitters: Louise and Gary (my mom and dad), my mother-in-law Joanie, my sister-in-law Sarah, and Jenny. This book would literally not exist in its present form without you!

Thanks to my dear husband, Aaron, for riding the emotional roller-coaster that is writing a book with me once again, for your support and encouragement, and for keeping me supplied with ice cream and excellent hugs.

And thanks to Arthur for making writing—and life—an even bigger adventure than it was before. Love you, munchkin.

ABOUT THE AUTHOR

J OANNA RUTH MEYER is the author of *Beneath the Haunting Sea*, which Kirkus described as "epic, musical, and tender." She wrote her very first story at the age of seven—it starred four female "mystery-solvers" and a villain in a gorilla suit, and remains unfinished to this day.

Since then, she's grown up (reluctantly), earned a bachelor's of music in piano performance, taught approximately one billion piano lessons, and written nine novels, many of them during National Novel Writing Month.

Joanna hails from Mesa, Arizona, where she lives with her dear husband and son, a rascally feline, and an enormous grand piano. When she's not writing, she's trying to convince her students that Bach is actually awesome, or plotting her escape from the desert. She loves good music, thick books, loose-leaf tea, rainstorms, and staring out windows. One day, she aspires to own an old Victorian house with creaky wooden floors and a tower (for writing in, of course!).